"LOOK OUT, DAVE!"

Dave dropped on his face as a shot blazed from the corner of the cabin. He landed on his stomach, rolling on his side, his free arm whipping out his gun. Only the edge of a hatbrim showed, but Dave emptied his gun at it. He leaped to his feet, lunged for the shelter of the cabin, and drew his other gun.

Flattening himself against the wall, he waited. No more shots came and he poked his gun barrel around the corner to see if it would draw a shot but it didn't. He swung out, gun ready, and saw the outlaw leaning against the wall as if asleep. Dave lifted the outlaw's hat and saw a neat purple hole just above his right eyebrow.

Dave shuddered and looked away. In the course of a few hours he had made himself a killer six times over. He shrugged wearily, and dragged the body into the burning house. . . .

Dell books by Luke Short

BOLD RIDER	FIRST CLAIM
BOUGHT WITH A GUN	HARDCASE
BOUNTY GUNS	THE STALKERS
BRAND OF EMPIRE	THE OUTRIDER
THE BRANDED MAN	HARD MONEY
KING COLT	AMBUSH
THE MAN ON THE BLUE	SILVER ROCK
MARAUDERS' MOON	LAST HUNT
RAW LAND	THE DESERTERS
SAVAGE RANGE	STATION WEST
RIDE THE MAN DOWN	TROUBLE COUNTRY

THE FEUD AT SINGLE SHOT

THE FEUD AT SINGLE SHOT

LUKE SHORT

A DELL BOOK

Published by
Dell Publishing
a division of
Bantam Doubleday Dell Publishing Group, Inc.
666 Fifth Avenue
New York, New York 10103

ISBN: 0-440-20633-2

Reprinted by arrangement with the author's estate

Printed in the United States of America
Published simultaneously in Canada

June 1990

10 9 8 7 6 5 4 3 2 1

RAD

Contents

I	Gold for Single Shot	1
II	Whistle Stop John Law	11
III	Guns for the Dry-Gulchers	15
IV	Saddle Bum's Salary	29
V	Sitting on Dynamite	35
VI	Dead Man's Clue	41
VII	Nester Negotiations	51
VIII	Thunder Over Old Cartridge	58
IX	Water and Gold	66
X	Showdown at Midnight	75
XI	Rosy's Hunch	86
XII	Boot Marks	101
XIII	"We've Got You, Turner"	115
XIV	Kidnapped	127
XV	Murder Charge	133
XVI	Boot Trail	142
XVII	Death in the Canyon	149
XVIII	The Fight on the Ridge	165
XIX	Gold Bits for Every Horse	172
XX	Gambler's Trap	180
XXI	"Fill Your Hand!"	184
XXII	Crowell Sees His Boss	191
XXIII	Tangled Trails Turn Straight	206

1
Gold for Single Shot

On the second seat from the front of the coach, facing forward, two cowpunchers were hunkered down, apparently asleep, for it was night. Their backs were to the poker game being played across the aisle by three cowpunchers and a professional gambler on two upended suitcases kept upright against the lurching of the train by four pairs of knees.

The gambler, a young man, glanced up the dimly lighted aisle and muttered quietly:

"Here comes Hoagy and he's on the prod."

The players did not betray they had heard him until the middle-aged brakeman, Hoagy Henshaw by name, paused beside the game and placed a proprietary hand on the back of the seat. His not unamiable face was fretted under the stiff cap of authority he wore.

The cowpuncher whose back was to Hoagy slapped his hand down.

"Three johns, gents, and a pair of bullets. Bury the dead." Then, as if he had interrupted himself in the midst of a story, he continued: "—And this jasper with the feet the size of a loadin' chute turns to the brakie, real polite-like, and says: 'So there's a law agin' playin' poker on a train, is they?'"

"What did the brakie do?" a second cowpuncher, seated next to the speaker, inquired innocently.

"The brakie, he said: 'It's a law, my friend. Not that I care if you play poker on a train. You can play it anywheres. I'd like to play it with you.' And this Big Foot whips out a plow handle and sticks it in the brakie's belly and says: 'Now, ain't that fine! I reckon we can make a place for you. Jest set down.' The brakie sets down and they dealt him a hand after he'd bought in the game to the tune of a couple of two-figger bills."

"Then what happened?" his mate asked.

"Well, when the brakie'd been cleaned, Big Foot says: 'Mebbe you'd like a loan?' real meanin'-like. The brakie says he wouldn't and Big Foot sticks the gun in the brakie's belly agin and says: 'Mebbe you didn't hear me. I ast you if you wanted a loan?' The brakie says sure, he wants a loan. They plays for another hour, the brakie still losin' and still tryin' to get away. When they comes to Big Foot's stop, he looks around. 'How much am I into you?' he asts the brakie. 'Fifty dollars, ain't it?' The brakie says yes and Big Foot looks around the car. 'Danged if old Henry Crossman couldn't use these here plush cushions on that ore-wagon of his,' Big Foot says. Well, he thunk another two minutes and come to find out almost everybody he knew was freightin' ore. He just helped hisself to half the seats in that car."

"What did the brakie do?" the second cowpuncher asked.

"I reckon he let him. Big Foot was a mean man."

The second cowpuncher nodded sagely, then looked at the floor.

"What size boots you wear, Finney?" he asked casually.

"Elevens," the story-teller replied, just as casually.

The second cowpuncher looked up and saw Hoagy, whose arm was slowly withdrawing from the back of the seat. "Hello, Hoagy. Like to sit in?"

"Me?" Hoagy said, with well-feigned astonishment. "Hell, no. I was never so busy in my life. You fellers go ahead and have your fun."

He retreated, shaking his head soberly.

The gambler, seated next the aisle, laughed silently at Hoagy's back. He built a cigarette with quick and sure fingers, shaking his head.

"What size boots *do* you wear, Finney?" he asked.

The broad-faced, good-natured puncher across the seat chuckled. "That's what's funny. I wear size elevens."

Again the gambler laughed. His wide-set blue eyes roamed across the aisle to include the two cowpunchers in the joke, but they were still asleep. His eyes traveled to the one figure seated against the end of the car. He saw only a surly-faced cow-puncher looking out the window into the night. From a loose mouth a soiled cigarette drooped, curling smoke up into unblinking eyes. Cupped hands held a match preparatory to lighting the cigarette.

The gambler's eyes narrowed a little as he watched the man light his already burning cigarette. Observed now, the gambler was still-faced, quiet. He was perhaps in his early thirties. A black flowing tie accentuated the whiteness of his linen, which showed above a checkered vest. The lapels of his black coat were edged in braid and his trousers were striped.

A close observer might have noticed with surprise that the wrinkles around his eyes were of the kind that spider-webbed from the outer corners, sun-wrinkles, instead of the kind that pouched the lower lids, the wrinkles bred over a faro table in the uncertain flicker of an overhead saloon lamp.

When the gambler saw the cowpuncher light still another match, he turned to his seat mate, his mouth open to speak. Suddenly, he closed it, shrugged a little and his face was still again, incurious.

The sight of the man next to him had changed his mind, evidently, for the man had a sullen, almost chinless face, so clean-shaven it looked raw. He was a cowpuncher, in his middle thirties, whose continual scowling had worn creases in his forehead and soft loose face. He had been waked up from a doze two hours back to make up a fourth at poker.

"Let's play stud," he growled, picking up the deck. "This ain't poker, it's drop-the-handkerchief."

Finney eyed him speculatively and spat precisely into the aisle. He yawned, stood up.

"I'm startin' a game of draw back here if anybody wants to buy in," he announced.

The chinless cowpuncher flushed, but did not make a move. Finney cashed in a few chips, nodded to the gambler and left, followed by his companion.

The gambler nodded, also, then lounged back in his seat. He heard the door behind him open, and idly guessed that the match-lighting smoker had gone out. The door had not swung shut five seconds before one of the sleeping cowpunchers, a six-foot red-head, the gambler noticed, stood up, wide awake, stepped over his partner and went out also with a kind of tense haste.

The gambler's companion moved to the seat facing the gambler and picked up the cards.

"How about a showdown?" he asked. His face was still flushed from the words Finney had dropped so casually.

The gambler shook his head. "Finney's startin' a game down in back if you still feel like it."

"You're a gambler, ain't you?" the man asked truculently.

"When I'm at a table, yes. When I'm not, I do what I please."

The gambler looked indolently across the aisle. When his eyes turned, they were staring into the steady muzzle of a Colt in the hands of the chinless puncher.

"I say we'll play cards," the cowpuncher said in a low voice.

"I reckon not." The gambler's speech was a quiet drawl.

He saw the eyes of the puncher smear over and watched the thumb start to slide off the hammer. The trigger was pressed flat against the back of the guard.

"Gamblers don't come high in this country, stranger," the puncher replied thickly.

The gambler shrugged, but made no movement. He knew the train was going slow enough that the cowpuncher could release the hammer point-blank in his face, make a dive for the door before any one realized what had happened and be swallowed up in the night. He could feel the hackles rise on his neck.

"Once more," the cowpuncher said softly. "Let's you and me play cards."

The gambler shook his head slowly.

From across the aisle a gun lanced fire in a deafening explosion. It was followed by a sharp cry from the cowpuncher who drew a bloody, gunless hand to his chest. The gambler was out of his seat like a cat and drove his fist into the face of the cowpuncher.

Turning, he saw a sleepy-eyed cowboy sitting erect, a six-gun drooping across his knee, a slow grin creasing a long, lean face under raven-black hair.

When the red-head stepped out the train door on to the front platform, the man squatting over the coupling from the platform of the baggage car ahead looked up. He was the man who had left the passenger coach a half minute before.

"Howdy," the red-head drawled. The train was going so slow that his voice carried distinctly.

"Whadda' you want?" the man growled, still squatting, his guns hanging down from his hips like fins.

"Air," was the brief reply. The red-head lounged his even six feet of height against the end of the car, his gray eyes narrowed a little and suddenly wary.

"Passengers ain't supposed to ride the platform," the man said.

"Reckon that hits us both, don't it?"

"I'm one of the train crew," the man replied evenly.

"So am I," the red-head replied.

Slowly, the man came erect, his figure squat and shadowy in the light of the turned-down lamp that hung between the cars.

"Want me to call the brakie?" the man asked slowly.

"Sure. Call him. Mebbe he could tell me a lot of things I'm wonderin'."

A pause.

"For instance?"

"I been watchin' you in there for the last ten minutes," the red-head said. "You was smokin'. You lit that cigarette eight times when it was still goin'. Who's out there?"

He jerked his head out toward the night. A shot rang out from inside the coach. Neither man took his eyes off the other.

The train gave a sudden buck as the brakes screamed on. The red-head felt himself lifted from the wall. His hands streaked to his guns, swiveled up and exploded as he felt himself lunging across the space between the two cars. The man on the baggage-car platform slid abruptly to a sitting position, coughing pulpily, his hands locked on the butts of his guns, as the red-head crashed into the end of the baggage car. He took an accurate snap shot at the lantern, then opened the door to the baggage car.

"Blow them lights! It's a stickup," he yelled.

He did not even wait for the startled baggageman to obey him, but swung himself to the top of the car.

The train had come to a stop now, almost at the top of the grade. The red-head could see horsemen ahead in the glare of the engine light. Realizing he was skylined, he crouched low on the roof, raced forward, leaped to the tender, then crouched down, waiting to see if he had been discovered.

"Let 'em know we're here," a voice growled from the ground beside the baggage car.

"You damn fool. Wait till we're inside. They'll slam that door shut on us and we can't blow 'em out. Wait'll Snipe and Chinch cut that passenger coach off."

Stealthily, the red-head made his way over the coal until he could see down into the engine cab. Two masked men stood facing the fireman and engineer, who had been backed into one window seat cringing away from the menacing guns. The red-head's action was quick.

He slid down the heaped coal, both guns roaring at the two bandits silhouetted against the fire-door. One man pitched his length on the floor plates and the other made a wild, crippled dash for the steps. The red-head heard him sprawl on the ground, loosing a string of bitter oaths. Suddenly, the night around them came alive with shots, winking orange in the darkness.

"Get goin'!" the red-head commanded briefly to the engineer. "Will she run?"

"I dunno. We ain't made the top of the grade yet."

"Blow the damn thing up foggin' her over!" Then: "Look out!"

The three of them crouched in the shelter of the cab as a sweeping fire from horsemen racked the engine.

"Your track all right?" the red-head asked the fireman.

"Yeah. No blockade. Them two swung up just as we started nosin' over the grade. They made us slam on—"

"Then get this damn thing fannin'," the red-head interrupted him.

The engineer leaned against a lever which brought forth a rumbling shudder. The red-head dragged the limp form of the bandit from in front of the fire-door and dumped him off the train.

There was a running fire as the train labored into motion, most of it directed toward the engine. Glass tinkled down to the floor and the engineer swore wrathfully. The red-head sent a couple of shots into the night, then looked ahead as he did so for the top of the grade, which was close now.

As they nosed over it, he turned and faced the engine crew. The train was gathering speed steadily as it swung over the top. All of them listened as the shots seemed to diminish and grow dimmer in the distance.

"What do you reckon is on behind?" the red-head asked, holstering his guns.

In the light of the fire-door, his hair seemed alive and flaming. His hands, riding easily on the hips of waist overalls, were big, his fingers spatulate, and the easy crinkling grin of the wide mouth beneath his snubbed and freckled nose brought an answering smile from the engineer.

"They're all there. I can tell by the way she pulls," the engineer said. He mopped the sweat from his brow with a grimy handkerchief. "There was three mine payrolls in that baggage-car safe, and if they don't give you one of 'em, son, then—"

The sentence went unfinished, for the red-head had waved carelessly and disappeared over the tender.

"Now, just who the hell is he?" the fireman asked slowly.

The red-head made his way uncertainly over the catwalk atop the baggage car to the far end, where he swung down upon the platform. The door to the baggage car was open and he lounged in.

"That's the ranny," some one said from a group collected around a man lying on the floor. One lamp flickered dimly overhead and the red-head noticed that every one on the train was collected in this car.

Hoagy Henshaw turned around and peered through myopic eyes at the figure in the doorway. His gun nosed up unsteadily at the sudden apparition. "How'd you know this stickup was comin' off?"

The red-head shrugged and pulled a tobacco sack from his shirt pocket. There was a glint of amusement in his eyes as he looked at the brakeman, then at the dark man who had been his seat-mate in the passenger coach, now standing beside the gambler.

"I was tryin' to sleep and I seen that jasper in the seat ahead of me signalin' out into the night with matches. He got up. I followed him out. He was tryin' to uncouple the car. That's all I know." His voice was low, good-humored, calm under the threat of the brakie's gun.

"Well, he's dead," Hoagy said, "and nobody saw him do nothin' out of the way. We got only your word for it, and it seems to me you know a little too much about what was goin' to happen."

"He's right, Hoagy," the gambler put in. "I saw the man lighting matches myself and wondered about it."

Hoagy's eyes swiveled to the gambler and the nose of his gun dropped.

"All right, Quinn. I'll take your word for it." He looked at the red-head. "But I'm goin' to talk to the train crew first, before I let you go. There's somethin' funny about this." He turned to Quinn again. "I'll expect you to answer for him."

"He don't need to," the red-head drawled mildly. "I ain't goin' to jump the train."

Hoagy nodded grimly and addressed the group.

"You better clear out now. If the gov'ment knowed I let you in here, I'd lose my job."

Back in the passenger coach the black-haired puncher introduced the gambler to the red-head.

"Rosy, this is Martin Quinn." To the gambler he said: "This

here is the hero of the train robbery, or the robber. I dunno which. Name's Rosy Rand."

After shaking hands, they all sat down in the gambler's seat.

"What was the shot in here, Dave?" Rand asked his partner. "Didn't I hear one?"

"Turner here—" Quinn began. Suddenly, he stood up and glanced around the car. "Well I'll be damned," he said, amazement slowing his voice. "He's gone. He hightailed it while we were out of the car." He laughed, then explained to the redhead what the shooting had been about. He turned to Turner as he finished. "I'm obliged to you for that, Turner. He'd have let that thing off in my face in another second."

"Who was he? Ever seen him before?" Rand asked.

Turner shook his head. "There's not a stuffed Stetson yet that didn't think he could choose a gambler on any grounds of his own makin'."

Quinn nodded, smiling. "That's about it. I used to know an old-timer who said if a gambler changes his name once a month and keeps on the move, he's got an even chance of outlivin' a dumb rustler."

Turner laughed. "And I've heard him say it. It was Dipper-Mouth Hartley, wasn't it?"

"He's the one," Quinn said. "I thought he'd be before your time. I'd been led to believe he was in the Yuma pen."

"That's where I knew him," Turner said briefly.

"Sorry," Quinn said. "That was none of my business."

He studied the two men before him with the acuteness of a man shrewd in the judgment of men. Turner was perhaps ten pounds lighter than Rand, two inches shorter. But they both bore the same stamp, that of quiet men, young, slow in judgment, quick in action. He knew the kind. Steel toughened in the fire of experience, old beyond their years, wanting nothing so much as to be let alone.

It mattered not at all to the gambler that Turner had been in prison. A glance at him told Quinn that it had left him untouched, with none of the sourness, the bitterness, and the hate that prison breeds. They were both young, perhaps twenty-five, dressed in the soft, oft-washed range clothes of waist overalls and blue shirt.

They looked up to see Hoagy shuffling down the aisle intoning to the car: "Single Shot. Five minutes to Single Shot."

He stopped by their seat and looked judiciously at Rand.

"I been up to the cab talkin' with the boys. They tell me you pulled 'em out of a tight spot."

Rand squirmed. "All they needed was to run the engine."

Hoagy shook his head and persisted. "I'm goin' into Walpais on this run. I'll tell the super. There may be some money in it for you."

Rand's face flushed uncomfortably. "They can keep it."

But Hoagy was persistent. "Look here. He'll want to do somethin' for you. There was three mine payrolls in that baggage-car safe."

Rand thought a minute. "All right. If he wants to do somethin', have him write the warden at Yuma and tell him."

"Warden? Yuma?" Hoagy said slowly.

"I'm out on parole," Rand told him. Hoagy shook his head, but took Rand's name and left.

"He doesn't believe you," Turner said.

"Neither do I," Quinn put in.

"It's a fact," Rand said.

Turner's nod confirmed him. Quinn shook his head slowly, looking from one to the other.

"If a gambler's word in a tight place will do you any good, let me know. I'll be at the Free Throw in Single Shot."

"We'll be neighbors then," Turner said. "My dad's got a spread near there."

Hoagy's voice droned through the car. "Single Shot. Single Shot."

2
Whistle Stop John Law

The Sierra Blancos, towering the hundred miles of their east-west length in snow-capped aloofness, must have looked at the town of Single Shot with a degree of tolerance, since this irregular and shabby cowtown had been allowed to remain at the mouth of its deep valley for more than forty years. The valley cut a deep gash back into the mountains, a gigantic knife-thrust that had for its core only a wide and gravelly stream bed.

At the foot of the valley on the bank of this dry stream bed lay the town, an affair of one main street and two weak cross streets. South of the town lay the foothills sloping in three stippled swells to the semi-arid plains many miles below.

Looming up as a mountain in its own right, to the west of the town and a little to the south lay Coahuila Butte, a spur of Old Cartridge, itself one of the proud members of the Blancos. To the east, more mountains, but low, over which the train had labored this night to coast triumphantly and noisily into the station.

Dave was glued to the window, Rosy behind him, lifting down their warbags.

"See her?" Rosy asked.

Dave's answer was long in coming. "No. Reckon she didn't get my letter after all."

"She'll likely be at the hotel," Rosy said. He stooped down to look out the window at the town. A glance was enough. The station fronted the main street, a broad, string-straight road fetlock deep in dust, flanked by boardwalks under wooden awnings and an almost unbroken line of hitchracks. A good many of the false-front stores of weathered clapboard were lighted, hip-shot ponies and teams harnessed to buckboards blinking in the light they cast out into the street.

"I don't think so," Dave said quietly. "If I hadn't seen my sister for eight years, I reckon I wouldn't wait for her in a hotel. I reckon Mary wouldn't wait for me there, either."

They were the last two out of the car and as they descended to the station platform, Dave's eyes roved the small crowd for a sign of his sister. An uncontrollable bitterness came over him as he realized she was not there. She, too, then, had been ashamed to be seen in public with a jail-bird brother. He felt a hand on his shoulder.

"Ain't you Dave Turner?" a slow, flat voice asked him.

Dave turned. Confronting him was a fat, shapeless man, looking like nothing so much as two hundred-odd pounds of soiled clothes topped by a greasy Stetson. He wore ragged, saber mustaches below a thick-nostriled nose and his eyes were colorless, unblinking, red-rimmed. Where his chest sloped to his belly, a star reposed, the only neat thing about him except the twin butts of Colts that sagged just above his knees. Dave recognized him at once.

"Sure. I'm Dave Turner. You're Sheriff Lowe—still," Dave said dryly. Neither of them offered to shake hands.

"Uh-huh. Still." The sheriff's eyes did not blink. "Come on this train?"

"Yeah," Dave drawled. He waited a moment. "I bought a ticket, if that's what's worryin' you."

"It ain't worryin' me," the sheriff said in his flat, unemotional voice.

Dave's eyes ignored him as they searched the platform again for Mary.

"Lookin' for your sister?"

Dave looked at him, waiting a moment before he answered. "Uh-huh. I figgered she'd meet me here."

"She won't," the sheriff declared flatly.

Dave's eyes narrowed a little. "No? She knew I was comin'."

"I reckon she knew. Everybody does."

"Then where is she?"

"Soledad."

"Soledad? Why there? I asked her to meet me here."

"That's what she said." The sheriff's statement was careless, almost agreeable.

Dave looked at him curiously and when he spoke his voice was soft, mild. "What's all this about, Hank? I asked Mary to meet me here. She doesn't do it, and you do."

"Got any objections to me meetin' a train?" the sheriff asked.

"I'd object to you anywhere," Dave said slowly, "and you know it. You say Mary's at Soledad. I'm asking why."

"Ain't Soledad as close to your spread as Single Shot?" The sheriff countered, ignoring Dave's thrust.

"Sure. What of it?"

"Nothin'. If I was you, I'd go to Soledad and meet her there."

"Did she tell you to tell me that?" Dave asked quietly.

"Huh-uh."

There was a carefully guarded edge of exasperation on Dave's voice as he asked: "Then how do you know she'll be there?"

"I don't. I just guess she will. I told her you'd meet her there."

Dave was quiet a long moment. "You haven't got the guts to say it right out, have you, Hank?"

A small group of loafers had collected in a wide circle around them listening.

"I reckon I have. Get out," the sheriff said flatly.

Dave laughed softly, his eyes sultry and smouldering.

"Why?" he asked bluntly.

"I got enough trouble without lettin' more of it walk right into town."

"I'm out," Dave said slowly. "I didn't escape from prison. I was pardoned. You were never very sure of the right in that case in the first place, were you, Hank?"

"The jury was. I'm not here to row that over agin," the sheriff said.

"Neither am I," Dave said softly. "I took my whippin'. Eight years of it, for killin' a horse-thief that deserved killin'. I'm out now." He paused, watching the sheriff. "I'm goin' anywhere I damned well please."

"I reckon not. Not if you aim to come here," the sheriff persisted.

A new voice broke into the conversation, Quinn's.

"These two men fought off a train robbery tonight, Sheriff. If that's not law-abiding enough for you, what is?"

The sheriff turned his expressionless gaze on Quinn, who held it steadily.

"Who tolled you in on this?" he asked quietly.

"Nobody," Quinn said mildly. "Somebody's given you a bum steer. I'm tryin' to give you a right one."

"If I was you and had business to mind, I'd mind it," the sheriff answered.

"That's good advice," Quinn conceded. "It might apply to you, too." He turned to Dave. "When I see some of these whistle-stop John Laws, I sometimes wish my old man had been hung for rustlin'," he drawled insolently. "Mark of honor in some cases, I'd call it." He waved a negligent farewell to Dave and Rosy and turned on his heel.

The sheriff's eyes barely flickered. "You only been in this town two weeks. Mebbe you'd like to ride out with Turner?"

Quinn stopped and turned deliberately to face the sheriff. Very slowly he placed on his head the black, shapeless Stetson he had been carrying. "When you run Turner out of town for good, Sheriff, then you can start on me," he said in a low voice. "Very likely by that time I'll be willing to go."

"I'll remember that," the sheriff said.

"I doubt if you will," Quinn replied. "I doubt if you'll be in any condition to." He turned and walked slowly off around the corner.

At this moment the train bell clanged, announcing its departure. Hoagy, who had been listening to the argument, laid a hand on Dave's arm.

"If she's waitin' in Soledad, you better climb on."

"Thanks, Hoagy," Dave said, without taking his eyes from

the sheriff's fat face. "Hank, I dunno when I'll be in Single Shot, but when I take a notion, I'll be in."

"Try it," the sheriff drawled.

"I don't savvy this," Dave said slowly. "You tryin' to make fight talk, Hank?"

"Huh-uh. Not me."

"Then what's wrong with my goin' in to Single Shot if I don't start trouble?"

"Try it," the sheriff reiterated.

Dave's jaw clamped shut with a little click.

"I'll do that. I'd do it now if Mary wasn't waitin' in Soledad."

He paused and regarded the sheriff, breathing a little deeply.

"Hank, I got a lifetime to live in this country, about twelve miles from Single Shot. I aim to be peaceful. But if you think I'm goin' to stay out of this town just because you don't happen to like me, take another guess."

"This ain't a guess," the sheriff said.

The train gave a jerk. Rosy was already on the steps, watching. Dave swung up.

"You can't make it stick, fat man," he said, his drawl thick and slow. "I don't reckon I'll have much business in Single Shot, but when I do, I'm coming in."

The sheriff stood flat-footedly, watching the train pull out, a look of mild surprise on his face.

3
Guns for the Dry-Gulchers

There was no reason why Soledad should not have been the prosperous town that Single Shot was. By rail they were twelve miles apart, both nestled high in the foothills. Legend had it that a prospector coming in from the west on the train had spent all his available cash to reach Soledad. He disliked Mexicans, and when he saw that he was being put off at a town composed mostly of Mexicans he traded the conductor a prospector's pick, a compass and a plug of tobacco for a ride on to Single Shot.

There, he traveled up the canyon to the north, found gold, and started the rush which had lifted the sleepy cattle town into a mining town also and left Soledad a clean, sunburnt huddle of adobes squatting around a frame general store and a small whitewashed church.

The sun-blistered station seemed to have part of the prospector's arrogance, since it too had decided not to settle in town, but lay aloof four or five hundred yards from the nearest building, turning its back on the town, preferring the blue mists of the far mesas and the low-lying dry plains below it and to the south.

Even at night it kept its individuality, burning two bright lights at train time, while the windows of the few adobes gleamed soft and mysterious and humble behind it.

When the thrashing locomotive had labored its way around Coahuila Butte, the chief physical obstacle separating the two towns, it subsided into the station, disgorging two lone passengers, cowpunchers, warbags in hand.

A small figure ran quickly from the shadows of the station, saying one word: "Dave!"

She was in his arms, laughing a little with the sudden easing off of a tension that had been growing for eight years. Dave held her at arm's length, his hands on her shoulders.

"Mary," he said simply, huskily. "Why, I reckon—I—why you're beautiful, sis. But where's the corn-colored hair? It's brown and nice and crinkly now. Those same eyes, though; only a little of the mischief has gone out of them."

A slight flush diffused the girl's face and her wide moist eyes looked at him with affection, with a serenity in their brown depths. She was half a head shorter than Dave, but straight, erect as a cavalryman in her riding breeches and white, open-necked shirt. Her body was slender, yet full and rounded, and her unconscious movements were quick and graceful. She laughed huskily, deep in her throat, a laugh full of emotion.

"But Dave, my hair turned, just like mother's. But you haven't changed. You've filled out, but you still look as if you were going to play a trick on the devil himself. Those eyes give you away."

They laughed together.

"Haven't you forgotten something, Dave?"

She didn't wait for an answer, but turned to Rosy, who was standing politely a few yards away.

"You're Rosy Rand Dave wrote about. I'm Mary." She extended her hand and Rosy took it, mumbling something that was lost in the sudden thickness of his tongue.

"Did you come alone, Mary?" Dave asked.

"Yes. I like to ride alone. Don't you remember?"

Rosy looked at Dave and grinned. "There you are, big brother."

They walked behind the station to where the horses were hitched. Mary stopped her chatter long enough to laugh a little.

"I brought a big bay for Mr. Rand. You wrote me he was so big, Dave."

"I didn't lie, did I?"

They found their horses. Dave's hand rubbed up against something slung from the saddle-horn and he looked at it.

"What's this, sis?" he said slowly. "Guns?"

Mary hesitated a moment before answering. "Yes. I didn't know whether you'd have any or not."

Dave looked through the dark at her, trying to see her face. "Is there anything wrong?" he asked.

"No. Not especially. I—I just didn't know whether you'd have them or not."

Thoughtfully, without talking, Dave tied his warbag on the saddle. There was something behind this he didn't understand yet. He'd have to find out.

Mary kept up a continual stream of animated talk as they rode through the town, headed north in the direction of the mountains. Everything that had happened on the spread that Dave might want to know, she told him, including Rosy as if he were an old friend. Dave listened contentedly, laughing occasionally at Mary's excitement, loving her spirit and brightness.

Soon he found his opportunity to speak. They were far from town, riding abreast, the night was warm and friendly, a smell of sagebrush was in the thin air. It seemed as if nothing could be wanting on this night to make it complete, but a nagging doubt goaded him.

"Is there something wrong, Mary? What is it? Why did you bring the guns?"

"Is that so strange in this county, Dave?"

"For you, yes. Remember, it was a gun that sent me to jail, Mary. I'm bein' a little careful how I use one after this."

"Well, it was a combination of everything, Dave. The sheriff warned me not to meet you in Single Shot because he wouldn't let you off the train there. I thought there might be an argument. If it was a bad one, it would be pretty wise to carry a gun, wouldn't it?"

"You've got to do better than that, Mary," Dave said quietly. "Sheriffs don't bushwhack. Besides, I'm twenty miles from needin' a gun right now. What is it?"

Mary sighed. "All right. I'll tell you." Her voice was grave, and Rosy noticed a little of the life had gone from it when she spoke. "Do you remember those three sections on our south line right against the badlands that dad always wanted to ditch for hay?"

"And never did. Sure."

"There are five families of nesters on there now," Mary said slowly. "They hate us. Finnegan—one of the hands—went down and they took his gun away from him when he ordered them off. I don't know whether they're really bad or not, Dave, but maybe they think your coming home will mean they will be kicked off. They might—"

"—take a notion to take a crack at me," Dave finished. "Is that it?"

"Now you know," Mary said quietly.

"Maybe," Dave said dubiously. "Why haven't they been kicked off?"

"Who would do it? None of the hands seem interested."

"What about the sheriff?"

"Help our family? He barely speaks to me on the street. You see, he still holds that kid's foolishness against you."

It was the first reference to Dave's prison term and he was glad Mary was open about it. He began to realize bitterly that the years of prison had been torture for some one besides himself. Evidently people thought they could run over his sister or else ignore her because he had been in prison. Things would change then, and mighty quick.

He thought about the nesters, reflecting on what Mary had told him. So they were tough enough that Mary thought they would try to bushwhack him? Nesters, those poor, hard-working, stubborn men who wished nothing so much as to be let alone. It didn't fit. He tried to see Mary's face in the dark, but he couldn't. A deep doubt urged him to speak again and when he did it was calmly, quietly, probingly.

"And what else, sis? What else made you bring the guns?"

"I told you."

"What else besides that?" he persisted.

Mary sighed. "You were stubborn as a kid, Dave, and I see you haven't changed. Must I tell you everything tonight?"

"Sure. Now." And Dave grinned in the dark.

She laughed a little. "Well, it's Hammond. You've not heard of him, have you?"

"Who's he? Another nester?"

"No. He's a mine owner. He's bought up land just above Single Shot. You know where the trail goes into the notch just behind Coahuila Butte and down the mountainside into Single Shot?"

"Sure."

"And you know how steep the mountainside is? How the only way you can get down it is through that dry wash? Well, he's built a mine, the Draw Three, right at the mouth of that wash at the bottom of the slope."

"What about it?" Dave said.

"Wait a minute. Do you remember, too, that little lake just below Old Cartridge that's so close to the edge of the rimrock?"

"Of course. That's all our water, isn't it?"

"It still is," Mary said. "Well, the lake is only a few yards from the rock rim and our boundary. Hammond, when he bought the mine, said that in the deed there was a lake mentioned. He claims his land comes over the rock rim to the lake."

Dave's mouth sagged. "Lake? Why, it's ours. When dad registered that land, he took a hundred and sixty acres off the west and put it on the east so as to include the lake. Why doesn't Hammond look it up?"

"Oh, it's all so stupid, Dave. The maps show that section perfectly square, shows the lake off our land. I've shown him the papers and everything else, but the map is drawn wrong and he won't believe me. He threatens to take it to law if we haven't given in by the time he needs the water."

"When will that be?" Dave asked grimly.

"I don't know. When he gets the mine along further and gets into gravel. He wants it for sluicing then."

Dave laughed softly. "That's gall for fair. Just because he let some forked jasper sell him a lake with the help of an inaccurate map, he thinks he can take it away from us. We're supposed to give him all our water because he got the worst of a horse-trade. Is that it?"

"He seems to think so," Mary said wearily.

"And what does the sheriff think about that?" Dave asked sardonically.

"He won't have anything to do with it," Mary said. "He says that fight belongs to the land office and if the Turners are crooks, then it's up to Hammond to catch us at it."

"That slob," Dave said bitterly. "So the Turners are crooks. I'd like to have dad here to tell that to."

"I don't think I like that sheriff," Rosy drawled.

"He's all right," Dave said. "A good man. He's dumb and patient, but he's honest. When he gets riled, though, watch out.

You'd never know it, but that big fat jasper has got a draw that's as soft and quick as a whisper. He's never been afraid in his life. Never will be, I reckon."

"Some people are too dumb to be afraid," Rosy said.

The far yipe of a coyote came to Dave's ears, interrupting his thoughts. The night was soft and quiet, the far, countless stars semaphoring silently. Trouble, and more trouble. Hammond's claim was too preposterous to be considered. But the nesters. They must go.

"What about the courts, Mary?" Dave asked presently, out of a reverie. "Those nesters haven't any right there, have they?"

Mary laughed slightly. "We have no money, Dave. I guess I forgot to mention that. The two men we've got left haven't been paid regularly in a year." A sudden huskiness caught her throat. "It's not much to hand over to you, I know, but I just couldn't do better."

"Never mind," Dave said quietly. "We've got the land and the water and the grass. Banks loan money, so we'll have cattle."

"The bank has loaned money, Dave," Mary said. "They won't loan us any more. A good slice of the paper is due in a few days, too." Her voice was suddenly bitter. "That's another present for you, Dave, from a loving sister."

"Stop it, Mary," Dave said softly. "I hate to hear you bitter like that."

"I know," Mary said contritely. "I'm sorry. You're the one that has the right to be bitter." She looked at him. "And you aren't and I'm glad, Dave. It would have spoiled you."

Dave wondered if he wasn't. Surely, the past eight years had been enough to make him bitter, as he looked back on it now. But all that was past. He was free now, had land of his own, and a future ahead of him. And he was with the two people he loved and respected above all others.

They fell into single file now as the road narrowed between two canyons and slanted steeply up-hill. He remembered the place. These were the small badlands that announced the deep gently sloping plateau—the Soledad Bench, it was called—on which the D Bar T, his spread, was located. Behind the Bench, mountains begin to lift into jagged, rocky foothills, then into peaks.

He recognized each landmark. Here was that arroyo across the road, bridged, now, where he had piled up the buckboard with those two fuzz-tails he had been breaking in and was foolish enough to try to drive to town. Right here by this pinnacle rock, just over the bridge, and a ways into the badlands was where he had found those five little wolves that he took home and nursed to Dinah, the ranch dog, until they got so wild and savage that he reluctantly killed them and collected the bounty.

All of it, every inch of it, barren land and fertile, held some such association. How could he be bitter coming back to this?

Mary was ahead of him and he spoke to her softly. "Don't worry, sis. The black days haven't come to the Turners yet. Not for—"

Crash!

A spouting mushroom of fire winked from the high rim-rock and Dave felt a searing slap on the top of his head that swept him off his horse into falling unconsciousness.

Rosy's gun streaked up in coughing savage lances of flame and a thin, wailing scream took up the echo of the shots.

Mary was kneeling by Dave as Rosy fought his horse quiet and leaped off.

"Get him?" he asked hoarsely.

"I can't tell," Mary answered in a tight frozen voice.

Rosy struck a match. In its light they could see a raw smear of red on the top of Dave's head, the blood oozing out from under the thick, black hair. Rosy put his ear to Dave's chest, listened a moment, then raised up.

"Pumpin' like a locomotive," he announced cheerfully.

"He's out cold and lost some skin. I reckon that's all."

Mary was sobbing softly and Rosy patted her shoulder tenderly, awkwardly.

"It's all right, Miss Mary." He gulped. "If they killed him, I reckon I'd just go hog wild."

Mary nodded. "So—so would I."

"There's a *hombre* up on the hill, I think," Rosy said. "I'm goin' to take a *pasear*. You tie this handkerchief around his head. He'll come to pretty quick."

Rosy left the road and scrambled up the steep canyon wall, sliding back occasionally as the soft rubble gave way with him. On the rim he saw a sprawled, prone figure, resting face downward on the stock of a shotgun. Rosy turned him over and struck a match. He was a thick-set man, dressed in soiled denim pants, greasy shirt and tattered vest. A wreck of a hat lay by him.

He was unshaven and just where the stubble of beard ceased to grow on his neck, a thin stream of blood trickled from a hole. He was dead already, his surly face shrunken and blue from the loss of blood. Rosy let the match die, waited until his eyes became accustomed to the dark again and peered off into the night, listening.

A scraping hoof gave him the clue he was waiting for and he walked over to a ground-haltered horse. He led the horse over to the rim-rock, loaded the man across the saddle and after walking south for a hundred yards found the arroyo which led down to the road.

Mary was waiting for him.

"He hasn't come to, yet," she said, fighting the tears back.

"He will. Don't worry. The best thing we can do is hurry on to the spread, where we can do somethin' for him."

"Yes," Mary said weakly. With an effort, she spoke again. "Who is it?"

"Dunno," Rosy said, then added quickly, "He ain't much to look at. Better wait and see if Dave knows him."

"I want to see," Mary said firmly.

Rosy reluctantly struck a match, wondering if the man would turn out to be some one she knew. Mary peered at the man and Rosy let the flame die quickly.

"Is it one of them nesters?" he asked.

"I've never seen him before."

Rosy's scowl gave way to a look of surprise.

"You know all them nesters?"

"Yes. This man is not one of them."

Rosy shrugged. "Reckon you can lead this horse? I'll put Dave up in front of me and lead his horse. How far we got to go?"

"Three miles."

Together they managed to hoist Dave to the saddle while Rosy mounted behind him, his left arm encircling Dave's body to hold it upright and rein the horse, his right holding the leading rein of Dave's horse. Mary led the dead man's pony and took the lead.

The Turner ranch lay on the sheltered side of a large draw with sloping grassy sides which served as a windbreak. Tall sycamores mushroomed up in the black night, hiding everything about the house but the two spacious and lighted windows. Rosy could make out a broad creek below the house and the barns and outbuildings to the rear against the hill.

No one greeted them as they dismounted. Rosy took Dave in his arms and followed Mary into the house. They entered a broad, low-ceiled room, a huge fireplace at one end, the dark floor brightened by Navajo rugs, its timbered ceiling glowing darkly with the fire's reflection. Rosy did not see the man seated in a deep chair before the fire as he laid Dave on a davenport next to the inner wall of the room.

"Well, Mary," the man drawled.

Rosy looked up. The speaker was young, perhaps thirty, with a dark, coolly appraising face. He was dressed in whipcord breeches and shiny boots, slouched comfortably on his backbone in the easy chair. He had just laid down a book and was stroking a carefully clipped black mustache, a look of amiable curiosity on his face.

"Oh, Ted," Mary said, a little catch of fear in her voice. "Some one shot Dave—!" She looked at Rosy and flushed a little. "Excuse me. Mr. Rand, my husband, Ted Winters."

Winters nodded lazily. "Welcome, Rand."

"Howdy," Rosy said. He looked curiously at Mary and she interpreted his look correctly.

"I wanted to surprise Dave," she said, flushing a little deeper.

Rosy nodded indifferently. "Better get some water."

"What happened to the favorite son?" Winters drawled.

He lounged out of his chair and came over beside Rosy, looking down at the unconscious figure on the davenport. Mary left for the kitchen.

"Some whippoorwill on the dry-gulch," Rosy said briefly.

"Where?"

"This side of the bridge. Forted up on top the ridge with a shotgun."

"The devil!" Winters exclaimed, frowning. "Who would want to do that?"

"I dunno. He's out there on a horse now. Take a look at him and see if you know him."

"You mean you got him?" Winters asked, a light of admiration and surprise creeping into his eyes.

Rosy nodded.

"Alive?" Winters asked.

"Dead," Rosy said dryly.

Mary returned with the basin containing warm water and a mild disinfectant. She kneeled by Dave and bathed the wound, her face white and drawn with strain.

"Ted, it was awful," she said in a low voice, not taking her eyes from Dave. "We were riding single file, just over the bridge put in last summer. The man must have had cat's eyes. He—"

"Rand told me," Winters interrupted. "I can't imagine any one who would want to kill Dave."

The disinfectant Mary had put in the water was biting into the raw flesh of Dave's wound and he groaned and writhed under the pain. His eyelids fluttered, then opened. He stared blankly around the room a moment, then his gaze fell on Mary. He smiled weakly.

"What happened? Somebody shot at me." His eyes traveled to Rosy questioningly.

"Some whippoorwill up in the rocks tried to blow your head off," Rosy said grinning.

Dave nodded weakly and shifted his eyes to Winters, who was still regarding him in silence.

"You the doc?" Dave asked him.

"No, Dave. This is Ted Winters, my husband," Mary said. "I wanted to keep it a secret and surprise you. I would have, for—" her voice trailed off as she searched Dave's face for a sign. Dave looked at her steadily.

"Well, sis, this is a surprise." He stretched his arm out to Winters and they shook hands, Dave smiling weakly. "You got the best girl I ever knew, Winters," he said simply.

"I know it," Winters replied. He put his arm around Mary's shoulder and she hugged him tightly, looking down at Dave.

Rosy was searching Dave's face, keenly, silently, wondering.

"How do you feel?" Mary asked.

"Good. I'll be up tomorrow. What was this all about?"

"He's out there dead—on a horse," Winters said. "Rand brought him home to stuff." He laughed easily, showing fine, even teeth.

"Who was he? Doesn't any one know him?"

"I'm going out and take a look," Winters said. "I'll put up your horses while I'm at it."

"Want some—" Rosy began, but Winters waved him away.

"No. I'll put our friend in the tool shed. You stay here, Rand." He left by the front door and Mary and Dave looked at each other.

"You little devil!" Dave said. "Why didn't you tell me?"

"I didn't want it all to come at once," Mary replied, laughing shyly. "Can you walk to bed? I think some sleep would do you good and we can talk it over in the morning."

Dave nodded. Leaning on Rosy's shoulder, he walked with dragging footsteps down the middle corridor of the one-story house. Mary opened a door to a bedroom, containing a broad white bed in one corner, a cot in the opposite corner, and a simple, unpainted chest of drawers.

"It's not been changed, Dave," Mary said.

She drew back the bedspread and shook the pillow. Dave

looked around the room with weary eyes, noting every familiar detail.

"Mr. Rand, you have the room next door—or you can sleep here on the cot. We're just across the hall, so don't think we won't hear him if anything happens in the night."

"Meanin' if I die," Dave teased her.

Mary laughed and kissed him, bid them both good night, and left the room. Dave looked around the room thoughtfully.

"A little different from a ten by six cell, eh? You'll like it here, Rosy."

Rosy sat on the cot, drew a Durham sack from his pocket and rolled a cigarette slowly, careful to keep his eyes from meeting Dave's.

"A little different," Dave echoed himself. He strolled to the bed and sat down.

Rosy lighted his cigarette slowly, then looked up at Dave.

"I'm hittin' the grit tomorrow, pardner," he announced calmly. Dave stifled the surprise in his eyes and looked long at Rosy.

"What's the matter?" he asked presently, quietly. "Is it what Mary said about our bein' broke?"

Rosy's eyes dropped evasively. "It ain't that. I reckon I ain't ready to settle down yet. I want to wear out a couple more saddles before I pick me a corral."

"And leave me here, stuck with a bunch of land-grabbin' nesters, a water-thievin' fool, a proddy sheriff, and a bush-whackin'?" Dave said.

Rosy flushed and his freckles seemed to fade under the sudden rush of blood to his face.

"You don't need me. I can't help. I'd be in the way."

"All right, you red-headed ranny," Dave said. "We'll go together. Tomorrow mornin'."

"And leave things this way for Mary?" Rosy asked, unbelievingly. "You wouldn't be that low-down ornery."

"If you go, I go," Dave said firmly.

Rosy regarded him a moment, rubbing his chin thoughtfully. "Look here. It's this way. I'm goin' because I don't hanker livin' off folks that ain't got enough to spare. I'd stay, Dave, and work, but my work would bring you in nothin' and you'd feel bad because you couldn't pay me wages."

"Part of that's true," Dave said. "But give us a chance. I can't get this spread runnin' again with no help. We still got everything we ever had and one day we'll have her where she was; ten men workin' plenty, not countin' the cook and blacksmith. How am I goin' to do it if you run out on me?"

"You can do it," Rosy insisted stubbornly.

"I can, but I won't. You go, I go," Dave said. "We planned this thing out together and then you run out on me. All right, I can run out on Mary."

"You jughead, you will not," Rosy growled. He crossed to Dave's bed and gently shoved him back into a lying position. "Stick up your foot and I'll pull them boots off. If you leaned over, the dang few brains you got would trickle out in a half-inch puddle through that hole in your head. Git some sleep. We're up by sun-up. You want a bandage on that head?"

"If it'll make you any happier to play nurse, go ahead," Dave prodded him.

"You go to hell. And you can pull off your own boots."

Rosy undressed slowly, thoughtfully. When he was ready to climb into bed in the cot he spoke to Dave.

"Just why do you reckon that jasper shot at you?"

No answer. He looked up, in the act of blowing out the light. Dave was asleep.

4
Saddle Bum's Salary

Dave and Rosy were up before sunrise the next morning. Save for his paleness, Dave seemed none the worse for the events of the night before. After building a fire in the big kitchen range, he and Rosy strolled out to look the place over. A feeling of depression came over them both when they had looked around.

The house was as it had always been and always would be, so long as any one was living in it. It was a stone affair with a low, sloping slate roof. It was planned roughly in the form of an I, the long living room being the base, the four bedrooms along the corridor the shank and the dining room and kitchen the top. The sycamores and cottonwoods, old and gnarled, spread their canopy high above it. From the front of the house the ground sloped gently to the willow-shaded creek a hundred yards distant.

The buildings were different. The board cook-shack was empty, its windows gray and filled with cobwebs. The adobe bunkhouse, a long straight building runneled with rains, the bricks showing in places where the mud plaster had cracked off in sheets, lay between the cook-shack and corrals.

The barn itself seemed falling to pieces, its door sagging, wisps of hay sticking out the weathered cracks like hair out of a battered sombrero. The corrals were awry, some of their bars down, their space clotted with manure.

"Looks like some one had just moved out," Dave growled.

"Lot of work ahead," Rosy conceded. They went over to the corrals and looked at the horses, perhaps a dozen in all. They were fat, but uncurried and shaggy, giving them a dispirited and crestfallen appearance.

"Which horse was Little Bo-Peep ridin'?" Dave asked.

"That black with a white stockin'. Let's see the brand."

They cut the horse out, and while Rosy stroked his nose, Dave looked for the brand.

"Naked as a baby," he announced. "That don't help much."

"That horse is five years old if he's a day," Rosy said. "Who's loco enough to let his horse go antigodlin' around without a brand? He must be rich."

"Or dumb."

"Want to see that jasper?" Rosy asked.

"Not till I've eaten," Dave said, making a wry face. "Besides, if sis don't know him I won't."

At that moment, Mary called them from the kitchen door. Inside, they found she had breakfast nearly ready. Dave looked at the round table in the kitchen and noticed five places.

"Who's comin' for breakfast, sis?" he asked, after Mary had inquired after his health.

"No one," Mary said brightly. "Those are for the hands."

Dave was silent a moment. "You cookin' for the hands?"

Both were well aware of the tradition that draws a line between a big ranch and a little one, a cow outfit and a farm, a cattleman and a homesteader. It dictated that the rancher's wife did not wait on, cook for, or serve the ranch hands.

"Of course," Mary said lightly. "We haven't had a cook for three years, Dave."

Dave nodded and was silent, prowling about the kitchen.

"Can I do anything?" Rosy asked uncomfortably.

Mary turned to him and laughed.

"You can, Mr. Rand. I haven't much wood and there's none split. Would you mind splitting enough to get through breakfast on?"

"Not Mr. Rand to you, ma'am," Rosy said. "I ain't ever been called anything but Rosy all my life. Sometimes I think I'll wake up some mornin' and find myself a girl." His grin was friendly.

"All right, Rosy. Then I'm Mary to you, and not ma'am. It makes me feel forty anyway. The wood is out at the end of the cook-shack. I think you'll find the axe there too."

Rosy dodged out the door, and Mary and Dave were alone.

Dave's face was clouded. Mary looked up at him and saw he was scowling, looking out the window.

"Rotten homecoming, isn't it?" she said in a low voice.

Dave nodded. "Seeing a ranch in this shape almost makes me want to howl." He looked at Mary and grinned, then shook his head. "You must have a couple of prime knotheads for hands, sis. Most people couldn't let a spread get in this shape if they tried."

Mary flushed. "They do most of their work all right. What they're told to do anyway."

"Then why is everything so rundown?" Dave asked gently. "Why there's stuff here that wouldn't take twenty minutes fixin' but nobody's done it. Why?"

Mary was bending over the stove and she did not look up. "It's Ted, Dave. He's been running the place for two years now, ever since old Link died. But he's no cattleman." She looked up and her face was flushed. "But I guess you've noticed that already."

"Sorry," Dave muttered.

"He's a mining man, Dave, not a rancher. He's pulled us through the best he knows how, and I guess he'd be the first to admit that he hasn't done a good job."

"Sure," Dave said. "Forget it."

He wished now that he hadn't mentioned it at all. He listened a moment.

"Where is he this mornin'? Around the place?"

Mary was still bending over the range. "He's in bed," she said quietly. "He's a city man and thinks we're barbarians to get up with the sun."

Dave wanted her to look at him, but she didn't. He laughed uneasily.

"Maybe we are," he conceded lightly. "Tell me about him, sis. Where'd you meet him and when did you marry him? All I know is that you've got a husband."

"Dad met him one day. He was an agent for a mine and he was scouting around looking over this country. Dad liked him and offered him a string of good horses because his own were

pretty poor. He used to come over quite a lot after that and—
well, we just liked each other and decided to get married."

"After Dad died?"

"Yes. A couple of months." She turned to Dave and he could
see the pain in her eyes. "Oh, Dave, it was awful. I was lone-
some and discouraged and—I don't know. It just seemed as if
Ted was something sent from heaven. He was so kind and sym-
pathetic and helpful."

Dave nodded, rolling a cigarette.

"I know. It was pretty tough. Dad dead and me in jail and
this spread on your hands to run alone." He paused, frowning.
"What about the place, sis? I'll have to go to Single Shot today
on business. Maybe I could talk to the bank."

Mary looked at him searchingly. "Do you think it's wise?
After last night?"

"Likely not," Dave said grimly, "but I don't always do wise
things. I'm goin' into town. Now what about the place, the
cattle and all?"

"There's hardly a corral count, the men tell me," Mary said.
"Ted never has been able to get the right tally, but it's low. And
there's the paper on the place."

"I'll go to the bank."

"You'll have to. Pearson is still there. He's been awfully good
to us. Maybe he'd give us a sixty- or ninety-day extension, but I
don't know what good that will do."

"Plenty," Dave said. "Time's what we need."

"But if nothing happens, Dave, what will we do? And what
can happen? We'll have to sell some land to pay off the paper
and get enough cattle to stock the range decently. And what if
Hammond takes his claim to court?"

"He can't win. It's foolish. We've got the papers to prove it."

"But it will cost us money to fight it, Dave."

"No, it won't," Dave said doggedly. "It'll never get that far.
All that jasper needs is to have some one talk salty with him.
He'll find out he can't run a sandy on us, then he'll shut up."

"There's always one thing we can do," Mary said speculatively. "We can sell out to him after he finds out he can't bluff

us, because it's the only water he can get. I got a letter from a man a while back—Crowell, I think his name was, asking me to put a price on the ranch. It was just after Hammond threatened to take the case to court, so I put two and two together and figured he was trying to buy the place—that Crowell was Hammond."

"What did you do?"

"Nothing. I didn't answer him. I got several more letters from him offering money for the place, but I ignored them all."

"Good girl," Dave said, grinning.

"But we could sell to him if we're up against it."

"We won't be," Dave said decisively. He looked at her. "I'd feel like a stray pup anywhere else and so would you. I'm glad you didn't bother to answer him."

"I hoped you'd say that," Mary said, smiling warmly. "I never, never would have sold my half unless I thought you wanted to. And I knew you didn't."

"We won't sell it," Dave said, determination in his voice. "Nobody'll get this place out from under us unless they want to lose some tail feathers doin' it. We've got everything here that it takes to make a ranch. Grass, water, land, buildings—everything but the cattle. And it'll last, Mary. It'll be here when both our kids are old men. That lake up there by Old Cartridge will always assure water on the place. As long as we don't overstock the range, we're safe."

Mary laughed. "Hardly a chance of our overstocking it now."

Dave laughed with her.

Rosy, loaded with wood, entered just then with two strangers whom Mary introduced as Sod Harmon and Lew Finnegan, the two remaining hands.

Harmon was a tall, bony man of an indeterminate age, with hair so white, skin so pale, that at first Dave thought he was seeing his first albino. All Dave noticed about Finnegan was his dirt and his shifty black eyes. He was small too, Dave noticed afterward, and of course unshaven.

They sat down at table, Mary taking the hotcakes out of the warming oven and setting them on the table.

"Where you ridin' today?" Dave asked Harmon pleasantly.

The blond man looked up and a twisted smile creased his face. "Ridin'?" he growled. "I'm goin' fishin'."

"Not today," Dave said carelessly. "You're cleanin' out that corral first, and rightin' those poles. After that, you can fix that barn door so it don't swing like a rusty beer sign. If I was you, I'd shift that hay in the loft this afternoon, then rustle some boards and patch that barn. After that, I'd get that hayin' machinery—"

"Wait a minute," Harmon said, laying down his fork. "If you was me, you said. Well, you ain't. When I git paid, I work." He turned to Mary. "More flapjacks," he ordered curtly.

"Please," Dave said softly, laying down his fork.

Harmon stared at him.

"I said, say please when you ask my sister for anything." His voice was thick in a drawl.

Harmon laughed silently and turned to Mary.

"I'm waitin' for those flapjacks, sister."

Dave was out of his chair in a leap. Grasping Harmon by the shirt-front he yanked him to his feet, turned him and drove his fist into the blond man's face, catapulting him over a chair and crashing him full length on the floor.

Finnegan stood up. "Whaddaya' think—"

Rosy's fist smashed his jaw and he sat down abruptly on the floor, his head meeting the stove with a resounding crack.

"What do we owe these saddle bums, Mary?" Dave asked in a strained, thick voice.

"Sixty dollars apiece, I think," Mary said.

Dave reached in his pocket and drew out some bills, counting them with trembling fingers. He threw them to Finnegan.

"Clear out of here in ten minutes, both of you. If I ever catch you on D Bar T land again, so help me, I'll pistol whip you both until your own mother'll be sick to look at you. Now get out!"

Finnegan half-carried, half-dragged Harmon out of the

kitchen and across to the bunkhouse. Rosy followed them out, watching while they got their few possessions, roped two scrawny horses from the corral, saddled them and rode off.

He leaned on the corral fence, watching them disappear down the dusty road toward Soledad.

"Maybe them black days of the Turners is only gray," he mused.

5
Sitting on Dynamite

Dave had gone behind the cook-shack out of sight, to strap the gruesome, tarpaulin-wrapped load on the white-stockinged black. Rosy saddled two horses and joined him.

"What's your guess?" Rosy asked.

"Dunno," Dave replied thoughtfully, regarding the wrapped figure. "No brand on his horse, no letters in his pockets, no clothes with a tag. I reckon he's one of those forked coyotes you'll find in any dive that would cut a throat for a square meal."

"Somebody paid him. Who?"

Dave shrugged. "Every one in the country knows I was comin' home."

"Reckon that *hombre* you cut down on the train would have put him up to it?"

"Couldn't," Dave replied. "He wouldn't have had time to get out there and wait for me."

"The sheriff?"

"Hell no. Not him. Not because he wouldn't like to, but he's too straight."

"Maybe," Rosy said laconically. "A man can hide a lot of cussedness under a tin star."

"No. It wasn't Hank Lowe," Dave said firmly.

They swung into the saddle and headed northeast up the slope behind the house. The trail which Dave had chosen was an old and familiar one, used since he could remember as the shortest way to Single Shot. It wound up and across the Soledad Bench to the notch between the base of Old Cartridge and Coahuila Butte, then dived angling down the steep mountainside to the dry stream bed in the valley and into Single Shot.

Rosy noticed the country had none of the sunbaked gauntness of the plains below. Instead of the canyons there were gently rolling, grass-covered swells with only an occasional rock outcrop. As the trail lifted, piñons gave way to Navajo pines and cedars. The country lay spread out behind them, a series of varied plateaus and mesas mottled with splotches of timber that stretched interminably into the blue haze of the semi-desert far below to the south.

He could see that the D Bar T had the pick of the range, the tall mountains behind it, the small badlands immediately in front of it, Coahuila Butte, in reality a low mountain to the east, and broad stretches of grassland to the west.

Soon it was noticeable to Rosy that the timber was thinning out and that rock outcrops were more numerous, and they seemed almost at the base of the towering peak of Old Cartridge.

"Up there"—Dave pointed ahead on the trail and a little to the left—"is that spring-fed lake. That's what waters our whole range. She winds through it, back and forth, and it runs water the year round."

Rosy turned in his saddle and looked back again at the country. It was a rancher's dream, he thought, as he pictured these vast grasslands permanently watered by a full creek.

"You can't help but have a ranch here," he said.

"But no cattle," Dave said. "I've got an idea. After I see the banker today I'll spill it to you. If it works, we'll have the range stocked in two years."

Through the notch, a level stretch perhaps a half mile in

width, they reined up on the rock rim and looked down into the valley stretching below them. It was a deep valley, perhaps a thousand feet below the rock rim, a dry ribbon of wash marking the bottom. The side of the valley they were on, formed by the slope of Old Cartridge and Coahuila Butte, was craggy and rough, rocky hog's-backs criss-crossing into a maze of black canyons; sudden outcrops of wind-eroded and, where there was a pocket of soil, wind-gnarled piñons clung tenaciously.

The other side of the valley was a marked contrast. It was heavily wooded, the contours of these lower mountains smoothed into gently flowing lines by centuries of rain on the soil.

They looked at the scene in silence.

"You mean you got a trail down this slope?" Rosy asked, doubt in his voice.

"Sort of," Dave said. He pointed over to the base of Old Cartridge. "There's the lake, up there, close to the rock rim. Over the rock rim just below it is a wash cut deep in the rock. We can follow that wash down to the valley floor. I reckon a goat couldn't make it without that."

Ten minutes of perilous descent and they were on the pebbly floor of the wash, which twisted and writhed down the mountainside, angling imperceptibly off the south between high walls.

An hour's ride brought them almost to the valley floor. Dave was ahead and as he rounded a sharp bend in the steep-walled arroyo, an exclamation escaped him and he reined up to wait for Rosy who was leading the horse with the corpse. Before him, the arroyo widened out like the mouth of a funnel, and square in its middle was a cluster of board buildings, tin-roofed, unpainted.

Rosy pulled up beside him and whistled in exclamation. "That jasper don't mind sittin' on dynamite, does he? He the one Mary told about?"

"Yeah. Hammond," Dave said. "The gent that thinks he owns the D Bar T lake." He looked the place over carefully, then pointed. "See how he's run ditches around the buildings, blasted 'em out of the rock? If it wasn't for them, he'd be buildin' new shacks after every shower. This wash goes hell-for-leather in a rain."

As they circled the buildings and picked up the road leading from them, they heard the hum of activity in the place. Across the front of the main building was painted in uncertain black letters: "Draw Three."

"He must have won that outfit in a poker game," Dave said.

Rosy looked at the buildings, at their precarious position in the middle of the very mouth of the arroyo down which tons of water would hurtle in a rain. He shook his head.

"He likely lost that land and had to take the mine," he said dryly. He looked at Dave. "You stoppin'?"

"Later," Dave said.

The mine road now, as they swung into it out of the wash, was rutted deep from ore wagons and followed the bank of the wide, dry stream bed heading for Single Shot and the railroad three miles away.

Rosy looked at Dave uncertainly, wondering what his plan was. As they came in sight of Single Shot he felt he had to speak.

"All right, Big Augur. How you goin' to talk to the sheriff without ropin' and hog-tyin' him? I got sort of a hunch he ain't goin' to be glad to see us."

"Ride in and see 'im," Dave said quietly. "Might's well get it over with. I'm goin' into Single Shot from now on, whenever I take the notion. If he aims to keep me out, he won't have to cut trail to find me. If he's just runnin' a sandy, then it'll do him good."

"One thing sure," Rosy said. "He'd be a damn sight proddier if we didn't bring this bushwhacker in to him."

The streets of the town were filled with the early morning hustle of a mining town. Buckboards at the hitchracks almost outnumbered the saddle-horses. No one paid any attention to the two horsemen leading a loaded black as they threaded their way down the street to the main corner.

The Free Throw saloon on the main corner a block up from

the station was doing a booming business in its two-story frame building, the front of which, on the main street, contained the bar and gambling tables. The back half contained the dance-hall, and a tinny refrain was issuing from it at this early hour.

The other three corners contained the bank, a tight one-story affair of brick across the street from the Free Throw; a hard-ware store which was also the post-office; and another saloon, the Mile High.

Behind the bank lay the single adobe building that housed the office of the sheriff. The courthouse, where the officers should have been, lay up the street.

Dave and Rosy turned by the bank and half-way down its length so as to be well out of view of a glance from the sheriff's window, they turned in to the hitch-rack. They left the body of the bushwhacker on his horse and covered the fifty steps to the sheriff's office, wondering if he had seen them.

Dave knocked firmly, paused for a sound of a voice and, hearing it, entered. In the far corner, his back trustingly to the door, sat the sheriff, laboring at something in the depths of his rolltop desk. He did not even turn.

"Take a chair," he said, over his shoulder.

Rosy closed the door and took the chair nearest the sheriff. Dave stood in the middle of the floor, his thumbs hooked negligently in his belt. His dark face was still, his black eyes wary. His Colt swung loosely at his hips. Rosy looked around the room swiftly. A deal table, a gun-rack, some fly-specked reward posters on the smeared white-washed wall was all there was to see.

"Got a package for you, Hank," Dave said.

At the sound of the voice, the sheriff swiveled his chair, his little eyes sweeping the room, noting the positions of the two men before him, then settling blankly on Dave's face. His gaze stayed there a long time.

"Have you ever been to a zoo?" he asked Dave mildly.

Dave's forehead wrinkled a little. "No."

"I thought so," the sheriff said slowly. "They got signs around the cages sayin' 'Please don't poke the animals with umbrellas.' " He paused, his eyes never leaving Dave's face. "No, that ain't right. It don't say please at all. It says: 'It is forbidden.' "

"Well?" Dave asked.

"If you ain't got holes in your head, you'll take a tip," the sheriff said meaningly. "When I say stay out of this town, I mean it."

Rosy hadn't seen him move since he turned, yet his hands were resting placidly, close to his guns, which were both clear of the chair arms.

"I say I got a package for you out there," Dave said calmly, ignoring the sheriff's remarks.

"I'm talkin' to you," the sheriff said flatly, his monotone rising a pitch higher and a shade thicker. "You're not talkin' to me."

Dave's face was dark. "I heard you. I'm still tellin' you I—"

Rosy saw it first. Maybe it was the flicker of the red-rimmed eyes or the throbbing of the large vein in the sheriff's temple. Rosy leaped out of his chair, throwing his body across the fat belly of the sheriff, pinning his hands down tight against his gun butts.

"You big tub of guts," Rosy said savagely, "I oughta bend a gun barrel over your thick skull. We ain't makin' fight talk and we ain't takin' any either. There's a dead man out there on a horse. Pull your thinkin' pants on and talk sense."

The sheriff was breathing heavily. "Lemme up."

"Get his guns, Dave," Rosy said. Dave slipped the guns out from beneath the fat and pudgy hands and laid them on the desk.

Rosy stood up cautiously, a shadow of a grin on his face. "If you're goin' to say it ain't wise to talk sass to a sheriff, you can save your breath."

6
Dead Man's Clue

"You say you got a dead man out there?" the sheriff asked.

"If you wasn't so knot-headed, you'd have known that two minutes ago," Rosy said. "You reckon we're goin' to camp at the edge of town and whistle for you?"

"Show me the body," the sheriff said.

He picked his guns off the desk and leathered them. It was a gesture of peace.

The dead man was brought in and taken into a back room of the office, and laid on a cot. Sheriff Lowe listened to the story of the bushwhacking, then looked at the man.

"Nothin' in the pockets and no brand on the horse, huh?" he growled.

"No. You seen him around town?" Dave asked.

When the sheriff replied, it was as if the incidents of a few minutes ago had not occurred. "Nary once. I don't aim to fergit birds like that, but you can't always be sure. People's driftin' in and out all the time since this gold's been found. Might be he's been votin' here for three years and I'd never know it, but I don't think so."

"Ever see the horse?"

The sheriff shook his head.

Rosy stood up. "Well, sheriff, we got business. If you think of any more questions, you'll run into us around town."

All Rosy's rancor had gone, but there was a quiet and assertive challenge underlying his statement that the sheriff did not miss. He smiled a slow, crinkling smile that made his fat face look amiable and pleasant.

"I reckon I will," he said. "If you could be on eight corners at once where I was passin', I reckon you would. Go ahead.

Seems to me you'll do any dang thing you please anyway. So long's you don't let any blood doin' it, help yourself."

Outside, on the street again, Rosy took a deep breath and looked at Dave. "Did you ever get that crawlin' feelin' sittin' around a camp-fire alone at night when you felt like some one was drawin' a bead with a Winchester on your left ear? There's just nothin' you can do about it except wait. But instead of that, you send a couple of quick shots into the brush and find you've scared out a nosey jackrabbit. That's the way that fat sheriff hits me. I reckon I just had to jump him."

"I'm glad you did," Dave said. "It was either that or a gunfight. I reckon he never took such a combin'-out in his life and I'm danged sure he never will again."

"I hope not. Not from me, anyway. I was never so danged scared in my life," Rosy admitted honestly.

They stopped at the corner.

"Take a look around," Dave said. "I'm goin' to parley with old Pearson in the bank here. Drop a few questions about this bushwhacker. Maybe you'll get an idea."

Dave went into the bank and Rosy sauntered across the street to the Free Throw, and shouldered through the doors. After the hot dusty glare of the street, the saloon was cool and dark. The bar lay to the right, the gambling tables to the left, the door to the dance hall in the rear. He bought a drink at the mahogany bar, scrutinizing mildly the soaped legends on the mirror, the dead-faced bartenders, and the idlers at the bar.

A hum of conversation was loud and steady through a slowly rising fog of tobacco smoke. Only one of the faro tables was playing, and that lackadaisically, Rosy judged, from the thin crowd around it. The gamblers, mostly men from the gold mines, would be in after work. He crossed the big, box-like room to the faro table against the wall and mingled with the watchers.

Martin Quinn was at the box, his movements lazy, almost indifferent. In one of his occasional glances at the crowd, he caught sight of Rosy, called to another gambler who was idling

at a beer to take his place and came out from behind the table
to join Rosy.

"Howdy, Rand. How's things?" Quinn greeted him, extending his hand.

"Piddlin'. How's yourself?"

"Poco-poco," Quinn answered. "Let's have a drink. That's
the only way I keep awake."

They picked an uncrowded spot at the back end of the bar,
Rosy ordering Bourbon, Quinn beer.

"Did I see a question breakin' out in your eyes when you
looked at me?" Quinn asked, after they had received their
drinks.

"You did," Rosy said.

Quinn listened carefully while Rosy told him of the events
which had brought them in to Single Shot.

"He gets off the train and somebody slams him?" he said
softly to Rosy. "Why?"

"Dunno. I don't suppose he's got more'n two hundred dollars to his name. He's got a good ranch, a plenty good spread,
but she's spavined. Land mortgaged, no stock, buildin's poor.
Other hand, good grass, plenty water and a big range. Now you
tell me."

Quinn shrugged. "Describe this bushwhacker again."

"Sandy hair, cut with a drawknife about three years ago, I'd
say; three weeks' beard; blue eyes, four inches shorter'n me;
square face; missin' a few teeth. He was wearin' waist overalls,
dirty blue flannel shirt, black vest. Black Stetson."

"Cut it finer," Quinn said.

Rosy laughed.

"Hell, I can't. I'll pick six men in this room right now that
look like him—and yet they don't. Only one thing different,
maybe not so different either. Carried matches in his hatband
and wore his hat flat-crowned. He had ten fingers, ten toes and
not a scar."

"Any clay on his clothes?" Quinn asked.

Rosy looked at him keenly. "Now you mention it, there was.
Not much though."

"Look at the books out at the Draw Three then," Quinn said.

"Draw Three?" Rosy asked, his voice quiet, his eyes suddenly stilled.

"Sure. They're working in clay out there. There's men in here from a whole bunch of mines to the south and some to the east, and prospectors too, but you can tell a Draw Three man every time if he hasn't changed work clothes. They're covered with clay to their ears."

"Wonder if the sheriff savvies that?" Rosy inquired mildly.

"He might. If he didn't want you to know though, he'd sure make out like he didn't," Quinn said. He smiled. "Some people will tell you that old-timer is dumb. But I've found out that whatever gets by him has got to fight shy of a long rope. Twenty bucks will get you forty, he's got a note out to the Draw Three now checking up on that."

"I believe you," Rosy said, suddenly smiling. He finished his drink. "Have another?"

"No, thanks. I'm due back at the box. Let me know what you find out."

"I'll do that. Much obliged."

Rosy strode out the door, shouldering them aside roughly. So this bushwhacker might be a Draw Three man. Hammond —the lake. It was all pretty plain, too damned plain. He thought of picking Dave up at the bank, then decided he could see the sheriff alone just as well.

When he walked into the sheriff's office the fat man was sitting in the same chair, bent over the same papers.

Rosy slammed the door like a gun shot, and the sheriff wheeled like a cat, his hands at his gun butts.

"Watch it," he growled, "I'm a nervous man."

"I got a tip on that bushwhacker," Rosy said, ignoring the sheriff's words. "He had clay on his clothes, didn't he?"

"Yes," the sheriff said, his eyes small and shrewd, his tone doubtful.

"The Draw Three is workin' in clay, ain't they?" Rosy said. "How about askin' Hammond about that whippoorwill?"

"I was expectin' that," the sheriff said calmly. "I got a man on the way out there now to check up."

Rosy built a smoke carefully, looking at the sheriff. "That give you any ideas?" he asked slowly.

"You think Hammond figgered it might be a little easier to do business with Mary Winters if Dave was out of the way, is that it?" the sheriff asked.

"That's damn near it," Rosy said grimly. "When'll this messenger you sent out be back?"

"In an hour."

Rosy turned and strode to the door, his cigarette unlit.

"Just a minute," the sheriff said. Rosy turned. The sheriff picked a paper up, laid it down, searching for words.

"If I was you—" he began.

"If you was me," Rosy cut in, "you'd just wait and let the law take care of this, wouldn't you? Well, you ain't me. If Hammond thinks there ain't a man out at the D Bar T to argue this out, with guns, fists or words, he's loco. I've heard of the law runnin' hawg-wild in some cow-towns and when it does, it's a pretty good idea to not to leave it to the law."

"Don't you reckon the jasper might have been some one Dave knowed in prison and that had a grudge agin' him?" the sheriff asked gently.

"I know he isn't," Rosy said flatly. "That's the kind of excuse these small town laws start lookin' for."

The sheriff's eyes narrowed a little, but he did not move.

"How do you know it ain't?" he said.

"Because I was Turner's cell-mate."

The sheriff blinked. *"You* was?"

"Uh-huh."

"What for?"

"I run afoul a tough-talkin' law," Rosy said. He turned and started for the door.

"Wait," the sheriff said. He hoisted his bulk out of the chair. "I'm comin' with you."

Rosy did not talk as they walked together down to the corner and turned into the bank. Inside, he saw a partitioned-off room at the front of the bank, a frosted glass door marked "Private" opening on to it behind the wire wicket which ran the whole length of the bank.

Dave soon came out with Pearson and they walked over to Rosy. The sheriff hung back, as if he were not with Rosy.

"Mr. Pearson, this is Rosy Rand, the D Bar T's new foreman."

Rosy slid a surprised glance at Dave, then looked at Pearson. The immaculate clothes of the banker covered a spare, thin body, and in shaking hands Rosy noticed the banker's hands were thin, almost boneless, and a dead white. Sparse graying hair covered an intellectual head, the eyes were sharp, probing, black and deepset. Rosy guessed at once he was a New Englander and the clipped speech of the banker soon verified it.

"Rand," he said, bowing a little stiffly. "A pleasure." He regarded the two younger men with warmth. "So you're the young man who prevented the train robbery last night?" he asked Rosy.

Rosy flushed uncomfortably.

"I reckon I just walked into it," he drawled. "I couldn't very well back out without shootin'."

Pearson nodded agreeably.

"Well, I had the payroll money for three mines coming in on that train. Of course, they were insured, but then,"—he shrugged and smiled meagerly—"it saved a very costly delay. As soon as I heard about it this morning, I wrote the insurance company. I think there will be a reward for you, young man."

Rosy started to protest, but Pearson held up his hand.

"I know. But insurance companies like to reward men just as much for the prevention of the crime as for its cure." He laughed thinly at his own joke. Turning to Dave again, he said: "Well, Davy. Things may brighten up. At any rate, I wish you both luck. Come in and see me whenever you're in town."

Pearson turned and left them and before Rosy could speak, the sheriff was beside him.

"That bushwhacker likely come from the Draw Three," Rosy told Dave bluntly.

"Maybe," the sheriff said.

Dave looked at Rosy. The sheriff saw the jaw muscles in Dave's face bulge a little.

"From the Draw Three," Dave said quietly.

"Maybe," the sheriff repeated.

"The sheriff thought so enough to send a man out to ask," Rosy said. "The clay on his clothes gave him away. The Draw Three is the only mine working now in clay."

"So that cheap—" Dave began, then clipped off his speech, turned on his heel and strode to the door.

"Where you goin'?" the sheriff asked.

"Get a horse if you're comin'," Rosy told him.

The sheriff had a horse at the hitchrack and they mounted and headed out for the Draw Three, all of them sober and quiet.

"Seems to me you're doin' a lot of guessin'," the sheriff said, when they had gone a mile.

Dave looked at him bleakly.

"And it seems to me you got a damn thick skull if you can't see through that. Hammond is the only jasper in this country that would want to see me dead. The man he sends to do it for him gives it away that he's been workin' in Hammond's mine. I wouldn't call that exactly guessin'," Dave finished bluntly.

"All I got to say is make sure of it before you do anything," the sheriff said mildly. "And when you start, you can count me on Hammond's side."

"Suits me," Dave said bluntly. "I thought that's where you'd be on any deal I figured in. On the other side."

"You don't think Hammond done it?" Rosy said to the sheriff.

"No."

Rosy nodded briefly and they fell silent again. As they were in sight of the mine, a rider swung into the road and headed for them. When he was even with them, he reined up, and the sheriff spoke.

"Well?"

"Name of Freeman. Fired three weeks ago. Hammond could tell by that scar you found under his chin."

Dave looked at Rosy and they both looked at the sheriff, who was sucking his teeth complacently.

"Better come along," he said to the rider, obviously a deputy. Then he turned to Dave. "Go on. We might's well get this over with."

"Got any more John Laws you can scrape up to throw down on us in there?" Rosy asked tauntingly.

The sheriff turned to the deputy.

"You go back to the office," he told the man.

The deputy, puzzled, waited a moment until the sheriff repeated his order, then he turned and started slowly back to town.

"I never needed a gang yet to keep me on my feet," the sheriff said. "I ain't aimin' to now."

Silently, they rode up to the mine and dismounted. The main building was tall and angular, one corner of it containing a door and two windows. The sheriff unloosed his guns, and took the lead, Dave and Rosy following.

The door was open and the sheriff strode into the office without knocking. It was a long affair, with a wide desk at the far end, at which Hammond was seated, bent over a ledger. He looked up at their entrance and rose.

Dave was a little taken aback by Hammond, as was Rosy. The mining man was tall and grizzled, with kindly blue eyes. He had a mane of almost white hair, and a full mustache to match it. His face was seamed, weather-burned, his eyes deepsocketed and widely spaced under bushy white brows. He was dressed in a baggy and unpressed suit of black, and his movements were slow, but certain.

He shook hands with the sheriff and his voice rumbled in this small room. Then he turned to Dave and Rosy and eyed them quizzically.

"These gents have got some questions to ask," the sheriff said, and thereupon introduced them.

They shook hands, the older man warmly, the two younger

perfunctorily and without speech. Hammond bid them be seated, but Dave stood up.

"You don't know me, Hammond, I reckon," he began. "Leastways, you didn't seem to recognize the name. I'm Dave Turner, D Bar T."

Hammond nodded quietly, his gaze searching, his face a little stern now. Rosy noted idly that Hammond's ivory-handled guns jutted up conveniently close to his hands which were resting on his thighs.

"Some whippoorwill took a crack at me with a greener last night," Dave said slowly. "Rand killed him. The deputy we met on the road just said he used to work for you. Is that right?"

Hammond's eyes were blue, cold marbles as he stroked his right leg with a big, rough hand.

"That's right," he said quietly. "What about it?"

"That's what I'm wonderin'," Dave said, just as quietly.

Hammond leaned forward a little.

"Yes, he used to work here. He was canned because he tried to run a high-gradin' dicker with my forearm, Shed Martin. What about it?"

"And you want the D Bar T water," Dave said slowly. "You tried to bully my sister into givin' it up and when she wouldn't you threatened to take her to court when you know damned well it's our water and has been for forty years. I'd like to hear you do a little talkin'."

The sheriff spoke up quietly. He had moved off his chair noiselessly and now stood in a corner, his six-guns resting steadily in his palms. "And without any leather-slappin'," he said. He looked at Rosy. "That goes for you too, red-head. You've tried to put a saddle on me too many times today."

Rosy settled back a little in his chair, flushing. He had been caught flat-footed. But Dave and Hammond glared at each other, and Hammond slowly rose in his seat.

"Turner," he began, hoarse with suppressed passion. "I've killed men for less than that. And damned sudden."

"Easy," the sheriff purred.

Hammond glared at him blankly, his hands clenching and unclenching, then he swung his gaze back to Dave, who was standing with legs spread a little, thumbs hooked in his belt.

"I bought that water," Hammond said slowly, "paid for it in hard cash. I need it to mine with and I'm goin' to take it. The map shows it's on the section I bought, and by Harry Hell I'll use every drop of it if I have to drink it!"

"And I say you won't use a drop of it if I have to build a raft and live on the lake to see that you don't," Dave said.

"Don't make a move," the sheriff said softly.

"We've got the papers for that land," Dave said. "There's a hundred and sixty acres taken off a section on our west line and tacked on our east line to include that lake. It's in writin'. Come up and take a look for yourself some time."

Hammond's face had gone from a dead white to a deep red of flushed blood. Rosy watched his every move with a tense readiness.

"That ain't all you can do," Dave said. "You can go into Phoenix and look in the Land Office files of the year 1893. If they've got 'em back that long, you'll see for yourself. Whoever sold you that land was runnin' a sandy on you, from the ground up. And if you think you can take it with a bunch of killers—"

Hammond, in his rage, forgot he had guns. He lunged at Dave's throat as Dave leaped to meet him, his face contorted with fury. As soon as the sheriff saw that Rosy was trying to part them, he holstered his guns and stepped in. It was a full minute before Dave and Hammond were separated, the sheriff pushing his grunting bulk against Hammond and forcing him against the desk. Rosy held Dave's arms. Hammond's face was almost purple as he struggled with the sheriff. Then he gave in, but his eyes were murderous.

"Turner, I'll kill you like a damned coyote the next time I see you. That's a warnin'. Pack your guns loose and don't talk the next time we meet!"

"If I don't hunt you down first, Hammond," Dave rasped,

his voice hoarse with fury. "Next time, I might have a fightin' chance if I kill a couple more of your whippoorwills off."

Hammond lunged forward with a furious string of oaths, only to be held by the sheriff. Dave struggled with Rosy.

"Get him out!" the sheriff ordered.

Dave realized how futile the scene was and he ceased struggling. Rosy loosed his hold.

"Remember," he said quietly to Hammond. And he turned and walked out, Rosy behind him.

7
Nester Negotiations

They left the trail at the notch an hour after noon, heading more west than the trail would have taken them. Rosy had not spoken since they mounted at the Draw Three. Dave's face had been dark with fury, but he had ridden off his anger.

Now he turned to Rosy and smiled, a little sheepishly. "I reckon I lost my temper," he said.

"Plumb," Rosy said briefly. "I figgered you'd be sorry if you done anything to the old man. After all, we didn't have no proof. All he had comin' was a warnin' and I reckon he got that."

"It took me a long time to see that," Dave said slowly. "We haven't proof that he paid the man. All we can do is guess." He looked at Rosy again and grinned. "He didn't take to the idea much, did he?"

"He took to it so danged little that I'm wonderin' if we ain't shoutin' down the wrong barrel."

"Mebbe," Dave said. "You can look at him gettin' on the prod from two ways. He might not have done it and was mad because I said he did, or he might have done it and was mad because he got called."

"Whatever he thinks," Rosy said grimly, "he ain't goin' to buy you a drink the next time he sees you."

"Nor me him," Dave said briefly. He rode on in scowling silence before he spoke again. "What beats me, Rosy, is how Hammond knew I was comin' home. How'd he know I'd get off the train at Soledad instead of at Single Shot?"

"I been wonderin' when you'd think of that," Rosy said slowly. "When the sheriff said on the way out to the Draw Three that he never thought Hammond done it, I got to thinkin' maybe he was right. How would Hammond know you'd be passin' there in that draw at that time of night? How'd he know about it?" He crooked a leg over the saddlehorn and looked at Dave.

"This is a hell of a time to be tellin' me," Dave growled. "After I've riled Hammond."

"You wouldn't have stopped for anything I said," Rosy said with a grin. "You had to get it off your chest. Besides, I ain't sure who's right."

"Well, there was Mary, Ted, probably Harmon and Finnegan and whoever they told, and Sheriff Lowe and whoever he told, that knew I was goin' to get kicked out of Single Shot and would be in Soledad," Dave said.

"And the sheriff don't run off at the mouth," Rosy answered, looking at Dave.

"Then how'd Hammond know?"

"You tell me," Rosy said.

"Well, Harmon or Finnegan could have picked it up around Ted or Mary and then went to town and got a couple of drinks under their belts and spilled it."

"They could," Rosy admitted. "So maybe it wasn't Hammond at all. Maybe it was some one that wanted it to look like Hammond done it. Say, them nesters."

"I'm hopin' it isn't them," Dave said seriously.

"Why? You got to kick 'em off anyway."

"I'm hopin' I don't even have to do that," Dave said. He

turned to Rosy and looked at him for a long moment. "Who do you think was behind it?"

"Everything points to Hammond," Rosy said. "And I hate to say it, because he don't look like that kind. But even without seein' those nesters, I'd say it was him. He's got more at stake than them farmers."

"I hope so," Dave said. "I'm hopin' those nesters are reasonable people."

Rosy stared at him. "Why?"

Dave drew a long breath and cuffed his hat off his forehead. "Here's the scheme. I thought of it last night, but didn't say anything until I'd seen Pearson. He gave me a ninety-day extension on the paper he's holding against the spread."

"Well?"

"Those nesters are squatted in good black land," Dave continued. "They're probably pretty good farmers. All right. I can get a crew of Mex's to ditch water down to them from the creek. It only runs about a mile from that bottomland, but it's shut off by a low hill." He looked at Rosy. "Let those nesters raise alfalfa on shares with plenty of water."

"You turnin' farmer?" Rosy asked slowly.

"No. But look. There's a bunch of mines around here, besides these two towns. With water we could get three crops of alfalfa in the summer. Contract some of it, hold the rest and get skyhigh prices for it later. In ninety days, I'll have enough from that to clean off the paper and start in stockin' the place."

"Sounds good," Rosy said, "providin' you can convince the nesters."

"That's where I'm headed for now," Dave said. "You wait and see."

A two hours' ride brought them to the lip of a grassy hill and they reined up. Before them a broad basin stretched, sandstone cliffs forming the south and west rim where the badlands began. At the bottom of the basin lay orderly checkerboards of fields, now fallow, waiting for the spring plowing.

Dave took the scene in at a glance, letting his eyes roam to the south cliff. There, small in the distance, at the base of the cliff, lay a cluster of buildings.

"Mary never said they had a town here," he said. His eyes narrowed a little and he frowned. By the looks of things, it was time somebody put a stop to their land-grabbing.

They rode point to the cabins, skirting the fields a little. There were six houses that Dave could see, log shacks. Sheds and pole corrals at the rear abutted squarely to the cliff. As they approached the first shack, Dave saw a man step out the door. He noted passively that the man was so tall he had to stoop to get through the door. He was unshaven, hatless, wearing dirty bib overalls and a flannel shirt.

They reined up before him and Dave let his eyes wander casually around the place before he brought them to bear on the nester.

"Howdy," he said amiably.

The nester leaned against the door-jamb of the house, regarding him hostilely with squinting, narrow eyes. He spat noisily.

"Lookin' for some one?" he growled, ignoring the greetings.

"Six of you," Dave said laconically.

"I'll do," the nester retorted.

He turned to spit and when he looked up again he was staring into the barrel of a steadily held Colt in Dave's hand.

"Close that door," Dave said softly. "You got a gun there just inside the door, so move slow."

The man did not move, did not take his eyes from Dave's face.

"I said 'move,' " Dave said thickly.

The nester continued to stare insolently at him, his hands in his hip pockets.

Dave's gun exploded, bucked up in his hand, and a chip of wood behind the nester's head splintered off.

Dave saw the nester's face set a little as he leaped away from the door. At first slowly, then suddenly, he reached in and got the rawhide latchstring and swung the door shut.

"Now step out here," Dave said. He leathered his gun and the nester stepped close to his horse.

Dave folded his arms across his chest and leaned on the saddle horn.

"I'm Dave Turner," he announced.

"Yeah."

"How would you like to hitch up a team and load your wagon and clear off my land?" he asked softly.

The nester's eyes shifted from Dave to Rosy and back to Dave. With the quickness of a cat, the nester drove his fist into the nose of Dave's horse. The horse jerked his head high, reared, and Dave slid out of the saddle. The nester turned and ran toward the house. He had a head start but he was heavy. Dave tripped him and the nester crashed into the door. The latch held and his head bumped resoundingly against the pine planking.

Dave stood a little ways off from him, unbuckling his cartridge belt and holsters, letting them fall to the ground.

"Get up and take a beatin'," Dave said softly, kicking the guns out of reach.

The nester looked at Rosy, who was sitting placidly, a leg crooked around his saddle-horn, smoking, watching.

The nester rose and faced Dave evilly, his arms hanging gorilla-like at his sides. Suddenly, he rushed in, head down. Dave stepped aside and straightened him up with a looping left to the mouth. The nester shook his head, wheeled, charged again, his chin couched in his great bull neck. Dave let him walk into a straight right arm three times, then avoiding a low kick and flailing arms, he sank a body swing into the nester's stomach, doubling the heavier man up. Dave crashed a left full into his face, then hooked over a vicious slug to the ear that stretched the nester heavily on the packed dirt around the doorstep.

Dave stood over him, breathing heavily. The nester groaned, raised himself on an elbow, looking at Dave.

"If you want any more, stand up," Dave said.

The nester shook his head dizzily and got to his feet.

"Well?" Dave asked.

"Not me. That's enough."

"Look what I got in the round-up," Rosy's voice said from the corner of the house.

Dave turned and saw four men standing sullenly before Rosy who had dismounted and made the rounds of the other shacks while Dave was fighting.

"You *hombres* want to curl your tail too?" Dave asked them. He got only sullen stares in reply.

"Get in the house," Dave said. "I got some turkey to talk."

The beaten nester threw open the door and Dave entered, picking up the rifle that leaned against the wall just inside the door. He stood it behind the door. The nester was evidently a bachelor, for his house consisted of one large room, a double-decked bunk at one end, a stove and table at the other. Four home-made chairs and a shelf comprised the rest of the furniture.

"Sit down," Dave ordered, standing in the middle of the room.

When they were seated he rolled a cigarette casually while Rosy slouched against the door.

"I reckon you know why I'm here," Dave said, looking them over.

They nodded.

"I can run you off this land right now and burn your shacks. I reckon you know that."

"Sure," one of the nesters, a small wiry man in middle age, replied.

"I could shoot your horses and smash up what machinery you got, and you couldn't do much about it, could you?"

They looked at each other.

"I reckon not," the same man replied.

"You been squattin' on this land how long?" Dave asked.

"Three years or so," the big man replied. He was holding a bloody and soiled handkerchief to his face.

"All right," Dave answered. "I got a proposition to make. You can take it or leave it. You five *hombres* can farm on a sixty-forty split here on an alfalfa crop. Startin' tomorrow, you can break up all the land you can. I'll get a crew of Mex's to blast an *acequia* through that low hill at the bend and put in lateral ditches. In a week and a half you can be ready to put in the crop if the weather's right. With plenty of water, we'll get three crops this summer and a good market for the hay with all the horses there are in these two towns and the mines. Suit yourself. Stick here and take a forty percent share and work like hell, or clear out—way out."

"You mean you're puttin' water down here?" the middle-aged man asked incredulously. "Ditchin' it?"

"That's it."

The nester gave a brief glance at his companions. "Hell. I dunno about the rest of 'em, but I'll stick and glad of it. Damn glad of it. My son-in-law—he owns the place on the other side of me—will too. He ain't here, but I'll swear he will."

"I'll stay," the big nester said. "Hell, that'll be more money than I've made in three years since I been here."

"Me too," the third said.

"Same here," the other two joined in.

"Here's another thing," Dave said. "We been missin' cattle, my sister says." He paused and looked each nester in the eye. "If what she says is true, you'd better get the runnin' iron out for those *oreanoed* calves. There won't be any questions asked —unless the tally's way short of what she says it should be. I'll give you range now, so long as our tally is so low. When we get the range stocked, you'll have to see me or move your stuff out."

The nesters nodded uncomfortably.

"If things go right," Dave continued, "there's no reason why this arrangement can't go on. It's up to you all. You've got more good bottom land here than you can ever farm. You've got water—or will have it. I'll have the seed ordered in Single Shot and delivered to Soledad and you can haul it up from there some time next week."

"I don't feel right about this," the middle-aged nester said. "I never have. I've usually paid for what I took, but this here spread had so danged much land—good farmin' land too—that they wasn't usin' that I reckon I hated to see it go to waste. But from now on, Turner, I'm payin' my debts. You'll get nothing from me but work. My name's Rourke."

"All right," Dave said, grinning. "Let it ride that way, Rourke. If there's anything you need, and I can give it to you, come up to the house."

As they rode away in the dusk, they saw the women and children standing in the doorways of the shacks watching their departure.

"I wonder what Hammond is goin' to say when he hears about this?" Rosy said.

Dave laughed. "I reckon he can't say much more than he has already."

8
Thunder over Old Cartridge

By lantern light—for it was past ten when they reached the ranch—Rosy rubbed down the horses, grained them and was forking some hay when he heard some one let down the corral bars and lead in a horse.

The stable door swung open and Winters stood in the doorway, his dark face scowling against the light.

"Oh, it's you," he said amiably, when he saw Rosy. "Mind forking down some hay for my horse?"

"Sure," Rosy answered.

Winters led the horse in, a big bay with a Roman nose, still breathing heavily, his sides wet with sweat. Rosy was about to speak, but held his tongue. If the *hombre* didn't know enough to walk a horse after lathering him, then let him lose a couple of horses in the process of finding out. Maybe it was lucky Dave was in the house. He would have spoken, maybe lost his temper.

The hay forked down, Rosy sat on the feed box and stroked the ear of the ugly sorrel Dave had been riding. He watched Winters tend his horse. His nostrils were drawn a little at the ammoniac stench of the barn and Rosy guessed that he didn't like it and never would.

"Look over the range today?" Winters asked.

"Took that jasper into town on his horse," Rosy answered.

"What did you find out?"

"Name of Freeman. Used to work for Hammond."

Winters leaned against the bay's shoulder, frowning a little. "Freeman? I don't remember the name. Did you see—that is—was—"

"Sure. We saw the sheriff," Rosy said casually. "He didn't say much."

"And you say this man used to work for Hammond?" Winters said, eyeing Rosy shrewdly.

"That's it."

Winters snorted, then smiled knowingly. "I don't suppose Dave has told you what Hammond's trying to do about the lake up here."

"He told me," Rosy said. "We saw Hammond too."

"What did he say?"

"He's shootin' on sight at next meeting'," Rosy said dryly.

Winter's mouth gaped a little. "Well, I'm damned! What's Dave going to do?"

"He'll do the same."

"Well, I'm damned!" Winters repeated. He whistled an exclamation and looked pleased. Rosy watched him, wondering why.

"I wouldn't tell Mrs. Winters if I was you," Rosy said. "She might worry."

"No. Of course not," Winters said. "Not a woman's business anyway. Well, I'm damned!"

As if to punctuate his speech a dim roll of thunder came to their ears. The first tentative slaps of rain, dull and widely spaced, echoed hollowly on the barn roof and Rosy went to the stable door to make sure there were no saddles on the corral bars.

Winters followed him into the corral and stopped, hands on hips, looking at the sky.

"Glad I'm finished with that hole," he said. "It'll have two feet of water in it."

"Prospectin'?" Rosy asked.

"Yes, I putter around some. I got some color up in those canyons to the west of that rock slide on Old Cartridge. May not be much, but it keeps me on my toes in case I want to get back in the minin' game."

"Sure," Rosy agreed. He let down a bar and stepped through, holding it up for Winters.

"I got so interested there this afternoon I worked till way after dark by lantern light. You'd never guess, but—"

"We better highball it," Rosy cut in. "We're goin' to get wet."

In the house, Dave was talking with Mary. She smiled at Rosy, gave her husband a fleeting kiss, and set the long delayed supper on the table as she listened to Dave's story.

"So with any luck," he was saying, "we can clean up that paper with three crops of hay. The nesters'll work. They'll make a nice stake doin' it too."

Mary nodded. "As soon as it's clear, we can get some registered stuff from Jerry Boardman. He told me he's overstocked and wants to get rid of some. Long terms too. He isn't crowded for money, but he doesn't like the paper on the place."

"Don't blame him," Dave said briefly. "And we won't take any unless we see our way ahead. It may be a slow pull, sis, but we got what it takes: land, water, and grass."

"We can't help but make out," Mary said excitedly. "Now you have it settled with the nesters and they'll leave our cattle alone."

She suddenly seemed to realize that she had indirectly cast reflections on Ted's ability to deal with the nesters, and she flushed. She sat silently by Ted, listening to the small talk of the day's experience from which was carefully omitted any mention of the quarrel with Hammond. Rosy thought she looked pale and her face tired, but he laid it to the worry about the ranch and its prospects.

The meal finished and cigarettes smoked, Dave helped Mary with the dishes. Finished, he yawned, stretched and informed them that he was going to bed. Rosy followed him, leaving Winters and Mary in the kitchen.

"Tomorrow we split up," Dave informed him as they undressed in their room. "I'm goin' to locate all the cattle and get ready for a count. You go to Single Shot, order the seed for them nesters and round up a couple of riders. Then ride over to Soledad and get hold of Pablo Manero at the frame store there. Tell him I sent you and that we want about ten Mexicans, tools and all, to put in that ditch. Put what stuff you need—dynamite, tools, headgates and such—on the books. He'll carry us into the next century if he has to. And—oh, I'll tell you in the mornin'. I'm talkin' in my sleep now. G'night, you sheriff prodder."

"G'night, you nester-spraddler," Rosy answered sleepily.

It was a dull gathering, earth-rocking, window-rattling roar that woke them.

Rosy raised up on his elbow. "Dave," he called softly.

"I heard it," Dave said.

"What was it?"

Another report came booming through the rainy night.

"Dynamite," Dave guessed.

"Goddlemighty!" Rosy whispered. "There must be a ton in each shot."

They lay silent as three more vast detonations in quick succession seemed to shake the house.

"Where'd it come from?" Rosy asked.

"Up by the mountain, Old Cartridge way," Dave replied. "I'm takin' a *pasear*. You comin'?"

They dressed in the dark and left the house noiselessly, first picking out slickers from behind the back door. A steady drizzle was beating down and the first faint lights in the east announced approaching day.

They saddled their horses swiftly and swung out through the mud up to the trail to the notch. A raw wind hurried the rain, bringing with it occasionally a fleeting smell of burnt powder. They rode in silence, giving their horses their heads and letting them pick a footing up the long up-grade. When they reached the timber, gray daylight allowed them to see. Dave rode ahead, urging his horse.

A half mile from the notch in the rock rim, Dave left the trail and started up the rock-strewn steeper grade that announced the mountain. Rosy, puzzled, reined off after him. A cold, piercing wind was coming off the mountain, making his slicker wooden.

"What's up here?" Rosy asked innocently.

Dave's eyes swept him and in them Rosy saw a strange bleakness.

"Maybe you'll never see it," Dave said.

Suddenly, it dawned on Rosy where they were going and why Dave had ridden so unerringly for this point.

The timber was thin now, the grade steeper and their horses had to fight for a footing.

They mounted a hog's-back and Dave reined up, staring. Before them, a basin seemed to have been scooped out of the very base of the runneled mountainside. It was roughly oval, quarter of a mile in length. Its bottom, slanting steeply to the center from all sides, was a thick, black, shining-wet slime of mud. Steady trickles of water seeped up thinly in some places. Rosy's eyes followed the level rim around and there, toward the east edge nearest the rock rim, a chunk seemed to have been knocked out of the rim, leaving in its place a wedge of gray and storm-blanketed sky. The forty yards from the edge of the rock rim to the edge of the lake had been blasted out!

The lake was no more, nothing but this black pit of slime, a small pool at the very bottom mirroring the sky, left to mark it.

Dave's face was paper white, his eyes as cold and expressionless as marbles, his jaw muscles cording tightly above his neck.

"Damn Hammond!" His voice clogged with fury.

He wheeled his horse and rode the hog's-back up to the

wedge, then dismounted, Rosy at his side. Close to it, the gap was terrific. Perhaps fifty feet across, the rock had been blasted clean in a series of shots, leaving the bottom of the gap only a few feet above the bottom of the lake.

"Springs blown underground too," Dave muttered bleakly. Even in the short time since they had come up, Rosy noticed, the seepage through the slime had tapered off until now these spots that once marked bubbling springs were only spots of mud, a little more shiny with recent water than the rest of the lake bed.

Dave rolled a cigarette with trembling fingers as Rosy stared glumly at the scene.

"Since grand-dad's time that lake level hadn't varied three inches," Dave said slowly. "That creek out of it ran the whole length of our range, watered all our stock except some scattered water holes. Now the spread isn't worth the paper that covers it," he finished savagely, crumpling his cigarette in convulsed fingers. He laughed harshly, bitterly, casting savage glances at the sky, his eyes finally settling on Rosy. "That does it, pardner. We're hamstrung proper. Dry-gulched."

Rosy nodded mutely and walked out to the edge of the rock rim, looking down the long slope through the drizzle. Dave lagged over to him.

"He knowed dynamite," Rosy said tonelessly. He pointed down to the bottom of the gap which sloped sharply down. "The first shot was put about fifty or sixty feet down outside the rock rim on the down slope. It blowed a big gouge out. The next was put on the rock rim and it tumbled the top of the wedge out. The next two was put one behind the other and the rock was throwed down into the valley instead of the lake. A neat job," he finished savagely.

"He had this planned a long time," Dave said slowly. "He didn't have time to learn about that irrigatin' scheme of ours, but he'd had it planned. He had to single-jack holes in that rock, drill them. It'd take time. Plenty. Lots of night-work." Pausing, he looked at Rosy, pain in his eyes. "We was sleepin' two of them nights, Rosy. And I could have killed him yesterday."

Rosy nodded, "You can't be everywhere, pardner, and know everything."

"But dammit!" Dave said savagely, "we passed within a mile of this place twice yesterday. Why didn't I come up and look the place over? Or take you up there? After I'd had that row with him, why didn't I come up and make sure? Anything, just so I could have been here and spotted those drilled holes."

"Easy," Rosy told him soothingly.

He rolled two cigarettes and gave Dave one, which he accepted and had a hard time lighting with his trembling hand. He inhaled deeply and the smoke seemed to calm him.

"Well, let's go," he said quietly. "The sooner I meet him and kill him, the better I'll feel."

"You can't shoot a man in bed," Rosy reminded him. It was early yet. "Wait till he's on the streets. Choose him and cut down on him. We'll take him one at a time. He can't down us both."

"But I'm first," Dave said grimly.

"All right." Rosy stood up and looked over the scene, a wry smile on his face. "That comes about as close to bein' the bottom of low down as anything I ever heard. He knew when you got home, he couldn't bluff you out of the lake. He decided to kill you first, and if that failed, then he'd blow the lake out on you. He couldn't get it, so he didn't want you to have it either. There ain't been a rope made that ain't too good to hang that jasper with." He threw his cigarette away. "Let's go. The more I think of it, the more I'd like to kill that *hombre* in bed."

Rosy discovered that his own hands were shaking with anger. The more he thought of it, the worse it seemed. It was sheer spitefulness, much worse to Rosy's mind than if Hammond had lain in wait for them and bushwhacked them both. A man of that stripe would be the kind that would rowel his horse's guts out, then not even bother to shoot him. It was the work of a man who loved torture, and that, to Rosy, was as low as a man could get.

The rain was slanting grayly as they mounted again, Dave now in the lead. He slid down the small hog's-back and set off for the trail. He was a hunched, bitter-looking figure on the big sorrel, and he stared straight ahead.

Rosy took a last look at the slime-covered rocks and cursed again, long and passionately. He mounted, squirmed until his slicker was settled and nosed his bay down the hog's-back, paying no attention to the reins. The horse was dispirited too, and wet. Feeling Rosy slack in the saddle, the horse looked ahead for Dave's sorrel, but he was out of sight. The bay edged off the trail of Dave's tracks a way, then Rosy not responding, he headed for the shelter of a tall jackpine. Under it he stopped, and Rosy roused from his reverie.

"Stretch out, you jughead," he growled, pulling the bay over.

Suddenly his glance fell to the carpet of pine needles and automatically, he pulled the horse up. There, just where the needles thinned out and where the rain fell in a thin, broken mist, he saw a cigarette butt. It was a tailor-made.

Rosy dismounted. As he stooped to pick up the cigarette, he saw a track, which brought a low whistle from him. It was fresh, made during the night, and had not been washed out by the rain. It had the sole of a boot and the heel of a shoe. It was a freak track, one seldom seen in that country. He scowled over it for a minute, measured it roughly with his hand, picked up the cigarette butt and put it in his pocket and mounted again.

He had no doubt that Hammond had squatted under this tree to set off the charges of dynamite—Hammond, or one of his understrappers. It was just a bit more evidence that would serve to damn the mining man. A small pile of fuse scrapings near the trunk of the jackpine confirmed this.

Dave was waiting for him beside the trail. Together, they rode into the notch, the sky out over the valley gray as death.

"This will be a pleasure," Dave growled, looking straight ahead.

"Won't it?" Rosy grunted, also looking straight ahead.

9
Water and Gold

Shed Martin fumbled with wet hands in his pocket and drew out a moist plug of tobacco. He stood lost in the black vellum of night, listening to the ore rattle in the wagons, watching the rain channel off his hat brim, almost obscuring the lighted window of the office of the Draw Three.

"He'll have to like it," Shed muttered, wrenching off a sizable third of the plug, feeling its cold sponginess as he rolled it around his cheek. He cursed softly, soothingly, cursed the night, his luck, Buck Hammond, horses in general and his own in particular; then lifted reluctant feet and made for the office door.

"He'll have to like it," old Shed repeated.

Hammond looked up from his desk when the door opened.

"Hullo, Shed," he greeted the figure that slammed the door.

"Howdy, Buck," Shed grunted.

He felt his resolution failing. Hammond's fine blue eyes regarded him warmly from a square, craggy face. A trace of a friendly smile played on the wide mouth as the mine owner swung in his chair to face the freighter.

"How're you doin'?" Hammond asked. "Have it cleaned up by seven o'clock?"

"I reckon," Shed said. "Look here, Buck. If this ain't a hell of a night to—ah, hell!" he finished savagely. He couldn't do it. A man couldn't refuse Buck Hammond anything.

"What's the matter? Anything wrong?" Hammond asked, sensing what the grizzled old freighter was trying to get out.

"Naw. I just came in for a knife. You gotta have a knife to cut this damn dark if you git anywheres," Shed growled.

Hammond reached wearily for a bottle which was in the

depths of a bottom desk drawer. It was followed by a glass. He indicated them both to Shed.

"Have a drink."

Shed accepted enthusiastically, eyeing Hammond closely. He tossed off the drink, smacked his lips and set the glass down with a clatter.

"Have another, Shed," Hammond said.

"Thanky no," Shed said. He scowled a little. "You look a shade under the weather, Buck. You ain't lettin' this outfit get you down, are you?"

Hammond's grave eyes sought Shed's and he shook his head slowly. "Ever been called a murderer, Shed? A bushwhacker, or the man that hired a bushwhacker? Ever been called a water thief?"

Shed shook his head slowly in negation. "Not to my face, no. I'm just a tol'able scrapper and not so fast with a gun, but I don't reckon I'd let a man call me that. Why?"

"I got called all of them this afternoon," Hammond said quietly.

"Who?"

"Young Turner up at the D Bar T. Claimed I hired Freeman —remember him?—to take a pot at him last night from a dry gulch. He thinks I done it to get that lake up there we been quarrelin' about."

"The hell," Shed said softly. He could understand the hurt look on Hammond's face now. "What happened?"

"The sheriff stopped us before we got to our guns." Hammond's eyes glinted strangely and his jaw hardened for a moment, then he seemed to sag again.

"Dick Turner's kid? The one that's been in jail?" Shed asked. He spat. "Hell, Buck," he said in a voice which was strangely gentle, "I wouldn't take that to heart. He's a kid, and a crooked one, if what ever' one says is true. He needs a spankin' before he's very much older."

Hammond shook his head slowly.

"No, it ain't that, Shed. He looks like a decent kid, young and hot-headed, but clean." He looked up at Shed. "What hurts me, Shed, is that he believed it himself. He believed I was everything he called me and was willin' to back it up. He'd have filled his hand in a second if he hadn't been so dang mad he never thought of it."

"Was it over that lake?"

"Partly. Mostly on account of Freeman, though." Hammond sighed, and suddenly smiled a weary smile. "Years ago, Shed, I reckon I wouldn't have cared. Now I'm old, and I've lived as square as a man can in these times. It—hurt like hell."

Shed made an awkward gesture of sympathy.

"Don't think nothin' of it. Next time you see him, cut down on him like you would a sidewinder. Sooner some of these tough kids learn they ain't the men to back up their mouth, this country'll be worth livin' in again."

"I guess that's what it's comin' to," Hammond said slowly. "I told him next time we met not to waste any talk."

"That's it," Shed declared emphatically. "I dunno the kid myself, but any one that calls Buck Hammond forked has not only got him to fight, but me too."

"Thanks," Hammond said wearily. He got a hold on himself and straightened up. "Think you'll get her finished tonight?" he asked.

Shed raised a hand and they listened to the ore crashing out into the wagons. Shed smiled.

"We'll make it," he said grimly, "but damn me if I don't think we'll have to swim the last load into Single Shot."

"Boggy?"

"Plain hell," Shed said. "Ever try to drive a six-horse hitch through a danged swamp in the rain? It ain't no fun."

"I know it," Hammond said. "I'm sorry I had to work the men through tonight, Shed, but you know how I stand. If I have to pay demurrage on those cars, I wouldn't be able to meet next month's wages."

"I know," Shed said glumly. "Seems like a man can't make a livin' nowadays even with a gold mine."

"Not this one," Hammond said, and his eyes gleamed with humor.

Shed grinned, then suddenly became serious.

"Pull out of it, Buck. Take an old freighter's advice. I seen 'em come and go and I've hauled enough ore to fill the Rio Grande eighty miles beyond El Paso. You git it in the neck sooner or later. You've spraddled this outfit and it's bleedin' you dry. Sell it, and git you a hoss ranch. They tell me you've had a chance to unload it for a heap of money."

"Damned if I will," Hammond growled. "I've got every cent to my name in this, Shed, and it's goin' to pay big some day. Either that or it'll break my heart."

"And it'll break your heart four ways to hell," Shed declared emphatically. He buttoned up his slicker. "But it won't be my freightin' that does it. I'll have every danged pebble in them cars by seven or I'll pay them demurrage charges and a year's interest to boot."

He turned to the door and yanked it open. Standing just outside was a slim, slickered figure. He peered at it silently.

"What in tarnation hell are you doin' out on a night like this?" he asked sternly, but not unkindly.

"Why in tarnation hell shouldn't I be out?" a girl's voice mimicked his gruff one.

Shed guffawed and held the door open for her.

"Hello, Dad," she called to Hammond. She turned to Shed. "Here I am freightin' ore on a night like this while you sit in here warmin' your pants, Shed Martin. And you a mule-skinner." Her manner of speaking was such a perfect imitation of Shed's that all of them laughed. Shed went out, his loud guffaw trailing him.

Hammond's eyes were humorous as she went up to him and kissed him, then swung a dripping saddlebag onto his desk.

"You better look out," Hammond said. "Shed'll be askin' you to marry him."

"I like him," she said. Her short straight nose wrinkled a little as she laughed.

Hammond looked at the clock on the wall. "Four o'clock. What are you doin' up and prowlin'?"

She drew off her Stetson, revealing an unruly mass of corn-colored hair, the edges reflecting beads of rain.

"I couldn't sleep, Dad. After the man came in with your message that you'd stay out all night, I thought I'd get a long sleep. I ate supper alone and went to bed and couldn't sleep. Then I thought you might be hungry, so I decided to get up and bring you out some sandwiches and coffee." She winked solemnly at him, her blue eyes warm and sparkling. "No. I decided to come out and help you freight ore. Earn my keep."

"You shouldn't be—" Hammond started to growl.

"Now, Dad. Pancho knows his way out here from Single Shot in the dark, so there's nothing to worry about." She grinned and Hammond's scowl disappeared. "He did fall down though. You should see him. He's a palomino on one side and a buckskin on the other."

Hammond shook his head gravely. "And you might be out there now, pinned under him, waitin' for a freighter to find you."

"Pinned under him in this mud? All I'd have to do would be to fold my arms and I'd sink out of sight. I could swim out from under him."

Hammond laughed in spite of himself. He watched her seat herself on the desk top, extract a huge bundle of sandwiches and a whisky bottle full of coffee from the saddlebag and lay them on the desk. Suddenly, his eyes were grave.

"Do you mind bein' poor, Dorsey?" he asked gently.

Her hands paused and she regarded him soberly. "Of course not. Why do you ask, Dad?"

Hammond shrugged wearily. "I just wondered. We aren't makin' much more than poor wages out of the mine now and won't until we open it up more. Then too, it looks like I got a court fight comin' with young Turner up at the D Bar T."

"Has he been in?"

"Yes. Been in and—well, we quarreled."

Hammond told her about Dave and Rosy's visit, omitting the accusations Dave had made and the ensuing struggle.

"It looks like we'll be crowded," he finished. "It looks like I can't get the water without a court fight and I haven't the money for one. My water," he added bitterly.

A sullen, sudden gathering rumble shook the building, punctuating Hammond's speech.

"What was that?" Dorsey asked. "Thunder?"

"Sounded like blasting," Hammond said absently. He got out of his chair and started to pace the floor.

"But, Dad," Dorsey said, "do you think it will go that far?"

"I do," Hammond said emphatically. "Just as far as Turner can—"

A second detonation, louder than the first, came rocketing to their ears.

Hammond listened a moment, then strode to the door and opened it.

"Shed!" he called.

In the interval of waiting, he turned to Dorsey and she could see the concern in his eyes.

"Yeah?" a voice called out of the dark.

"Was that blasting?" Hammond asked.

"Dunno. It sounded like lightnin' hitting. You could hear the rock movin' up the hill, but there wasn't no light."

"Who'd be blasting now?"

Three more earth-shaking, coughing roars came to them in quick succession, the echoes slapping across the broad valley.

"Hell, that's dynamite," Shed said. He was standing in the doorway now before Hammond and Dorsey.

As the echo died out, a sullen, dim roar rose over the patter of the rain. They listened in silence a full minute, looking at each other.

"Sounds like water," Shed ventured.

Hammond stared at him, his face slowly draining of color.

"My God. Do you suppose it might—"

"The lake!" Dorsey cried. "The D Bar T lake!"

Hammond whirled, raced across the room for his slicker.

"Shed, get these teams away from the buildings. Drive hell for leather for high ground anywhere outside of this wash!" Shed disappeared and he turned to Dorsey. "Honey, you get

Pancho and make your way up the hill here. Be sure and stay out of the arroyo. Give him his head. And hurry."

He plunged out into the night and Dorsey called after him: "Dad! Dad!" There was no answer.

In the dark, Hammond made for the mine shaft, the entrance of which lay precisely in the forks of the two manmade ditches that were even now diverting the water on either side of the cluster of mine buildings. Six men down there, working nightshift. He cursed bitterly, striking blindly through the dark. Then something cut him savagely across the shins, checking his speed with a crushing pain. He fell forward on his face in a mass of cable. The winch, he knew now. He struggled to get up and found that he could not even stand, much less move. His lip bled where he bit it trying to check the pain.

"Shed!" he called out into the night. "Shed! Oh Shed!"

He repeated it until a voice answered him. He listened, a part of him almost aloof, hearing the sound which had started as a murmur now growing louder, more rumbling.

"Where are yuh?"

"Here. Come here." He could hear Shed slog across the stretch of mud, could see the freighters in the inadequate, rain-slanted light given off by the lanterns, fighting their six-horses in an effort to get them turned.

"Yeah?"

"There's men down in the shaft, Shed. Six of them. I've broken—my leg—I think. Shed—can you reach them?"

But Shed had already gone down the slanting shaft. Hammond could hear his great voice roaring, calling the men, dimmed now as the seconds passed. Thank God, the shaft went horizontally into the hillside and not vertically. They might have a chance to get out.

Then the full force of the accident hit Hammond. His mind went straight as an arrow to the cause.

"Dave Turner," he said aloud, and then he cursed viciously.

So Turner had been so damned contemptible that he had resorted to this—blowing out the lake on top of the Draw Three. Ruining it, endangering lives. And all because he knew that the lake was rightfully Hammond's and belonged on Draw Three property.

Turner, after their talk, had feared a court fight, because he knew he would lose it. Like the cur he was, he determined that if the D Bar T couldn't have it, then neither could the Draw Three. All the horror and viciousness of it came to Hammond like a blow and his eyes swam black with fury.

When he was calm again, he knew he would have to move, get out. The whole damned lake was coming down the hill from the sound of it, and he'd be caught. He crawled painfully on his hands and knees through the slime, the searing torture of his leg making the night dance in front of his eyes with countless stars. He heard a horse gallop away and dimly realized that it was Dorsey fleeing.

When he came to the diversion ditch, he knew the water was only a few inches from the top. He had to crawl through it and its chill seemed to clamp every muscle in his body to its nearest bone. He rested on the other side, feeling the air now and the rain as warm as soup to his skin.

The sound, the rumble, was closer now, more ominous. He began crawling again, feeling the sharp stones on his knees almost a relief from the pain that was stabbing up from below his knees. His right ankle dragged sickeningly, awkwardly: he could feel it trailing flatly out to one side. The rocks were bigger now, giving him some sort of handhold and leverage as he lifted himself among them fighting his way up the hill.

"Shed'll be lost," he thought miserably. "Lost, drowned. Seven of them, like rats."

He heard the first warning hiss of water off to his right as it raced along and slapped the arroyo walls, spreading out over the top of the diversion ditches in what he could imagine was a bubbling, tumbling fan.

Then the noise, a great welling roar, seemed to charge out of the night. He fought frantically to gain a greater height on the hillside as the thin scream of a horse rose above the din.

It opened up, this howling, furious bedlam. The unleashed lake had jumped the watercourse, lifted itself in a mighty surge over the surrounding land. He could feel its swift tug at him as it runneled off the rocks. He dimly saw the light wink out in the office, heard and felt the timbers of the building crash and scrape.

The water was bringing down boulders with it in drunken lunges. The noise of one as it gouged its way through the building came to him; the dissolving tinkle of crushed machinery was beaten down into the night by the still driving rain.

Thank God he could not see. It would have been a savage torture to watch it, watch the strangling horses tossed like straw on the torrent, the men who were free helpless to do anything for them.

In a great, screeching shudder, the main building upended and was dissolved in the flood. He could hear the water slap against the far bank of the creekbed a hundred yards below the mine. It became more calm as it spread out, finding its way down the bed toward Single Shot.

Then it died, almost as suddenly as it had begun. He could hear the arroyo running loud and full, but the bulk of the water had passed and had poured around him. The rain was still driving, monotonous, cold and unrelenting.

He waited, his ankle throbbing viciously. Were any of the men saved? Was Dorsey? He grew cold at the thought. She must have been. She had had time to get her horse and ride up the hill out of reach of the flood.

The bottomless black void of the night was graying a little over the mountains to the east. He called loudly and got no answer.

"Better stay here," he thought dully. "If I try to move I'll faint and will just as likely as not fall face down in a pool of water and drown."

He listened for sounds that would tell him of human activity, but the rain smothered everything. As the night slowly lifted he could make out the scene before him. Where the mine buildings had stood there was a sodden mass of the heaviest machinery. The buildings had been entirely swept from around them, even the floors. Part of the main building lay folded against the east bank of the wash far below him. The rest had evidently been carried down stream on the crest of the flood. He could see where he was now. He had managed to crawl up the hill perhaps fifty yards and a hundred yards away from the arroyo.

All the horror and desolation and cruelty of it was increased ten-fold by the weak dawn light. A murderous fury filled him. Turner would pay for this with his life as long as a drop of Buck Hammond's blood ran red. In his rage, he clutched at the jagged rocks until his hands bled.

They found him there unconscious.

10
Showdown at Midnight

It did not occur to Rosy and Dave as they rode down the mud-slimed wash that the lake had cascaded down this natural channel, or if it did they did not mention it to each other. The mud was fetlock deep and the going was slow. When they rounded the bend at the bottom that showed them the mouth, they reined up and stared.

"It's gone," Dave said, looking at the boulder-strewn ground where the mine had been.

"Insurance," Rosy said bitterly. "Insures the mine then blows a lake out on top of it."

As they pulled down into the mouth of the arroyo they saw men working frantically. One of the men spied them and waved them over. Three men were laboring steadily with crowbars and shovels. The fourth dropped his shovel and slogged through the mud to reach them.

"Give us a hand, will you?" the man asked, his face streaming with sweat.

"What's the trouble?" Rosy asked.

"There's seven men down this mine shaft," the man said, pointing to the spot. "The mouth's clogged with boulders and mud and there's a chance they may be alive. They was down there when the lake went out up above."

Rosy looked at Dave, who turned to the man. "Hammond isn't down there, is he?"

"No. He's in town, I reckon. He got hurt a little."

"How bad?"

"Not bad, I heard. Can you give us a lift?"

Again Dave and Rosy looked at each other. They had both ridden for the last half hour with a murderous hatred in their hearts, driving straight for a goal shrouded in gun-smoke and death. And now they were being asked to take enough time from killing to try and save lives. Neither of them hesitated.

"Sure," Dave said. They dismounted and followed the man over to his companions. "I reckon he can wait this long," Dave said to Rosy.

"Didn't even bother to get his men out of the shaft," Rosy said, his face still bleak and cold.

They worked with crowbars and shovels for an hour until help came out from town. It was hopeless to begin with, Rosy saw, but he said nothing. It was their duty to leave nothing undone if the lives below could be saved.

When other men and wagons and the pumps came out from town, they gave way to the fresher men, got their horses and started into town.

They had learned from the men at the mine that Hammond had been taken to Dr. Fullerton's and they rode through town to the main corner, turned left at the Free Throw and easily found the doctor's house a half block above. It was a frame house, neatly painted white, with a deep yard and a huge glassed-in porch at the side. This was the Single Shot hospital.

Dave felt a strange, icy calm as he knocked on the door and waited for it to be opened by the housekeeper.

"Is Hammond in here?" he asked the woman who opened the door.

"Yes. What do you want?"

"On the porch?"

"Of course. But he can't see any one," the housekeeper declared.

Dave simply shouldered past her. To his right was an open door which led into the darkened doctor's office. The door to the porch opened onto it. Dave strode into the dark room, hitching up his gun belt.

"I thought so," a flat toneless voice said.

Dave stopped. It was the sheriff's voice, and Dave waited until his eyes became accustomed to the dark room. He picked out the sheriff standing just to one side of the door, and he saw the warm glint of the two Colts in his hands.

"You can see I got guns throwed on you," the sheriff said. "You better hand over your own."

"Get out of the way," Dave said briefly, and took a step forward. The sheriff's guns tilted a little higher and his thumbs slid back a quarter of an inch on the hammers.

"I wouldn't if I was you," he said quietly.

Again Dave stopped. "Hank, there's two of us here. We can't beat you, but one of us will get you. Now clear out."

"I wouldn't go no further," the sheriff said flatly, and there was a deep, warning menace in his voice that arrested Dave in mid-motion.

"Give me them guns," the sheriff said recognizing his advantage. "Talk to him all you want, but give me them guns. There's a woman in there. And you can't kill a man in bed."

Dave sighed loudly, shuddering a little with the cold violence of his anger. He had a desperate impulse to go for his guns and take his chances of coming out alive with the sheriff. But his sense of justice prevented him. He had seen too much wanton killing and destruction on this day to want any more of it.

"All right, Hank," he said bleakly. "But I'm warnin' you. You and all the deputies you can swear in in seven years ain't goin' to keep me from killin' Hammond."

"I know that," the sheriff said. "I'm just tryin' to put it off until the fight's a little more even. Now hand them guns over, both of you."

He received the four guns and wedged them in his belt, then opened the door and backed through it onto the porch. "Now come on," he said quietly.

Dave stepped through the door. There were four beds on the porch and in the far one Hammond was lying propped up on a pillow. Dorsey was sitting on the foot of his bed, but Dave did not even see her.

He walked across the room slowly to the foot of Hammond's bed. The mining man's face was slowly flushing and his hands plucked the cover convulsively.

"You damned, murderin', bushwhackin', waterthievin' skunk!" Dave said slowly and distinctly, his voice quivering with contempt. He had hardly finished speaking before Dorsey was on her feet facing him. She slapped him sharply across the face, but Dave did not stir, did not even look at her, did not even take his eyes from Hammond. It was as if she were not there at all.

Hammond struggled to sit up, but his face twisted in pain and he sank back on the pillow again.

"Hank, give me a gun," he pleaded hoarsely.

"He took mine away," Dave said thickly, "or you'd be dead now."

Hammond groaned in his rage.

"You couldn't get the lake so you had to ruin it for me," Dave continued, his voice slow and thick. "Ruin it, and drown seven of your own men doin' it. Just for revenge."

"That's a damned lie!" Hammond thundered, suddenly, finding his voice. In spite of his pain, he lunged up in bed and pointed a blunt finger at Dave. "You did it yourself. You blew that lake out to ruin the Draw Three because you knew that water was mine!"

Dave's mouth slacked in amazement at Hammond's words, and he looked dumbly at Rosy who was standing just beside him. "Why—why"—he looked back at Hammond and his face was black with fury—"you think I—why damn you—"

The sheriff grabbed his arms and pinioned them behind him as he brushed Dorsey aside and started for the bed.

"Killed seven men!" Hammond roared. "Seven men, and you ain't fit to wipe the boots of a one of 'em."

Dave lunged again. Dorsey screamed and Rosy lunged at the sheriff.

"Get those guns, Dave!" Rosy clipped out, and he crooked his elbow around the sheriff's neck and pulled back.

"I did it! I did it!" the sheriff roared, half strangled. "Let me go. I did it!"

These damning words, shouted at the top of the sheriff's lungs, arrested Rosy and Dave in mid-movement. The sheriff twisted out of Rosy's arms, his hand streaking to his gun. His hand came up filled and he backed off a way.

"Thanks, Rand," he said dryly. He looked at Hammond and Dave. "I wondered when you two jaspers would tumble to this."

"What?" Rosy asked.

"Why, that neither Hammond nor Turner done the dynamitin'," the sheriff shouted.

The three men looked at each other blankly.

"You damned knot-headed fools," the sheriff continued, his voice scornful and suddenly quiet. "Calm down enough to look at it. Why would Hammond blow the dam out and ruin his mine and drown seven men?" He turned to Hammond. "And you, Buck. You're older. You should have saw it all along. Turner thinks that lake is his, whether it is or not. Would he blow out that dam and spoil every drop of water on his spread —ruin it—just to ruin you? Git some sense, you danged fools!"

Hammond looked at Dave, then at Rosy. The two younger men were staring at the sheriff.

"You mean," Rosy said slowly, "that some one else did it?"

"That's it," the sheriff grunted. "The *hombre* that did it wanted Turner to think Hammond done it, and wanted Hammond to think Turner done it."

"How do you know?" Hammond demanded.

The sheriff whirled on him. "You never done it, did you?"

"I was in my office all night," Hammond said.

The sheriff turned to Dave. "And you was in bed, wasn't you? Rand can prove that, and your sister and her husband."

"Sure," Dave said.

The sheriff shrugged and holstered his gun. "There. Now you start guessin'. I'm through."

Dave sank weakly on a bed and stared at Hammond. The guilt had been so obvious to them both that they stared at each other, trying to collect their wits. Dorsey was sobbing against the wall, and Dave, for the first time, noticed her. He blushed, but said nothing.

Hammond put his hand out to Dorsey and she fell on her knees, sobbing on his chest.

"I reckon we're a couple of fools," Hammond said quietly.

Dave nodded.

"There, there," Hammond said patting Dorsey's shoulder.

"Oh Dad," she sobbed. "They might have killed you. They might have shot you."

"And I might have shot them," Hammond said.

Dorsey looked up, her face streaked with tears. "But you're an old man. In bed. Without a gun." She looked at Dave and her eyes were bitter with scorn. "Is that a trick you learned in jail? Killing defenseless and innocent men?"

"Stop it, honey," Hammond said.

Dave flushed, but his eyes flashed.

"I reckon I didn't think of that, ma'am. It was whoever got a gun first."

"And dad with a broken ankle!" Dorsey flared up.

"I didn't know that either," Dave said.

"You contemptible, sneaking jailbirds!" Dorsey said, then started to cry again.

Hammond looked at Dave. "I reckon she's upset and don't know what she's sayin'."

Dave nodded and reached with trembling hands for his sack of Durham. Rosy sat beside him and cuffed his Stetson off his forehead. He was scowling fiercely, looking at Hammond occasionally. The sheriff took a chair against the wall and sat down.

Dorsey soon straightened up and wiped her eyes. Her eyes were cold as she turned to Dave.

"I—I guess I lost my temper," she said. "I'm sorry."

"That's all right," Dave said quietly. "There may be a lot of truth in what you said."

Again Dorsey flushed, but held her tongue.

"Mr. Hammond," Rosy began, "I reckon we owe apologies all around. We've all been barkin' up the wrong tree. Let's get together and try and settle this."

Hammond smiled and the warm gleam of humor came into his eyes. "That's sense. Whoever owned that lake, it won't do them much good now. I reckon all cause for our fightin' is over."

Dave nodded glumly. "We're in the same boat. The spread ain't worth the grass on it now, and your mine is just a pothole, from the looks of it."

"And it'll stay that way," Hammond said. "I couldn't raise the money to have the water pumped out of it."

Dave smoked in silence a moment, then looked at Hammond. "All this knocks me into a cocked hat. I thought you'd set Freeman onto me because you wanted that water and thought you could bully it out of sis." He smiled a little. "You see, Mr. Hammond, I didn't know much about you. Reckon that'll teach me not to think the worst of people."

Hammond nodded. "I was as much to blame as you, Turner."

"But who could have done it?" Rosy said. "Some one did. Was they wantin' to ruin you, Hammond, or us?"

"Did you two know any one in jail that might have wanted to get even with you?" Dorsey asked.

Rosy glared at the sheriff, who looked sternly back at him.

"You needn't look at me that way, Rand," the sheriff said. "I ain't even opened my mouth."

Rosy turned to Dorsey. "The sheriff asked that yesterday. I'll tell you what I told him. No."

"Then who could it have been if it wasn't that?" Dorsey asked. Rosy shrugged, and got up. He hitched up his belt.

"Dave and me don't know many people around here. Dave's been away eight years. I'm new. It looks like some one wanted to run you off that mine, Hammond—clean off. You got any enemies you think might do it?"

"The only enemies I've got are people I owe money to," Hammond said, smiling. "And I don't think they'd want to cut off the chances of gettin' paid back."

"No one else?" Rosy persisted. "Haven't you had any fights, good hatin' fights, during your life?"

Hammond shook his head. "Closest I ever come to a fight was this time, I reckon. I know people that don't like me and I don't like. Like Pearson, for instance. But that's nacheral enough."

"Sure. What about Pearson?" Rosy asked. "Ain't he the banker?"

Hammond nodded. "We were almost partners once. I got the Draw Three on a tip from a minin' man I did a favor for once. I was ranching about a hundred miles to the south, then, and I sold my spread and come up here. I didn't have enough money to swing the deal, so I tried to borrow money from Pearson. I had the option bought up, but I had to get the money to swing the deal. He wouldn't have anything to do with it at first, but he finally sent east for a minin' man to come and look the property over. I never heard what the minin' man said about it, but Pearson come around and wanted to buy up my option when it expired. I told him I wouldn't sell, and that if I couldn't get the money to mine it myself, I was goin' to sell the option to a minin' company."

Hammond grinned, as if remembering something.

"Well, that brought Pearson around. He agreed to put some money in it. We started work and Pearson was all for sinkin' a lot of money in it first thing. Open it up wide. I was for payin' as we went. Pearson kept puttin' money in until I tumbled to what he was tryin' to do. He was tryin' to put so much money in it that he'd get control. Loan me out of the mine, so to speak. Well, I set my foot down. Pearson didn't like it, and he hasn't been around since."

"Think he's forked?" Rosy asked.

"No," Hammond said immediately. "I don't think so. He's a sharp business man, is all. He wanted the mine. He tried to get it in a legitimate way. He couldn't and we disagreed." He looked at Rosy. "That often happens that business partners don't agree."

"Sure," Rosy said. "And some of his money is still in it?"

"Plenty."

"Then that's out, on that score alone. He wouldn't want to lose his own money," Rosy said.

"He wouldn't do it, anyway," Hammond said.

"Well, that leaves us about where we were, don't it?" Rosy said. "Can you think of any one else?"

Hammond shook his head. "No. I reckon the rest of the town hasn't got anything against me. Not enough to want to ruin me, anyway."

"Well, you're ruined right enough, Buck," the sheriff said. "You'll never work that mine again without puttin' in a lot of money."

"I know it," Hammond said glumly.

Dorsey patted her father's arm. "Dad, why buck it? Sell out. Sell out to Crowell. Take that offer he made you this morning and buy the ranch back."

Dave leaned forward, his eyes staring strangely. "Sell out to who?" he asked.

"Crowell," Dorsey said. "He's been interested in the mine. He happened to be in town last night and when he heard about the accident, he came over this morning and wanted dad to sell to him."

Dave looked at Rosy and back to Hammond. "Crowell, you say? Then you folks aren't Crowell?"

"I don't know what you mean," Dorsey said puzzled.

"You—" Dave began, then looked at Rosy. He shook himself and leaned forward, talking rapidly. "Listen to this. For the past year, Mary, my sister, has been gettin' letters from a gent by the name of Crowell, askin' her to put a price on the D Bar T spread. Those letters came about the time she was havin' that trouble with you, Hammond, over the lake. She thought it was you writin' the letters under the name of Crowell. She thought that you were so sure that you couldn't win the lake in a court fight that you were tryin' to buy it secretly. Under another name, that is, because Mary figured you thought she wouldn't sell to you if she knew it was you that was tryin' to buy the place. And you folks didn't write the letters at all?"

"No," Hammond said.

"And you didn't have this Crowell try to buy the D Bar T for you?"

"You know how much money I've got, Turner. I couldn't buy it."

Dave slapped his knee. "Then that's the *hombre!* Where is he?"

"I still don't see," Hammond said slowly.

"Why, he's the only man we know that wants both our spread and your mine," Dave said excitedly. "He's the only jasper that we know of. Chances are it was him that blew out the lake hoping he could buy both places after the water was gone. Don't you see?"

"Where is he now?" Rosy cut in.

"Gone," Hammond said. "He took the morning train out. He—"

"Gone?" Dave said, half risen off the bed. He sank back again and said: "Go on. What about him?"

"He come in here around seven o'clock, about ten minutes before the train went, and made me an offer for the mine. Said he just come on a hunch, after he'd found out what happened."

Rosy broke in. "What did he look like?"

Hammond thought a moment before replying. "Short, dark. Got a thin face and dark eyes. Wears dark clothes, city clothes. Got a funny habit of lookin' at your tie or your collar. Don't weigh more'n a hundred an' thirty. Why?" he asked. "You seen him?"

"Huh-uh," Rosy grunted. He stood and spoke to the sheriff. "Hank, wire his description down the line. Have him yanked off that train an' held for you."

The sheriff shook his head. "Wires is down after that storm last night. I tried to get through this mornin'."

Rosy groaned.

"But he's the ranny," Dave said emphatically. "It's the only way this whole thing makes sense."

Rosy rammed his hands in his pockets and paced the floor, smoking furiously. Suddenly he turned on Hammond and Dave.

"And he'll be back," Rosy said decisively, "if I got this figgered out right. First place, he thinks that you, Dave, and Hammond each think the other blowed the lake out. He's countin' on you fightin' on sight, or anyway not talkin' together peaceable like this. He don't think you'll be calm enough to talk it over. Second place, he hasn't seen Mary about the ranch. About her half of it anyway, and he'll come back and try to buy it from her. He'll come back to you, too, Hammond, and try to buy the mine again. He'll be back, all right, and if I ain't loco, he'll be back right *pronto*. While he thinks you and Dave are fightin' mad and when everything looks hopeless. He'll be back and he'll be back with cash!"

Hammond was visibly excited now. He looked around on a side table then asked Dorsey:

"Get my pipe, will you, honey?"

Dorsey went to the closet and opened the door. Hammond's clothes were inside and Dorsey fumbled around in his coat pocket. Rosy idly noted that Hammond wore half-boots, the tracks of which could not possibly jibe with the track he had seen up by the lake. And Hammond was smoking a pipe too, not tailor-made cigarettes.

"Hanged if I don't think you've got it," he said finally.

"And that ain't all," Rosy said, still pacing the floor. "There's somethin' behind this we don't understand. For instance, how could Crowell have been around these parts and kept hidden long enough to drill them holes for the dynamite? There was lots of them, and in hard rock."

"He couldn't," Hammond said.

Rosy looked at him a long time.

"That tell you anything?"

Hammond puffed savagely on his pipe.

"Lots," he said briefly, holding Rosy's glance.

"Right," Rosy said. "It means that Crowell ain't done the dynamitin' at all. It was done by some one he hired, some understrappers that could travel around in this country and not be noticed much."

Rosy paused in his pacing and leaned on the bed, looking at the three men.

"Gents, we've walked into somethin' that'll take a lot of blowin' up. I aim to start right now. There's tracks up there at that lake. We never looked for 'em, but there must be. We was so sure it was you, Hammond, that we never looked much. They'll be washed out bad, but we may pick up somethin'. I'm hittin' for the lake. You comin', Dave?"

Dave rose, and so did the sheriff.

"I dunno when we'll be back, Hammond," Rosy said. "Maybe not for days. But if this *hombre* Crowell shows up again, you string him along. You don't have to do anything except cuss Dave Turner and put off sellin' your mine to him. Tell him you're considerin' it." He grinned. "This has got the makin's of a first-rate chunk of hell."

11
Rosy's Hunch

After getting something to eat, Rosy, Dave and the sheriff set out for the lake. Rosy was silent all the way out to the Draw Three. When they arrived there, a crowd had gathered. The shaft had been opened and the seven bodies found, one of them Shed Martin's. Rosy hung back and let the sheriff dismount and look the place over. Dave waited patiently, noting idly that the rain had eased off now.

"I've changed my mind," Rosy said suddenly.

"What about?"

"Do you think you two jaspers can take care of the tracks up there at the lake?"

"Sure. Why?"

"I've got a hunch," Rosy said slowly.

"What?"

"I dunno, but I feel like I ought to play it." Rosy looked at him. "I've got a hunch about Crowell. I think he's either in town or will be in town in pretty short order, and I ain't aimin' to miss him."

Dave thought a moment. "There's no reason why we shouldn't split up. I've got a sort of hunch myself that I wasn't aimin' to spill. It's this. There's a heap of badlands behind Old Cartridge and a trail that goes around on the rock rim to them. I think those jaspers that did the dynamitin' hit for there. It's a canyon country, not good for much except hiding. I know it pretty well from when I was a kid, and I know where the likely places are. And they're places where a single man works better than two."

Rosy's eyes narrowed. "You aimin' to go alone—without Hank, even?"

"That's it," Dave said.

"Huh-uh," Rosy said. "I'm goin' with you."

"I'm goin' alone."

"Huh-uh."

They looked at each other. "Remember you're the foreman of the D Bar T and you're takin' orders from the boss. That's me," Dave said. "I'm orderin' you to go back to town and play your hunch and let me play mine."

Rosy's face was grave. "Leavin' all jokin' aside, Dave, I don't like it. No matter how good one man is, three or four men can down him. I better go with you."

But Dave was just as serious. "I can do it better alone. I'm goin' to have to move like a cat. I know the country. There won't be any shootin' that I don't do first, because it's a surprise party. If two of us—or even three went in there, we'd pick up trouble and plenty of it. They couldn't help but know we was there. But alone—well, you'd be surprised." He grinned. "And that's my orders. You go back to town."

"What about Hank?"

"I'll send him down to tell Mary the news." He smiled wryly. "I haven't the heart to do it myself."

The sheriff waddled over to them and mounted his horse. He accepted Rosy's news that he was going back to town without surprise.

"Don't look for me until you see me," were Dave's parting words.

They separated, Rosy headed back to town. Another horseman was looking at the crowd around the mine shaft and as Rosy pulled away, he saw the man pull his horse and head for the road toward Single Shot.

They took the road at about the same time and fell in with each other. The stranger was a small man, mounted on a big roan gelding that made him look like a wizened monkey-faced little jockey. He had great, drooping sandy mustaches that were generously shot with gray.

"Howdy," he greeted Rosy.

His hat-brim was bent up, so that he had the appearance of a man constantly riding into a stiff wind. His seamed face was stubbled with a week's growth of beard, so that its blurred, whimsical lines brought out by contrast the black, deepset eyes. Rosy felt the man's eyes coldly appraising him.

"Dave Turner's new boss, ain't you?"

Rosy nodded, wondering how the man knew.

"I'm Laredo Jackson, Boardman's foreman. We're neighbors." They shook hands. Jackson scowled. "That's a coyote's trick. I'd rather shoot a man in the back. Who done it?"

"You might 's well make a guess," Rosy said carefully. "Yours is as good as the next one."

"My guess ain't fit to speak," Jackson answered, looking keenly at Rosy.

Rosy looked at him, secret amusement in his eyes. Here was probably some crank of an old cowpoke that had a pet solution for every crime. "Whisper it, then," Rosy said.

The older man ignored this with dignity. "Mary don't know about this yet, does she?"

"Sheriff's ridin' up that way tonight," Rosy said.

Jackson looked at him. "Hank? Hell, he'll fergit to tell her." A pause. "That makes the D Bar T just about a two-man outfit, don't it?" He cursed savagely and long, Rosy's mild gaze upon him. "There's such a thing as havin' neighbors," the little man said. "Old man Boardman and Dave Turner's old man come in this country when it took a six day's ride to get tobacco. They split the bench just above Soledad between 'em and never put in a foot of wire. Now, by God, I reckon Dave'll start tradin' Boardman land for water-holes and crossin' his breed with camels."

"I reckon," Rosy said. That was a pretty accurate summing-up of what would happen to the Turner spread.

They rode on in silence, Jackson with his leg crooked over the saddle-horn. If he looked like a monkey, Rosy thought he acted more like one. He was as restless as one, certainly. He seemed to use his saddle for a bed, a table, a sofa and a rocking chair, squirming incessantly; but his horse, evidently used to it, did not even turn his head. Rosy had an idea that Jackson wanted to tell him something, but was holding back for some reason. As they approached town, Rosy decided to try and pry it out of him.

"You said back there a ways you had a guess as to what's behind all this. Mind tellin' me? I'm about as interested in this as you are."

"Mind tellin' you? Hell, yes, I mind tellin' you," Jackson said bluntly. "You won't be here very long before you begin guessin' the same thing. I'm one of these *hombres* that's careful with his guesses." His smile took the bluntness off his speech, but it did not satisfy Rosy's curiosity.

When they reached the Mile High, Jackson reined up. "Have a drink?"

Rosy shook his head. It was near dusk and he had several things to do before the night was over. "I've got some business. Later, if I see you around."

"Sure. I'm gittin' drunk. You'll see me all right, but if I can't see you and I don't remember it, Boardman wanted me to ask Turner for the loan of a man day after tomorrow."

"He's out—" Rosy checked himself. "Sure. I'll tell him."

He thought he saw a smile start on the smaller man's face, then disappear. Jackson nodded and swung off his horse. Rosy watched him dismount, stretch and swagger into the Mile High. Rosy urged his horse on thoughtfully. What did Jackson guess? He swung down before the Free Throw and debated between a drink and supper. He hadn't seen Quinn for a while. Maybe the gambler would have supper with him.

As he shouldered into the Free Throw, he wondered if it would be wise to tell Quinn the developments. The gambler had a level head and didn't let much get past him. The gambling was slack, but there was a small crowd around Quinn's table. He saw Rosy and motioned him over.

"Get a drink. I'll eat with you later."

Rosy sauntered over to the bar and ordered a whisky, moving off by himself so that nobody would interrupt him. He wanted to think about things. For some reason, he had a feeling that Crowell was in town or close around. Too much in the man's scheme depended on time. He'd have to get to Hammond's mine and the D Bar T before the anger of the two parties had had time to cool down. Had he really gone out on the train? What was there to prove it? Merely his word. Would the agent know? Probably not.

Rosy looked up and found a man staring at him. The look was fleeting, and Rosy looked at the man idly. He was standing at the far end of the bar, a squat man with curious, dead-looking eyes. Rosy couldn't remember having seen the man before, and he supposed it was just idle curiosity in the man that made him stare that way.

Quinn strolled over to the bar and they left the Free Throw together. They walked down five doors to the U-eata cafe, took stools, ordered beefsteak, fried eggs, fried potatoes, pie and coffee from the Chinaman, then rolled cigarettes. Quinn was the first to speak.

"This about cleans you two, doesn't it?"

Rosy nodded. "That's an understatement."

Quinn was quiet a moment. "Who was it meant for? You or Hammond?"

"Both," Rosy said. He suddenly decided he would tell Quinn. The gambler toyed with his cigarette, listening to Rosy's story. When Rosy was finished, he threw his cigarette on the floor and grunted.

"Can Winters afford to lose a thousand dollars at poker?" he asked irrelevantly. Rosy looked quickly at him, wondering what he was driving at. Rosy thought a moment before answering, thought of the D Bar T and the shape it was in, of Mary cooking for the hands, of the few scattered cattle on the range, of Winters' never working and simply living off what could be made at the ranch.

"No," he answered.

Quinn drew an envelope from his pocket and handed it to Rosy, who could feel the limpness of well-worn bills. Rosy handed it back to him, swearing under his breath.

"Keep it," Quinn said.

Rosy looked at him. "Hell no. It's yours. If Winters can't take care of himself, he shouldn't gamble."

"Give it to Dave."

"He won't take it."

Quinn laughed quietly. "Be sensible, man. That money wasn't honestly come by."

"You mean you used a cold deck?" Rosy asked slowly.

Quinn nodded. "I figured he couldn't afford to lose it. You see I'd heard about his wife."

"What about her?" Rosy asked carefully.

"Fine girl. Too fine for him."

Rosy didn't comment.

"I used marked cards," Quinn went on casually. "I figured I'd clean him and then talk to you. If he could afford it, all right. I'd let him win it back and then play him on the level. If he couldn't, it went back to his wife." He looked at Rosy with amusement in his fine, unwavering eyes. "It's better than lettin' him lose it at the other saloon, isn't it?"

"I reckon," Rosy said.

"Ever since I got in town two weeks ago," Quinn continued, "Winters had been ridin' me. I reckon he thought I was a tinhorn." He laughed. "He's wasted a lot of money findin' out I wasn't."

"What if he savvies it?" Rosy asked.

Quinn laughed again. "He won't. He might suspect, but he won't catch me."

The Chinaman brought them their food and they received it silently. When he was gone, Rosy said: "How'll you get it back to Dave? He won't take it."

"Shouldn't he know?" Quinn asked.

"I reckon. Not from me and not from you, though," Rosy said.

Quinn frowned in thought. He drew a clean slip of paper from his pocket and wrote on it. Finished, he handed it to Rosy, who read:

"Dick Turner staked me once when I didn't have a dime. It's taken twenty-five years to pay it back. Hear it is. I can't give my name, because I'm hiding, but the munny's clean. Good luck.

a friend."

Quinn took the paper, slipped it in the envelope with the money and then addressed the envelope to Mrs. Ted Winters.

"They can't question that," Quinn said.

Rosy nodded agreement. "When did Winters lose it?"

"Last night, early. He came in late in the afternoon and wouldn't play with the house men. I'm dealin' faro, but when things are slack I can sit in on a poker game. He waited for me."

"Early last night, you say?" Rosy asked, as casually as he

could. He felt his muscles stiffen, but he could not control them. "What time did he leave?"

"Eight-thirty or so."

Rosy took a slow, deep drink of coffee, fighting the slow horror that he felt. "Sure about that time?" he asked, when he was finished.

"Uh-huh. Why?" Quinn looked at him.

"Nothin'."

"You mean he might've passed the lake on his way home and there might have been men workin' there then?"

"He rode in from Soledad," Rosy lied. "I reckon he rode home around Coahuila Butte."

"Sure," Quinn said. Rosy didn't know what had made him lie to Quinn—perhaps a deep urge to protect Dave and Mary. For it was a lie. By way of Coahuila Butte and Soledad, Winters, leaving at eight-thirty, could not have made the spread by the time he did, not even lathering his horse like he did. Rosy wasn't sure what way he'd come home, but he was sure it wasn't by Soledad. And the thought made him a little sick. There was only one other way, and that was by the lake. Well, maybe the men hadn't started to work until ten o'clock or so. That was it. They had seen Winters in town, maybe, and knew he would be riding past the lake, so they waited until he had ridden home before they laid the dynamite.

The door to the restaurant swung open and two men entered, one the man whom Rosy had caught staring at him in the Free Throw.

"Know that *hombre* with the dead eye, the fat one that looks like his pants was comin' off?" Rosy asked Quinn. The gambler waited a few minutes before he looked.

"Don't know him. Does he look familiar to you?"

"Huh-uh, but he looks like he knows me."

Quinn had to be back at the faro table at seven-thirty, so Rosy left him and walked up the street to the hotel which was three doors past the Mile High. He engaged a room, went upstairs and washed. Winters kept forcing himself into his mind. If Winters could lose a thousand at poker, where was he getting the money? He couldn't get it from Mary's share of the ranch. Rosy doubted if Mary knew anything about it. And Winters didn't have a job. Had he saved money? Did he get it from the East? "It ain't a bit of business of mine," Rosy thought, "but yet it is in a way." He decided to look up Laredo Jackson and pump him. Maybe Laredo's air of mystery would vanish as soon as he had a few drinks under his belt.

He left the room. As he was going down the stairs he met the same strange still-eyed man that had come in the restaurant. The man nodded as men do who see a stranger so many times a day that they become almost acquainted.

Rosy nodded briefly in answer. Was this jasper following him? After all, there were only two restaurants in town and this man would doubtless pick the one nearest the Free Throw, just as he had done. And there was only one hotel in town, so if the man wanted to stop in town all night, he would almost have to choose this one. He dismissed it with a shrug. He was getting spooky. After all, why be concerned with a stranger when the important thing was finding out if Crowell was in town? And that gave him an idea.

Downstairs, he inquired of the clerk: "Anyone by the name of Crowell registered here?"

"A. J. Crowell? No, he left this mornin'," the clerk said. He was an old man, and seemed eager for conversation.

"You know him, do you?" Rosy asked.

"Never forget a face," the clerk said.

"You've been on duty all day?" Rosy asked. "I mean, he couldn't have come in and registered under another name?"

"No sir. I've been here every second since he checked out."

"Thanks."

Outside, he decided to look in the Mile High to see if Jackson was in a talkative mood.

Once through the swinging doors, the rank smell of alcohol and cheap tobacco struck him in the face like a thick, miasmic fog. Compared to the Mile High, the Free Throw was an aristocrat among saloons. The Mile High was large, but lacked the dance hall of the Free Throw. A glance around told Rosy that here was where the hard-cases of the town and surrounding country hung out. In one glance, he took in the faro and monte tables attended by sleek and soiled Mexicans; the two battered pool tables at the rear; the poker tables along the wall and finally the bar. He grinned. Planted smack in dead center of the bar was Laredo Jackson, five feet of elbow room on each side of him. The bartenders were eyeing him with silent disapproval.

Laredo was facing the bar and mirror and saw Rosy's reflection in it as the younger man joined him.

"Two whiskies," he said to the bartender without turning his head. Then to Rosy: "How's things, Red?"

"Good." Rosy saw the customers watching them. "Don't you like company or don't they like you?" he asked.

Laredo turned and faced the room, hoisting his elbows on the bar. He was so short it gave him the appearance of a hunchback.

"I got throwed out of this stinkin' pothole five years ago," he announced loudly. "I git drunk once a week here hopin' somebody'll try it again." He spat noisily and surveyed the room belligerently. "Y'see?" he said, turning back to his drink. The bartenders looked at each other and shrugged.

Rosy decided it was useless to try and talk with him. The little foreman was well on his way to being drunk now. Out of courtesy Rosy bought a round, examining the room behind him in the bar mirror. As he was watching, he saw the swinging door open in and the same man Rosy had seen watching him in the Free Throw, the restaurant, and the hotel came in. The man cast a hurried glance around the room, saw Rosy and sauntered back to the faro table. Rosy was sure now that he was being followed.

He leaned over to Laredo. "Know that jasper that just came in? Fat, stocky, with them cedar-handled guns. Got dead eyes in his face."

Very slowly, Laredo set down his glass and looked up at him. "Why might you be wantin' to know?"

"I think he's followin' me."

Laredo turned, and with difficulty singled out the man. Then he turned and grinned. "Sure I know him," he said loudly. "He's an understrapper for a coyote named Sayres."

"Easy," Rosy warned in a low voice. "Some of these hard-cases have got ears."

"Hell," Laredo said. "They know it too. That *hombre* over there, I dunno his name, but you can bet he's a primmer donner with a runnin' iron. His boss owns part of the herd of nigh every man in this room."

The talk at the bar dribbled off into silence, and the customers stared at the two.

"Wally Sayres, this jasper's boss—" Laredo began loudly.

"Let's go over to the Free Throw," Rosy said easily. The room was almost silent, and all eyes were turned on the two men.

"Jerry Boardman made Wally Sayres a present of fifty head of Three B steers last year," Laredo continued, his voice booming through the room. "They call it makin' a present in this country when you turn your back."

It was out. Rosy half turned toward the room, watching the faro table out of the corner of his eye. He saw the stocky man leave the table and come walking slowly toward the bar. The man stopped some ten feet from the bar, feet planted solidly.

"What was you sayin' about Sayres?" the man drawled quietly.

Laredo spat precisely and had trouble focusing his eyes on the man. "What was I sayin' about Sayres?" he repeated. "Why, nothin' much, 'cept he's the forkedest jasper west, east, north, south or in the middle of the Rio Grande."

Rosy swiftly calculated the lights. His gaze swiveled back to the man standing before them.

"And that ain't all," Laredo continued, his elbows coming slowly from the bar. "He feeds and runs the damnedest pack of buzzards that ever forked a bronc."

The man was leaning forward a little, and Rosy could see his features bloated with anger.

"Take it easy," Rosy told the man calmly. "Jackson's drunk." He felt his spine crawling, crawling.

"You been flappin' that chin of yours once too often, Jackson," the man drawled. "If you ain't yellow-bellied, back it up! Fill your hand!"

Rosy's hands blurred to his guns, which clicked swiftly as they settled, cocked, rock-steady, pointing at the man's belly.

"Better let it die," Rosy said silkily. The man's thick hands were wrapped around his gun butts, where they froze. Rosy stepped in front of Laredo, who had barely realized what had passed. This was no wise play, he thought swiftly. There were men behind them, besides the bartenders. The stocky man's hands did not relax off his guns. He was watching for a break.

Rosy's guns up-tilted a little and spoke in three lances of flame. The lights diminished in three sudden gradations, the last shot bringing darkness. Rosy pushed Laredo from him, then moved quickly after the little foreman. As Rosy expected, the insulted outlaw had drawn his guns and was shooting in the dark, his slugs slapping into the bar.

Rosy reached for Laredo's feet and lifted, heaving the slight body over the bar, then vaulted over himself, dropping behind it on his hands and knees. Some one else was shooting now from across the room and Rosy heard the first tinkle of glass which denoted a broken mirror. He felt for Laredo and discovered him in a heap, passed out. Gun in his right hand, Laredo's collar in left, he moved toward the back of the building. He bumped into some one and promptly slugged out with his gun.

"One bartender down," he muttered. There was a blind rush for the doors, shouts, muttered curses, more shots. Feeling his way along the wall, he swung Laredo to his shoulder, and made his way cautiously until he felt the door handle. He shoved the door open and fell forward. A whine of slugs sang over his head. He rolled out of range, dragging Laredo, and lunged to his feet.

Across the street fronting squarely on the alley was the sheriff's office. Rosy made for it, taking the alley between the office and the bank. In the lean-to, which had no door, he deposited Laredo on the floor and tried the door to the back room. It was locked. He shouldered against it, broke the lock and carried

Laredo into the room. He remembered the room contained a cot and without striking a match he found it. Laredo was sleeping peacefully as Rosy laid him on the cot. He struck a match, shielded its flare and examined Laredo. There were no wounds and he rose, laughing quietly, and left the building, closing the door carefully behind him.

He drew a deep breath. Things were shaping up. He knew now that the understrapper in the saloon had been following him, and that the fight with Laredo had merely been a pretense to shoot it out with him, Rosy. The man had wanted to kill him. Why? Who was Sayres? Laredo had told so little about him that Rosy was curious.

He built a cigarette slowly, leaning against the office wall in the alley. One thing was certain, now. He had a clue to work on. And it seemed to point to Sayres. He determined to do some prowling and find out some things. The commotion in the Mile High was dying out now and through the high side windows Rosy could see that the lamps were being lighted. That fat jasper would have cleared out by now. He'd pick him up later. First, he wanted to prowl and find out a little about Crowell—and Sayres. As he started to cross to the shelter of the dark alley behind the Mile High, he thought of something.

He fished around for a stub of a pencil in his pocket, tore the back off a soiled envelope and wrote: "Quinn: If I was you, I'd change my room tonight. Rand." Maybe it was unnecessary, but this fat understrapper of Sayres had seen him talking to Quinn, and Rosy didn't want the gambler pulled into the trouble.

At the bank corner, he flagged a young Mexican, gave him a dollar and told him to deliver the note to Quinn.

Then Rosy ducked back into the alley and headed for the north end of town where the livery stable was located.

He was taking a chance, he knew, but men who worked around horses and who ran livery stables were usually good men—if they would talk. And Rosy intended to hear some talk.

The office of the livery stable was lighted and Rosy strolled in. An old man was sitting at a desk, poring over a feed catalog.

Rosy sized him up in a glance. The man had good eyes, a kind, homely face, and was slow in movement as he looked up at Rosy while still leafing the pages. "Oh," Rosy said. "The other feller ain't here?" He looked around the bare room, at the cold stove and two rough chairs.

"The night man? Louie? No, I give him the night off. Anything I can do for you?"

Rosy pretended disappointment. "No, I reckon not. I hoped I'd git him in. You see, he sort of thought he had a job lined up for me. I'm new here," he said, by way of explanation.

"That so?" the old man said. "Set down." Rosy sat. "Where did Louie think he could git you a job? Here?" The old man was smiling now, and Rosy smiled back.

"No. He wasn't sure, but he thought a feller by the name of Sayres that's got a spread somewhere near here could use me."

Rosy saw the eyes change and the old man's jaw clamped shut. "Louie said that?" the old man asked. "Huh-uh. You must have talked to somebody else."

"Might be," Rosy said carelessly. "He was a sort of fat feller, with dead eyes and packed a couple of cedar-handled guns."

The old man laughed, and Rosy thought he detected a note of relief in his voice. "That wasn't Louie. Louie's tall and thin as a rail." The old man looked at him. "I think I know who you talked to, though. He works for Sayres himself. Hangs around here some."

"That so?" Rosy said, looking up. "Think he could get me a job?" The old man looked at him a long time before he answered. "You ain't a wild one, are you?"

"Not me," Rosy said. "Why?"

"That's the only kind Sayres hires. I don't reckon you'd like the job."

"What's the matter with him?" Rosy said bluntly. "Work's work."

"Not if it's—well, not if you have to do things that it's pretty awkward answerin' for," the old man said.

Rosy looked keenly at him. "Meanin' what? I'm a stranger here and I'd be much obliged for a straight steer."

"Meanin' rustlin', killin's, dry-gulchin', workin' with men that ain't ever earned a honest penny in their lives. Stealin' mebbe. Mebbe holdin' up banks."

"So," Rosy said. He smiled slowly. "If I tolled in with Sayres, I might see some of that, huh?"

"I never said you would," the old man said, and he smiled. They understood each other.

"Where does this Sayres hang out at?"

"Used to be up in them badlands behind Old Cartridge, but they tell me he's pulled out of there. You got to ride up the valley a ways, then turn east into them mountains. They say you can git acrost them, but I'm danged if I know how. Sayres does. Leastways, people think that's where he hangs out."

"Much obliged, old-timer," Rosy said. "I reckon I'll look somewhere else."

He swung out the door into the night. That helped. Could it be Sayres was the man who had done the dynamiting? It fitted in. Crowell could be behind Sayres, who had orders to blow out the lake, so Crowell could step in and buy the D Bar T and the Draw Three for a song.

He didn't know, but he was going to find out. He heard a train whistle far off and he quickened his pace toward town, using the alleys again. He headed straight for the station. The train was just a little ahead of him and was panting in the station as Rosy approached. Hoagy Henshaw was in conversation with the agent in the middle of the platform. Rosy waited until Hoagy was free then beckoned him out of earshot of the idlers. Hoagy greeted him with a slow smile.

"What can I do for you, Rand?"

"Dunno," Rosy said. "You on the morning run out of here?"

"Sure. Every other morning. Why?"

"This morning?"

"Sure."

"Was there a little short jasper got on here this morning? Dark, in black clothes, city clothes. Had black eyes, and pretty mouthy in his talk."

Hoagy shook his head slowly. "Can't remember him."

"Think," Rosy said. "When he looked at you, he always looked at your tie or your coll—"

Hoagy snapped his fingers. "Hell, yes. I remember him. I never did find out where he got off. I never seen him and I didn't get his ticket."

"Then he got off?" Rosy said eagerly. "Where?"

"Before Walpais, the first town east."

"That's all I wanted to know. Much obliged." And before Hoagy could blink, Rosy was gone into the night.

He jogged up the alley, turned at the bank, walked over to the Free Throw and got his horse. As he swung past the hotel, his bay was at full gallop.

"And me loafin' in town the whole damn day," he raged. "He's either seen Mary by now, or he's goin' to tomorrow mornin', I don't know which."

12
Boot Marks

Rosy reached the ranch well after one o'clock. The house was dark, still, and he wondered if Hank Lowe had stayed all night. If so, then it was encouraging, for if Crowell had already been to see Mary about buying the place, the sheriff would have got him. And if he'd got him, then he would have brought him into town. And Rosy had not met him on the road, so the chances were that the sheriff was staying all night, and that Crowell had not appeared yet.

Rosy let down the corral bars, unhooked his hull and slung it off his bay, whistling in a minor key the while. He heard a sharp object strike the barn and he stopped.

"That damn cinch buckle," he groaned softly. "If I don't find it tonight, I never will." He was impatient to get in the house and talk to Mary and the sheriff, but his caution kept him there.

He slung the saddle over the corral bars, after a glance at the clear sky for a night rain, then strode over to the barn and pulled a handful of matches from his pocket. Squatting, he struck a match and started looking for the buckle.

He had looked a half minute perhaps, when a low cry escaped him.

There, in the soft dirt of the corral, was the same footprint that he had seen at the lake!

He stared unbelieving, his mind racing. The match burned him and died, and he struck another. This time he measured track, but he knew it was the same. Whose could it be? His? No. Mary's or Dave's? No. The sheriff's? Hardly. Winters'? . . . Damn, yes! Now he remembered, Winters wore army boots, or eastern riding boots.

Rosy squatted against the barn, his heart numb. It was Winters, all right. Whether he wanted to believe it or not, Winters knew about the lake being dynamited. This, together with Quinn's evidence, was damning. And the cigarette butt. Of course, Winters smoked tailor-mades. Why hadn't he thought of it! Rosy rubbed a hand over his eyes and groaned softly. Good God, what if Dave knew it—or Mary? What if they found out, and sooner or later they would? Rosy felt sick and he hunched against the barn, miserable. He sat that way for fifteen minutes before he realized that he would have to pull himself together.

He tried to reason it out. Winters knew about the lake being dynamited, had perhaps talked to Sayres—if Sayres had done the dynamiting—that night. Maybe he knew why Crowell wanted to buy the place. Maybe he was in with Crowell. Rosy refused to believe it, but at the same time he felt it was true, knew it was true.

He strolled over to the corral bars and leaned on them. Why not chuck it, saddle up and light out? What business was it of his? A sudden shame swept over him as he thought of it. No. He and Dave were riding this out together. Dave and Mary would have to know about Winters in the end—but Rosy could make it as easy for them as possible. He didn't know how, but he would.

And the first thing to do was to keep it from them until it had to be spilled, until he could simply take Winters in and have him tell his own story.

Rosy looked at the house. He wondered how much Winters knew. How much had the sheriff told Mary and Winters about the conversation at Hammond's and what had been learned about Crowell? Very little, Rosy guessed, for the sheriff was as close-mouthed as they came. Winters, then, wouldn't know that they suspected Crowell. And if Winters was in with Crowell, and Crowell hadn't been to see Mary yet, then Winters would be sure to get the sheriff out of the house before Crowell came in the morning. And it was Rosy's duty to hear what Crowell had to say, and see if Winters was in with him. He turned his horse out of the corral and slapped him on the rump. Without seeing the horse, Winters wouldn't know he was here.

Sick at heart, he turned into the stable, crawled up into the loft to wait for dawn.

Rosy sat erect with a lunge. He had been asleep and it was already daylight. Was he too late? No, there was the sheriff's voice below, and Winters' genial laugh. He crawled softly through the hay until he found a crack in the boards and could look down into the corral. They were saddling up.

"You like a early start, don't you?" the sheriff drawled amiably.

"Sure. I'm up every morning before the rest of them are," Winters said.

"Well, if I didn't have to be at work, I'd like to ride down to Soledad with you and yarn with old Pablo."

"It's tough being a busy man," Winters said with a laugh.

"Busy but useless," the sheriff said.

Rosy saw Winters let down the corral gate, and both men led their horses through.

"Say," the sheriff said. "I might ride down with you at that. It's early yet."

"Yeah. Guess I better not at that. It'll put me in town pretty late. Well, so long."

"So long."

Both men mounted, the sheriff heading up the long slope to the notch, Winters to the south toward Soledad.

Winters had done a smooth job of getting the sheriff out of the way, Rosy thought bitterly. He'd risen three hours earlier than usual, then had kept the sheriff from riding with him to Soledad by that excuse that the nesters had to be informed. With a sinking heart, Rosy admitted that it looked as if Winters was expecting Crowell, and had gone down to meet him.

He climbed down into a stall and sat on a feedbox. If he had hoped the morning would clear things for him, he was wrong. It was still bewildering. And through all of Rosy's thoughts about Winters ran the refrain: "Why? Why is he doin' it?" But there was no answer.

He built a cigarette to steady his nerves before he saw Mary. What was he going to tell her? Just that he thought a man was going to come and try to buy the ranch from her, and that she shouldn't sell.

He gave himself another five minutes, then hitched up his belt and walked toward the house, his face bland, his heart filled with a damning misery.

Inside, Mary looked up from the table. She had been sitting staring out the window.

"Hullo, Rosy." She forced a weak smile. "Where's Dave?"

"He stayed in town. He had some business," Rosy said evasively.

"I didn't hear you come in."

"I'm part Injun," Rosy said and grinned. She smiled back. "Reckon you got any cold hotcakes I can have?" Rosy asked. He cursed himself for not brushing the hay off his clothes better. She would be able to tell he had slept in the loft.

"Sure. And the coffee's hot." She rose and went to the stove, while Rosy washed out in the lean-to. When he returned, freshened by the cold water, and minus some of the hay wisps, his face was inscrutable.

Suddenly, Mary whirled, her chin up defiantly, but her eyes lusterless and dull.

"Rosy."

He looked up from the table where he had been tracing the pattern of the oilcloth.

"What will we do, Rosy? What's it all about?" she cried. She was breathing deeply and Rosy wondered if she would cry. But he misjudged her.

"About what?"

"You too!" Mary said, stamping her foot. "Why don't you tell me? Isn't it half my spread? Are you afraid I can't bear to hear the truth? Is that it? The sheriff just hummed and hawed around and didn't say a word. It was awkward enough to have him here, anyway, after he wouldn't let Dave come into town. But to have him—oh, Rosy. Tell me!"

"What did Hank tell you?" Rosy asked.

"Nothing! Except that the lake had been blown out on top of Hammond's mine, and both it and our spread are ruined. Did Hammond do it, Rosy? Who did? Why? Don't you know?"

Rosy shook his head slowly, preparing his lie. "It's no wonder Hank didn't tell you any more. He couldn't. None of us can. We don't know who did it. But one thing we're sure of—Hammond didn't."

"Is that the truth?"

"Naked as a brandin' iron," Rosy said, and grinned. Mary sighed and turned to the stove.

That was over, but the worst was to come, Rosy thought. He put it off until fresh hotcakes were before him and he had put away a plateful.

"Some jaspers comin' to try and buy the ranch this mornin'," he announced and immediately stuffed hotcakes in his mouth.

"Who?"

"Dunno," he lied coolly. "Just heard. Dave heard about it too. He says not to sell just in case he wasn't home when this jasper got here."

Mary looked at him strangely. "What makes him think I would sell my half?"

"I don't think he did. He just wanted to be sure." Rosy went on eating, looking attentively at his plate.

"You're a poor liar, Rosy," Mary said quietly.

Rosy looked up at her and felt the blood creep into his face.

"I know it," he said just as quietly.

"Where's Dave?"

"I'm not lyin' now. He's ridin' and I'm not sure where." He smiled at her. "And if I did, I wouldn't tell you."

Mary's laugh was spontaneous and it warmed Rosy to hear it. "You're a funny man, Rosy—but a nice one."

"You'll think I'm a lot funnier when you hear this next," Rosy said doggedly.

"What?"

"I want you to hide me so I can hear what this jasper says that wants to buy the ranch. I got to." His serious tone impressed Mary, for she nodded mutely.

"It's none of my business, understand," Rosy said, knowing that he was blushing, but persisting anyway; "but I've got to hear him."

"Can you tell me why, Rosy?" she asked him.

Rosy shook his head and looked away.

"I wish—"

"Wait!" Rosy commanded, holding up his hand. They were quiet. The steady beat of hoofs came to them and Mary ran to the window.

"Why, it's Ted—and a stranger. Is that the man, Rosy?"

"I reckon," Rosy said shortly. "Where can I hide? And you better get these dishes cleared away."

Mary ran to the front room, Rosy following her. He picked the low davenport, over which a huge Navajo rug was thrown, for his hiding place.

Mary held it up while he crawled under. As he was on his knees he looked up at her. "Remember. Don't sign anything. And believe me, I'm trying to help you."

Mary nodded, and Rosy crawled under the davenport. He realized that Mary knew he was keeping things from her, but it couldn't be helped. He had been afraid to mention that the man

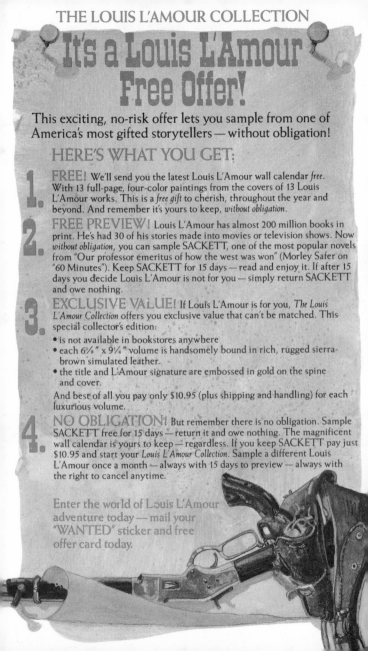

FREE — MAGNIFICENT WALL CALENDAR!
FREE — PREVIEW OF SACKETT
• No Obligation!   • No Purchase Necessary!

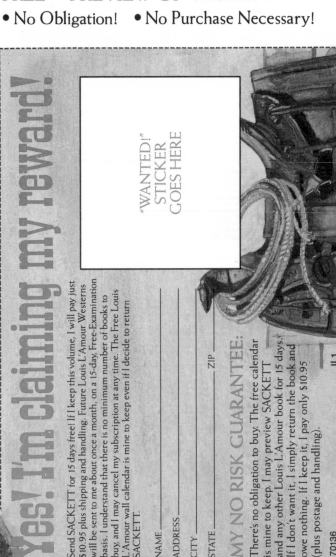

Yes! I'm claiming my reward!

Send SACKETT for 15 days free! If I keep this volume, I will pay just $10.95 plus shipping and handling. Future Louis L'Amour Westerns will be sent to me about once a month, on a 15-day, Free-Examination basis. I understand that there is no minimum number of books to buy, and I may cancel my subscription at any time. The Free Louis L'Amour wall calendar is mine to keep even if I decide to return SACKETT.

NAME _____

ADDRESS _____

CITY _____

STATE _____ ZIP _____

"WANTED!" STICKER GOES HERE

MY NO RISK GUARANTEE:

There's no obligation to buy. The free calendar is mine to keep. I may preview SACKETT and any other Louis L'Amour book for 15 days. If I don't want it, I simply return the book and owe nothing. If I keep it, I pay only $10.95 (plus postage and handling).

IL1

70136

Track down and capture exciting western adventure from one of America's foremost novelists!

• It's free! • No obligation! • Exclusive value!

coming to buy the ranch was named Crowell. He wanted Mary's surprise at the name to be genuine, so as to impress Crowell with the fact that none of them suspected him. He placed his guns at his head and lay sprawled on his stomach, listening.

He heard the two men enter the kitchen, the sound of voices, then Mary saying distinctly: "Come into the front room, Mr. Crowell."

Rosy heard them enter the room and take chairs around the fireplace, which was cold now. Crowell offered Winters a cigar, which he accepted with thanks, and lighted. Rosy resisted the impulse to lift the blanket and have a look at Crowell.

Winters spoke now, his voice thick with cigar smoke. "I met Mr. Crowell on the way to Soledad, darling, and he asked me to come back with him. I think he's going to give us some money, so listen carefully."

All of them laughed.

"Mrs. Winters," Crowell began, and Rosy noticed his voice was confident and smooth, "perhaps you didn't remember my name when we were introduced. I'm the Crowell that's written you about selling the ranch."

Rosy heard Mary's little gasp of surprise. "But I thought—I —I thought those letters were written by Hammond, and just signed 'Crowell.' "

"Hammond?" Crowell asked vaguely.

"Yes. He owns the Draw Three mine in Single Shot." And Mary explained their quarrel over the lake and the suspicion that Hammond was trying to buy the ranch under the name of Crowell. "Frankly, I was sure it was Hammond because no one ever came to inquire in person."

Crowell laughed genially. "Quite right. One for you. I was merely feeling you out because this ranching syndicate I work for wasn't quite sure it wanted the property. We are now, however."

"I'm sorry, Mr. Crowell," Mary said. "One letter from me would have settled this for good and all. I'm afraid you've wasted your time. I don't want to sell."

"That's strange," Crowell said. "When I talked with your brother last night, he was sure that you'd want to sell, too."

"Too?" Mary said, a little catch in her voice.

Rosy heard some papers rustle. "Yes. In my hotel room last night when he signed this deed, he told me he thought you'd be willing to let your half go for a reasonable price, now that the water's gone."

The paper rustled again, there was quiet for a second, and Rosy heard Mary gasp. "But—it's signed. Signed by Dave!" she cried.

"Is there anything the matter?" Crowell asked politely.

"No. I'm sorry," Mary said. "It—it was just such a surprise. I didn't know he intended to sell out. When did you see him, Mr. Crowell?"

"I can tell you exactly," Crowell said. "He had to run to catch the train."

"Train? You—you mean he's left town?"

"I presume so."

Rosy raged silently. Where had Crowell got Dave's signature? A forgery? And now Mary would think that Rosy had hesitated to tell her about Dave because he didn't want her to know that Dave had left town—run out on her. He felt his heart thumping wildly as he waited for her answer.

"But—but I don't understand," Mary said weakly.

"It's easily explained, Mrs. Winters," Crowell said. "Your brother realized that the place was worthless to him now. He decided on the spur of the moment to let his half go. He knew I would be out first thing this morning to tell you, so he didn't bother to send word out."

"But why are you buying it if it's so worthless?" Mary asked. Rosy strangled the desire to shout. Mary had got a grip on herself.

"Grass," Crowell said bluntly. "This close to the railroad, there's very little grass to be had. Our syndicate buys stock in Old Mexico, fattens it in the States near a railroad, and shoves it into market when the prices are right."

"But the water?"

Crowell laughed easily. "We have money, Mrs. Winters. Building up that wall again with a crew of men is a small matter for us. It takes money, of course, but then we have it."

Maybe, Rosy thought. There's that little matter of the springs blown under that you missed, Mister. But Mary wouldn't be expected to know about that.

"Of course," Crowell was saying, "I don't want you to sell against your will. There's no reason why you should. But—" and here Rosy imagined him leaning forward, emphasizing his points—"you realize, of course, that when your brother signed away his half, it included the house, barns, implements, horses —everything on the place. We intend to take the house and build it over into a large bunkhouse for forty men. Naturally, if you stayed here, we could only take over half of it, but then it would be rather uncomfortable for you. Then there's the water. If we damned up the lake again at our own expense, it wouldn't be fair for you to water your stock at our expense." He laughed shortly. "It would be quite uncomfortable for you, Mrs. Winters."

"I know. But I can't believe Dave would do it!" Mary cried suddenly.

"Very sensible, I should say, Mrs. Winters. He realized he didn't have the money to get the place on its legs again—dam the lake and everything, so he did the wise thing and took a good sum of money for it."

"Ted, what do you think?" Mary asked suddenly, her voice pleading.

"It looks like Dave has run out on us, Mary. Without him to run the place, I'd say we might as well give up and sell out to Mr. Crowell." Winters' voice was wistful, regretful, and Rosy could gladly have strangled him.

He heard Mary get out of her chair and walk to the window. When she spoke again, it was as if she was arguing with herself.

"But you'll have a court fight with the spread, Mr. Crowell. Hammond claims the lake too."

"But who owns it?"

"We do," Mary said.

"And you have the papers to prove it?"

"Yes."

"May I see them?"

Mary hesitated a moment, then said: "Surely."

Rosy knew she was wanting time to digest all this, to try and reason it out before she acted. Getting the paper would give her time. He heard her excuse herself and leave the room. Then he heard some one get up and say in a low voice:

"God, this is shaky! Do you think it's going to work?" It was Crowell speaking.

"Sure. Dave's signature convinced her. Now don't lose your head."

Crowell laughed softly. "I won't. But since Dave and Hammond aren't fighting each other, I don't know how much they suspect. And where's that red-head?"

"He hasn't been around here. We're safe enough," Winters said positively.

"And you couldn't get a thing out of that fat sheriff?"

"No, I couldn't pry a thing out of him."

"Well, there's only one thing to do. I'll register at the hotel today like I'd just come in. Then I'll see Hammond again and try to talk him into selling and then I'm disappearing."

Winters laughed. "You're getting spooky. They don't suspect anything."

"Maybe not. But I'm not chancing it. Every one is doing just what the Boss said they wouldn't. Except Turner. He walked right into Sayres' hand like I told you."

"Did Sayres have a tough time cracking him?"

"Not from what Chinch said when he gave me this paper."

"What does the Boss think?"

"He's satisfied with Sayres' work but he's on my tail to finish this."

"Don't worry. You'll—watch out!"

As Mary came into the room, Crowell was saying to Winters: "—and it can be done without too much expense."

Rosy had been listening until his ears rang. So Winters was in on it! And Sayres had Dave a prisoner! But more than that, *there was a boss behind them!* Even behind Crowell. A thousand questions raced through Rosy's brain. Was Dave alive? What was to prevent them from killing him now that they had his signature? But the one question that Rosy had to answer and couldn't—*Who was the boss?*

Rosy got a grip on his panic by a desperate effort. He heard Mary say to Crowell:

"Here's the land papers."

He heard Crowell take them. Rosy laid his head on his arms and shut his eyes, trying to rearrange his plan. He had hoped to be able to step out and capture Crowell and maybe Winters. Now it was useless, because they were only understrappers. There was a bigger man, a nameless, sinister, ruthless brain behind them. If he took Crowell now, Crowell would close his mouth tighter than an Indian's, because Rosy couldn't prove a thing against him. And that meant that the Boss would never be known. No, he couldn't tip his hand now. There was only one thing to do. *Follow Crowell until he led them to the boss!* He had to let Crowell walk out of here, let him go on with his scheming work until he betrayed the whole gang. And more important than all the rest, Dave must be rescued! Immediately, for God knows what that fiend of a Sayres would do to him.

"All in order, Mrs. Winters," Crowell said. "I think we can afford to pay an extra two thousand for that paper. It's fool proof."

Rosy heard Mary sigh. "I—I don't think I'll sell, Mr. Crowell. Not right away, anyway."

Rosy sighed so loudly that he thought he must have been heard.

"Well, I think you'll regret it, Mrs. Winters. But I won't insist. We'll give you exactly what we gave Dave, plus the two thousand of course. Won't you take time to reconsider before you give your refusal?"

"Why—yes," Mary said hesitantly. "How long will the offer be open?"

"Until tonight at train time," Crowell said, and Rosy heard

him rise. "I'll be registered at the hotel, at Single Shot, so if you change your mind you'll know where to find me."

"That will be fine," Mary said.

"Good-by, Mrs. Winters," Crowell said. "No. Don't bother to come out with me. I hope to hear from you by tonight. Good-by."

Rosy heard the outside door open and shut. He felt weak with excitement.

"Mary,"—it was Winters speaking pleadingly—"you can't be serious about not wanting to sell now that Dave has run out on us!"

"Let's go in the kitchen, Ted," Mary said quietly.

"Damned if I will!" Winters exploded. "I want to know if you're going to sell. Let's get rid of this ramshackle old place and go east where we belong."

Rosy heard Mary's heels on the floor, headed for the kitchen. Then they stopped abruptly and scraped, as if she had turned around suddenly.

"Look here," Winters said in a cold voice. "Cut out this sentimental nonsense. We'll have a fortune. Dave's out of it—"

"He isn't," Mary said desperately.

"Isn't he?" Winters said sardonically. "Are you doubting Crowell's word?"

"Please let's go to the kitchen," Mary begged.

Rosy was squirming in embarrassment for her.

"Answer me," Winters ordered harshly.

"No," Mary retorted heatedly. "I'm not doubting anybody's word. He's wrong. I know Dave too well to think he'd do a thing like that!"

"Take a fortune instead of a chance to run a bunch of mangy cattle?" Winters asked sarcastically. "You overestimate that jailbird's love for work."

Rosy heard Mary gasp and he fought back the impulse to fling off the davenport and beat Winters to a pulp. "If I do, the whole thing is spoiled," he told himself savagely, regretfully.

"Why not say it?" Winters said. "It's true. He's run off now and left us to share this place of sentiment and misplaced loyalty."

"Let's not talk about it, Ted," Mary said quietly. "After all, I'm the one to decide."

"Are you?" Winters sneered. "You're waiting for that no-good brother to turn up after another eight years and ask his advice."

Mary did not answer.

"You had chances to sell before Dave got here," Winters continued. "You refused. Now, since the place has been made worthless, you still refuse. Why?"

Rosy wondered if she'd break down and tell him. His ears thudded with the angry pumping of his blood.

"You wouldn't understand," Mary said calmly. "It's not sentiment. It's—it's just that I've lived here all my life and love it. If I had to leave it, it would mean half my life was gone."

"A cow-country gal," Winters sneered. "Just a calico sweetheart. All right,"—his tone was gathering confidence— "you'll either take the offer for the place or look for a new husband. I'm through if I have to stay!"

"I thought that was it, Ted," Mary said quietly.

"Then you won't take it?"

"No."

Rosy heard the sharp slap of flesh on flesh and Mary's startled cry of pain. Then the door slammed and Rosy hurled the davenport from him and scrambled to his feet. Mary was sobbing in a chair.

He walked up to her slowly and looked down at her a long moment.

"I'm sorry, Mary. I didn't mean to listen, but I couldn't help it."

"He hit me, Rosy," Mary sobbed out.

"I heard him," Rosy said quietly, too quietly. Mary looked up.

"Rosy, you won't do anything to him, will you?"

He studied her face before he answered. "He's your husband and you're my friend. I reckon I'll tell him"—his voice died as he watched her eyes. "No, I won't," he said softly. "It's not my business. I reckon if you want me to do anything, I'll always be here to ask."

"D-don't do anything to him," she sobbed, then added bitterly: "The beast."

Rosy didn't say anything more, but uncomfortably twirled his hat while Mary sobbed desperately.

"It isn't the first time, Rosy," Mary said brokenly. "He's done it before."

Rosy waited until she stopped crying, then laid a hand on her shoulder.

"Pack some stuff. We're going to town."

Mary looked up at him. "Where?"

"Hammond's girl is alone. You can stay there with her. But I don't want you in this place."

"Is it Ted?"

"Partly."

Mary nodded dumbly. "Did I do right with Crowell, Rosy? Has Dave—"

"Let's go," Rosy cut in on her. "Dave hasn't done anything. And I'm just beginnin' to understand some things." He started for the door. "Pack some stuff. I'll saddle up."

He looked at her sitting forlorn in the deep chair and a sudden wave of pity engulfed him. "You did fine, Mary. Sometime you'll understand how fine."

As Rosy raced for the corral, he already had a plan half formed. Laredo was in town. So was the sheriff. They could help him, could take care of Crowell, while he rode out to see about Dave. Maybe Laredo knew where Sayres' hangout was, and could tell him. Haltingly, painfully, a plan of action was fermenting in Rosy's mind. As he yanked the cinch tight, just as Mary came running out of the house, he smiled bleakly.

He had it!

13
"We've Got You, Turner"

Dave had argued with the sheriff at the lake. He hadn't mentioned his intentions until they had found the tracks, which were plentiful on the side of the lake against the mountain. They had been washed badly, but they could be followed. They led around the base of Old Cartridge to the rock rim, where they skirted the mountain. And here, where the trail was only a few feet wide, the dynamiters had placed a last charge, blowing the trail out behind them and cutting off pursuit. It meant that Dave would have to go down into the valley again and ride north for ten miles or so until the rock rim petered out and he could enter the canyons. He told the sheriff this, and said that he wanted to ride alone. At first the sheriff had objected, but Dave was firm. It was one man's work, and not to be attempted by two or twenty. Hank had given in grudgingly, but had agreed to ride to the D Bar T and stay the night, telling Mary of the dynamiting.

At parting Dave had borrowed a Colt from him, and a handful of cartridges. The gun he wrapped in his slicker and tied behind the cantle, for the rain was over. He rode down the wash again, past the Draw Three and headed up the valley. There was a rough pack trail to follow that skirted the dry wash, and he let his sturdy roan pick the pace, for there would be some rough riding further on in the canyon country.

He thought of everything that happened to him since he had come home. None of it made sense. Why would any one first try to bushwhack him, then destroy his ranch?

He knew only too well that he was ruined. With the water gone, the D Bar T was worthless. But what hurt him the most was that Mary was ruined too. It didn't matter so much to him, since he could get out and draw cowpuncher's wages, and so could Rosy. But Mary was different. He knew her affection for the ranch, and now that it was worthless and would scarcely support one person Mary and Ted would leave.

Winters would take up a position again as a mining engineer and Mary would follow him, maybe to Mexico, Alaska, South America, a wanderer on the face of the earth in pursuit of wages and a temporary home. Dave winced. It would be like penning up a wild horse in a dark barn and feeding him well, but watching him slowly pine away for the freedom of the open range.

Dave felt his weight shift against the cantle, drawing him out of his reverie. The horse was ascending a rocky ledge which rose up ahead. The trail had left the stream bed and had turned in toward the mountains. A limestone shelf, Dave reflected idly; first it probably backed up the water into a big lake which reached miles up the valley. Then the water from the outlet gradually sawed its way down through the limestone until the stream ran through a deep gorge. His horse settled into the muscle-stretching pull willingly and Dave settled back into his reverie.

He was yanked out of it by a dim warning whistle, a hissing. Automatically, his right hand streaked to his gun. He had it clear of leather when the rope settled around him and he was yanked from his saddle. He landed on his back, knocking the wind out of him, but he turned over. The rope had tightened above his elbows so that his forearm and gun were clear. Sixty feet off a rider, his rope dallied round the horn of his saddle, was just dismounting, oblivious to the fact that Dave could shoot.

Dave took a snap shot, saw the horse shy into the man and both disappear behind a rock as he was dragged forward helplessly on his chest. Then it was quiet, and Dave struggled to roll off his arm and get his gun clear.

"Better drop it, Turner," the man called from behind a rock. "We've got you."

Dave took as careful sight as he could, aiming where the

rope disappeared around the rock. He shot and the rope snapped. He lunged to his feet.

This time he didn't hear the rope. It came from behind him. Two of them, he thought. It settled from behind with the viciousness of a striking snake around his waist, yanking his gun arm down close to his body. He sat down abruptly as the rope was jerked taut.

Feeling the rhythmic tugs of the rope as some one came cautiously hand over hand up to him, Dave turned his head. He saw two men approaching, one with both guns out.

"Don't move, Turner," one of them called.

Dave was jerked erect, and his guns taken from him. The man who tried to rope him first came out from behind his rock, nursing a skinned elbow, and joined his companions. This man had still, dead eyes, Dave noticed, and his body was heavy, formless, and his pants sagged over a bloated belly.

"Maybe you'd like us to finish what Freeman didn't," this man said with a sneer.

"So you know about Freeman, eh?" Dave asked.

Another of the men started to speak. He was a swarthy individual, dressed in tattered range clothes, and he spoke around a cheekful of tobacco which dribbled down his unshaven chin in brownish-yellow streaks. "Why shouldn't—" "Shut up, Lew," the heavy man ordered. "Let's get off this trail before somebody comes along."

They walked behind a rock off the trail. The other man, a small vicious-looking hard-case with a rat's shifty eyes, prodded Dave with his gun.

Lew collected the horses, including Dave's, and brought them behind the rock. The man with the dead eyes looked at his horse and cursed. Dave's shot had creased the horse's neck, making it bleed.

"You better trade nags with me, Reilly," he said to the rat-face. "This blood is liable to cause questions."

"Why? You goin' to town?"

"Sayres said to get 'em both, didn't he? And the red-headed *hombre* ain't here."

"All right," Reilly grunted. They seemed to ignore Dave with callous indifference.

"What's—" Dave began.

The outlaw with the dead eyes wheeled and drove his fist into Dave's face, sending him back against the rock. Reilly gouged Dave with the guns before he could stand erect again.

"That's for cuttin' down on us," Reilly snarled. "I ought to let you have it."

"Don't be a damned fool," the heavier man said. "You better take him off the trail, tie him and git goin'. I'm leavin'." He walked over to Reilly's horse, mounted, and rode off in the direction of town.

Reilly and Lew took Dave away from the road, behind a small butte. Reilly sat down and regarded Dave silently. "Turner," he drawled, "you ain't got much sense fer a man your age."

Dave did not answer, wondering if this wasn't another ruse to taunt him into speaking so they could hit him again.

Reilly started to speak to him again but he turned to Lew instead. "We better take the Five Points trail to the shack, hadn't we? Stay off the trail?"

"Yeah. There's too many damn prospectors wanderin' the other trails." They ordered Dave to mount, then tied his feet in the stirrups and his hands behind his back. They seemed to be experienced at this sort of thing, Dave noticed soberly, when they ordered him on the wounded horse, and not on his own, which made any attempt at escape more hopeless. When he was securely tied, Reilly came up to him and grinned.

"You'd be smart if you had any brains, Turner. You figgered we'd blew out the trail behind us on the rim and then rode for them canyons, didn't you?" He laughed. "Well, there's another trail down that mountain. Try and find it if you ever get back."

The outlaws guffawed and mounted their horses. A mile off to the east of the road, they picked up a dim trail and rode it steadily. Dave expected them to cut across west to the canyons behind Old Cartridge. But they were going east up the mountain. He was between them as they angled single file up its side.

They left the sparse timber finally and headed into the broken country that Dave knew cropped out at the head of the valley.

Their ride was checked only once and that was when they had reached a pass that looked as if it would take them across the mountains to the east slope. The pass was narrow, guarded by two natural ramparts of rock, flat on top and higher than the jagged scarp of rocks stretching away from them. A dim trail snaked through the opening.

As they were about to enter it, a voice hailed them in the gathering dusk.

"Don't come no further."

"Shet up, Cassidy," Lew called out without raising his head.

"Where's the red-head?" Cassidy called down.

"Fat's after him," Lew growled. "Watch for 'em." He snapped a light to his cigarette and they rode through.

It was dark when they reached the ranch buildings. Dave could see nothing but several lighted windows in a building tucked in the folds of jagged rocky hills that made up these badlands.

The door was immediately opened and Lew called for a lantern. A sandy-haired cowpuncher came out with it and Dave, with a start of surprise, recognized him as the man who had stuck up Quinn on the train.

"Well, Turner, how's the hero now?" He sneered. His face slid into sullen ugliness. "Let's get that *hombre* off. I'm goin' to see how far my fist will go down his throat."

"I reckon you won't," a voice drawled from the door. The man who had spoken was lounging against the door, thumbs hooked in his belt. He was so big and tall that his head almost touched the top of the door. His light hair was closely cropped on a head as perfectly shaped as a statue's. His features were even and his lazy smile was as winning as a woman's. His presence in this bunch of riff-raff was surprising. Dave narrowed his eyes in bewilderment. Was this the Sayres that Fat had mentioned? Were Sayres and Crowell working together?"

The sandy-haired puncher took a step toward Dave, his fists clenched.

The man in the doorway spoke again, an edge on his mellow voice. "I said you won't, Chinch."

Chinch's hands unfisted and he whirled to glare at the speaker. "What the hell's the difference, Sayres, as long as—"

"Cut it," Sayres snapped. "Step in, Turner."

Dave went in. The inside of the shack showed an ill-kept bunkhouse, double-decked wall bunks surrounding a large table on which bottles, cards and glasses were scattered.

"Sit down," Sayres said politely. Dave sat, wondering what was in store for him. Sayres sat on the table and studied Dave, his handsome, careless face inscrutable. They sized each other up without a flicker of an eye. To Dave, Sayres was a misfit in this crew. His overalls were clean and neat, his boots expensive and well-kept. The guns which rode in soft leather holsters at his hips were worn, but oiled and shiny. Everything about him was attractive—too much so for Dave's peace of mind.

Sayres' opinion of Dave was summed up in a little narrowing of his eyes and the flip of his cigarette into the corner. He lifted a soft Stetson from the table and put it down again as if debating something.

"Like a smoke?" he asked Dave.

"I would," Dave answered.

Sayres lit a cigarette and put it in Dave's mouth. They sat quietly, Dave with tense muscles, until the three other men came in. Dave resolved to let Sayres speak first.

"Who gave Turner that shiner?" Sayres asked.

"Fat," Lew grunted.

"It's a good thing that you didn't." He turned to Chinch. "Saddle up. You got to take the paper to Crowell."

Dave's face remained set and watchful but his blood quickened. So it *was* Crowell, he thought.

Chinch glared at Sayres, who laughed softly. "If you're a good boy, Chinch, and don't sulk, I might give you a poke at him."

Chinch nodded and the attention turned to Dave.

"Wonderin' what we're talking about, Turner?" Sayres said.

Dave nodded. Sayres reached over and removed the cigarette

butt from Dave's lips. Dave nodded his thanks and laid his tied hands on the table.

"Especially the paper, eh?" Sayres continued good-naturedly.

This time Dave shrugged carelessly and watched Sayres take a paper from his shirt pocket, unfold it, and lay it on the table.

"That's a deed to your half of the D Bar T," Sayres said evenly. "You're here to sign it." He reached in his pocket for a cigarette, keeping his mild blue eyes on Dave's face.

"Maybe," Dave said.

Sayres laughed easily. "You take a lot of spookin', don't you?" Over his shoulder he said: "Take off your guns, boys, and untie him."

"Why?" Lew asked.

"He might grab one, you damned fool," Sayres said, without looking at him.

Dave watched them take off their guns, after which they gathered around him and watched Lew untie the knots of his bonds.

"Turner," Sayres began, "you might as well know what this is all about. You're goin' to sign your ranch over to a man named Crowell, shall we say? Names change. That name is liable to change too, because I doubt if it's his. But no matter. The point is, you have to sign the deed." He stopped, studying Dave's face closely. "I'm givin' you one chance. I'm askin' you to sign without bein' forced to. Will you?"

"No," Dave answered promptly.

"That's too bad," Sayres said softly. "Maybe I didn't make myself plain enough. We want the ranch. You sign your half away and the paper is produced to your sister. When she sees that you have signed we expect her to sign her half away. We're giving her quite a reasonable sum, Turner. Much more than the ranch is worth to you and her. Wouldn't it be better if you signed and not forced me to . . ." he left the finish dangling.

"No."

Sayres studied the tip of his cigarette. "You know," he began in a conversational tone, "I've often wondered at people who threaten torture and then don't carry it out. But I can swear I'd go through with it. Do you believe me?"

Dave did not answer.

"For instance," Sayres continued. "Suppose I got an axe and ordered you to sign that paper. You wouldn't. All right. I told you to sign or I'd cut your little finger off. Still you wouldn't." He paused. "I'd cut your little finger off then. After that, I'd give you another chance. If you still refused I'd cut your fourth finger off—and so on until you didn't have a finger left." He laughed easily. "Of course, you couldn't sign the paper with no fingers, but then I would still show you that I meant what I said. You see, it wouldn't do you any good to refuse, Turner, because you'd lose every finger on both hands. That's hardly worth a ranch, is it?"

Still Dave did not answer.

"I'm asking you once again. Will you sign?" Sayres said slowly.

"No," Dave said quietly.

"Get that hammer, Lew," Sayres said. Lew got a heavy hammer from one of the bunks and handed it to Sayres.

"Now spread his left hand out, palm down, on the table," Sayres ordered. Dave made a lunge to get up, but the four men pounced on him and he was borne down by their sheer weight. It took another three minutes to get his hand on the table. Lew held it with both hands, leaning his weight on it.

Sayres drew a ten-penny spike from his shirt pocket and looked at Dave.

"Observe this, Turner," Sayres said. "You see, I mean what I say." Placing the spike point on the back of Dave's hand just below the third finger, he drove the nail through the flesh and into the table with five savage, accurate blows.

Dave's face drained of color and he throttled the cry that rose in his throat as the nail seared through his flesh. His eyes blazed as he looked at the calm face of Sayres. Lew withdrew to one side and all of them looked at the hand nailed fast to the table, blood welling up around the shiny nailhead.

"Now get the axe," Sayres said. Lew, white-faced, disappeared outside and came back with an axe which he handed to Sayres. Dave felt every throb of his heart in his hand and the slightest movement was exquisite torture.

"I might as well tell you the rest, Turner," Sayres said. "I'm going to cut your fingers off, one by one. I'll start with the little finger on your left hand and I'll end up with the thumb on your right." His limpid, half-curious gaze settled on Dave's face. "Are you such a fool, Turner, that you think your sister can't be killed? If we wouldn't stop at torturing, do you think we'd stop at killing her? Winters too? Then the ranch would revert to whoever holds the mortgages and we'd buy it from them. You can't beat us, you see."

Dave's face was parchment-colored now, partly from the pain which he could endure, but mostly from what Sayres had just told him. He suddenly realized that he was dealing with a madman. He knew now that Sayres was not bluffing and that he could and would kill Mary and Winters after he had tortured him to death. Sayres' smooth voice cut in on his thoughts.

"I'm asking you again, Turner. Will you sign?"

Dave looked at his hand. Sayres had placed the gleaming axe-blade squarely on the base of his little finger. The hammer was raised. Sayres looked at him inquiringly.

"I'll sign," Dave said weakly.

Only then did all of them realize that they had been holding their breaths which now they exhaled in a small gust.

"Good," Sayres said jovially. He took a pen from a shelf nearby along with a bottle of ink. The paper was spread before Dave, the pen tendered him. He signed his name.

Sayres glanced at it briefly, nodded, then took the hammer and, stooping under the table, knocked the spike up. Then he pressed Dave's hand firmly on the table, took the claw of the hammer and yanked the nail out. Blood bubbled out of the wound as Dave drew his hand to him and tried to move the fingers.

"I reckon there's not much to say to a coyote like you, Sayres," Dave said, his voice trembling with a suppressed rage.

"Except this: If I live long enough, I'll kill you like I would a rattlesnake."

Sayres laughed pleasantly. "You better tie him up again, Lew."

Chinch stepped forward. "What about that promise?"

Sayres shrugged. "Go ahead."

Chinch stepped up to Dave, who was still seated, planted his feet firmly and drew back his hand.

Dave lunged out of his chair and drove his bleeding fist into Chinch's face, sending him sprawling across the room and into a bunk where he lay inert.

Sayres laughed boisterously and held up a hand to prevent the others from hitting Dave. "Leave him alone. It served that damn fool Chinch right," he said. Lunging off the table, he walked over to the bunk and slapped Chinch's face until the unconscious man groaned and sat erect.

"Still feel like curlin' your tail, Chinch?" Sayres asked. "We sort of like that rough and tumble way of fightin' you have."

Chinch glared at him, but made no move to get up.

"Now get saddled and hightail it," Sayres ordered. "Crowell's waiting. Get goin'." Chinch slunk out, not even looking up at the other men, and Sayres turned to Lew. "Take him out in the back room and put those leg irons on him."

"I thought—" Reilly began.

"Shut up," Sayres ordered crisply, his glance fleeting to Dave and then back to Lew. "Do as I say. Afterwards, come back here."

Dave was prodded into a one-room addition at the rear of the shack which served as a storeroom of sorts. He was handcuffed, seated on the floor facing the log wall and his feet were manacled with a logging chain to the drop log of the addition. He could lie down, but the semicircle in which he could move on the floor was bare of everything, even a blanket. When they were finished, Sayres came in to look over the job and after grunting his approval left with the other two. Lew, the last out of the room, slammed the door shut after him, but it swung open a couple of inches so that Dave could see them moving in front of the crack occasionally, and a dim shade of light filtered into the room.

"Get something to eat," Sayres ordered. Dave could hear him pull up one of the crude chairs to the table and pour a drink.

The outer door opened and Chinch spoke to Sayres. "Ready."

"All right," Dave heard Sayres say, "you better pour leather into it." The paper exchanged hands. "When you're finished look up Fat and by God if you get drunk, I'll drag you all the way from Single Shot to here at the end of a rope. Afterward, I don't care if you get the snakes, but lay off it now."

Chinch grunted and the door slammed. Dave could hear the rattle of a frypan, but the men were evidently smoking in silence. An occasional slap of a card on the bare table told him some one was playing solitaire. His hand throbbed achingly with the pumping of his heart and his fingers were stiff and numb. Lying on his back and staring at the ceiling he tried to read some sense into all that had happened to him. Headed, as far as he knew, by a man named Crowell (wrong name, he thought automatically) they were trying to get the ranch. Why? Reilly had admitted that he had blown the lake out, thereby ruining the ranch. Dave racked his brain for an explanation as to why they would want a spread that they had impoverished. Of course, if Crowell had the money he could build the lake up again and try to uncover the springs, but the money spent in fixing that and paying this gang of killers would not make the project worth while. Then too, Dave thought, they would have to face the music sooner or later from the sheriff, whosever hands the place drifted into. But would they? If he were dead, unaccounted for . . .

Lew's voice broke into his reverie. "When'll the gal be here?"

"Not very long now. We got to get him out of the way," Sayres said.

A short silence. "God, that's dirty work!" Lew said.

Sayres laughed. "Losin' your guts, Lew?"

"Hell, no, but I like to have a man wearin' guns anyway."

"You liar," Sayres said calmly. "In that job we pulled off on the other side of the mountains last month, you took a bead on that night-herder and laughed when he rolled off his horse like a sack of meal."

"He was wearin' guns, though," Lew insisted.

"Sure. And he might as well have been without them for all the chance he got to use them. Don't get pious, Lew. It doesn't fit you."

Lew didn't say anything for a moment. Dave fought down a cold wave of terror and fear. A girl! That would be Mary. They were going to get her, bring her up here, and they were on their way now. More than that, they were going to shoot him like a coyote. And what would they do to Mary when he was gone?

"Chief, who's the gent behind all this?" Lew asked.

"If I was you, I wouldn't ask that," Sayres said slowly. "I don't know myself. All I know is that Crowell is paying me, and paying plenty. If we live long enough, we can see who takes over the Turner spread."

"Who do you think it is? Crowell couldn't do it, because he knows we could take it from him and he couldn't squawk."

"I'm not asking, I told you."

Lew's voice was cunning when he spoke again. "Why can't we take it from the *hombre* that gets it, the *hombre* that's paying Crowell? He can't take it to law, because he'd have to tell how he got it. We can run him off."

Sayres snorted. "You think a man that can pull this off wouldn't think of that? No. Whoever he is, when he takes that spread over, and when he gets the Draw Three, he'll toll in about fifty of the toughest hard-cases he can find. We'll leave them plenty far alone, Lew. Just remember that. We've got a nice game here of our own without inviting trouble." Then: "Put that bottle down! You got work tonight, Lew, and you better not be drunk!"

"All right, all right," Lew said placatingly.

There was a clatter of dishes, then a long silence. Dave thought over what he had heard. There was some one behind Crowell even, a man who had money, brains, and the ability to keep his sinister identity a secret. And nothing, not even human lives, stood in his ruthless way.

Sayres' voice, a little clogged with food, came to him again.

"When you jaspers get back from this next job, you'll find the girl here. And if one of you mention Crowell's name in front of her, you might just as well give yourself up to the sheriff, because you'll be a dead man. Get that? She's got to be here without ever hearing the name of Crowell."

14
Kidnapped

Laredo set his glass down and eyed the bandage on the head of the bartender. His stomach was warming up anew.

"Where'd you git that?" he asked.

The bartender eyed him sourly. "I'm tellin' you for the last time, I think you give it to me last night. Now don't ask again because I won't tell you another time. Because when you ask again you'll be drunk and pick a fight with me."

Laredo nodded. There was truth in what the man said, he reflected.

"How sure are you I give it to you?" he asked mildly.

"Now quit rawhidin' me," the bartender whined. He was a pasty-faced individual save for his nose, which was blue-veined and bulbous. "If you're tryin' to make fight talk, then you didn't give it to me."

"I ain't makin' fight talk," Laredo protested mildly. "I'm just tryin' to get this straight. I don't remember it."

"Then it was that pardner of yours."

"Might be," Laredo said noncommittally.

The bartender shook his head. "It was a sorry day for Chris Lenning when he ordered you throwed out of the Mile High."

"I aim to make it a sorry one for him," Laredo announced. "Fill it up." He shoved his glass across the bar.

It was accepted with reluctance by the bartender. "Listen, Jackson. Do me a favor, will you?" he asked.

"I reckon not. What is it?"

"If you're gettin' drunk again, put it off two hours, will you? I git off at four. I reckon I've had my share of your hellery."

"Nope," Laredo said flatly. "That's somethin' I can't interfere with. That's delayin' the course of nature. If a horse is thirsty you let him drink, don't you?"

"Not if he acts like you do when he gits full," the bartender declared.

"You shet up," Laredo said quietly. "If you couldn't put up with me, I reckon you should never have took the job. I go with the place, ask anybody."

"Hell, I don't have to."

Laredo's gaze, a little befuddled, swept up to the mirror and what he saw made him blink. He turned slowly.

Rosy was standing by the swinging doors. He looked around the saloon, saw Laredo, and came over.

"Oh, Lord! Again," the bartender moaned.

"Hello, Red. Have a drink," Laredo offered, then saw the grim set to Rosy's jaw. "What's the matter?"

"You sober?" Rosy asked swiftly.

"Some."

"Where's the sheriff? I can't find him."

"Asleep, likely. What's the trouble?"

"Then you'll have to do it," Rosy said. "First thing, do you mind gettin' in a scrap?"

Laredo's eyes narrowed and he grinned. "I never turned one down yet."

"All right. Second thing. Can you tell me how I get to Sayres' hang-out?"

Laredo whistled softly and nodded. "You ride north up the valley until you come to a black lava bed on the east bank," he began. "When you git there you've gone too far, so turn back and watch the east bank. A half mile below the lava bed, you'll come to a big piñon on the bank that hangs clean over the creekbed. Got that?"

"Sure," Rosy said impatiently.

"There's a lightnin'-struck navajo pine a couple of hundred yards east of the piñon, toward the mountain. Line that piñon up with the pine and you'll see the line points right off the top of the pine to a little, dinky notch in them mountains."

"Well?"

"Head for that notch, and if you come acrost a trail keep off it. Sayres has got a bunch of them whippoorwills guardin' every trail and they'll cut down on you without askin' why. Head for that notch. It's a pass and it'll be guarded. I dunno how you'll get through that, but once you do, you won't have no trouble following the trail to Sayres' place."

"All right. Third thing," Rosy said. "There's a *hombre* here in town by the name of Crowell. Know him?"

Laredo shook his head.

"Hank Lowe is lookin' for him," Rosy said slowly. "He's connected with the dynamitin' of the D Bar T lake."

Laredo nodded attentively.

"Now get this careful," Rosy said slowly. "It all depends on how careful you get it. Crowell will be here at the hotel, registered. I want you to pick a scrap with him and fix it up with Hank so that Crowell is arrested and locked in jail. Got that?"

"Sure."

"Now here's what you got to remember, and to tell Hank. Crowell has got to be locked up, but he mustn't suspect that we know he's connected with the dynamitin'! Hank has got to lock him up on a phony charge and hold him till I get back."

"All right," Laredo said soberly, "but you better write Hank a note explainin' that."

Rosy called for some paper and pencil and wrote a short note to the sheriff. He hoped desperately that the sheriff would take his orders and not give everything away. Every minute counted now and he could not afford to waste time hunting him up. In his haste he had left Mary at the saloon door, with instructions for her to ride out to Hammond's and explain to Dorsey the circumstances that brought her. Dave's life might hang on the few minutes that it took to ride with Mary to Hammond's and tell the sheriff.

He handed the note to Laredo. "Make Hank believe it, Laredo," Rosy told him. "It's our necks if you don't."

"You git on," Laredo growled. "I'll take care of him and Crowell both. Time I'm finished with this Crowell he'll think he's been holdin' up trains in his sleep. How do I know him though?"

Rosy described Crowell quickly. "Hang around the clerk in the hotel and have him point Crowell out to you. And have Hank hold him till I get back. Remember, till I get back!"

Rosy started for the door, stopped in midstride, and hesitated a moment. Then he returned to the bar, picked up the pencil and wrote another note.

It read:

QUINN: Mary Winters is in town, and so is Winters. Keep an eye on him.

RAND.

He handed it to Laredo. "And give this to Quinn over at the Free Throw."

Laredo nodded. "Good luck, son," he called, his eyes suddenly anxious, but Rosy was through the doors.

When Rosy left Mary at the Mile High, she wanted to ask him a thousand questions, but his frown stopped her. She didn't even know why he was in such a hurry.

After asking at a store where Hammond lived, she mounted and rode down the street. The house was at the edge of town and she found it easily. It was small, white, with a neat yard. Cottonwoods lifted their lacework umbrellas over it and small cedars dotted it.

Mary dismounted at the gate and walked slowly to the door. This was going to be a little awkward but she hoped Dorsey Hammond would understand. The door was open a few inches, but her knock was unanswered.

"There must be some one here," she thought and swung the door open further.

A table lay squarely in front of the door, a white rectangle of envelope shining on its dark surface. She looked at the envelope lying there as if intended for her. On it was written in bold letters: TO YOU.

"How queer," she murmured. She picked it up, turned it over, then opened it. The note inside read:

To BUCK HAMMOND

You will never see yer dawter again until you pay 50,000$. We hav her and eny atemp to get her will meen deth for her

if you want to see her agen folow thees dreckshuns—we will giv you a day to get the munny on friday morning send sumwun with it on the eest bownd trane. the munny must be in wun hunderd doler bills. rap them in a wite sock and so it up. giv the man carying the munny a wach and hav him sit on the north sid of the car. after the trane has pulled over the graid at wagen wheel pass he will see a hors which will be yor gurls paynt hors puled clost to the side of the trax. hav him cownt too minutes by the wach frum the tim he pases the hors. when the too minuts is up hav him thro the sock owt the windo

if the trane slos up or ennywun gets of yor gurl will be put to death. if we get the munny she will be hom saturday or sundy.

you have only wun chanst so beter take it

be shur the sock is wite.

It was unsigned. Mary read it twice before she realized the import. She called Dorsey's name but there was no answer. Then she ran from the house and in one light spring was on her horse.

At Dr. Fullerton's the housekeeper answered her knock and took her to Hammond. He looked up at her, his kindly face curious.

"I'm Mary Winters," she said breathlessly, "I just called at your house and found this note on the table."

"Sit down, please," Hammond said, wondering at her anxious manner. He unfolded the note leisurely and read. Mary could see his hands tremble as he progressed deeper into the sinister message.

When he finished he groaned softly and let the note drop to the bedcover, and stared at the wall.

"I read it," Mary said quietly. "Oh, what can I do, Mr. Hammond?"

"What can any of us do?" Hammond asked thickly. "They knew I was in bed and helpless. They knew she'd be home alone." He broke off and looked at Mary with imploring eyes. "I reckon you better tell Hank Lowe. There's nothin' to do but pray they don't kill her before I get the money."

"Then I'll take it to him right now," Mary stood up. Impulsively she leaned over and patted his rough hand, trying to put encouragement and hope in her smile. "They'll get her back, Mr. Hammond." She hurried out to hide the doubt and fear in her eyes.

She mounted and rode swiftly down to the sheriff's office. He was unlocking his office door just as she swung into the hitchrack.

She entered as he was sitting down, and upon seeing her, he swung out of his seat with a grunt.

"Dorsey Hammond has been kidnapped!" Mary told him bluntly, offering him the letter. The sheriff merely blinked and took it, opening it and reading it slowly.

Finished, he called: "Van!"

The door to the back room swung open and a sleepy-eyed deputy walked in.

"Git a posse up," the sheriff said. "Meet me at Buck Hammond's place. His gal has been kidnapped."

The deputy got his hat and ran out the door and the sheriff turned to Mary.

"Mr. Lowe, will you—can you—will they get her?" Mary asked, her voice troubled and low.

"Damn, yes!" the sheriff exploded. "They will if I got to call the army out to git her."

"Can I help?" Mary asked.

The sheriff smiled wearily. "Ain't nobody that can't shoot can help, Mrs. Winters. I'm much obliged to you for bringin' the note to me. I'm goin' to see Buck Hammond right now."

The sheriff got his hat and waddled out of the office, leaving Mary alone. She stood looking at his vacant chair a moment, then shook herself and stepped out the door. The only thing left to do was to go to the hotel and wait for Rosy or Dave.

15
Murder Charge

After Rosy left him, Laredo finished his drink and started his search for the sheriff. He tried the office four times at five-minute intervals and found the door locked. Each time, his disgust increased.

"You'd think San Angel county never had a sheriff when you want to find the durn fool," he growled.

At the fourth try, finding the door still locked, he remembered the note Rosy had given him for Quinn. He went over to the Free Throw, delivered the note, bought a couple of drinks and went back to the sheriff's office.

This time the door was open. The sheriff had come and gone, evidently, for there was no one around.

Laredo made himself at home. He thought of Rosy's strange request to pick a fight with Crowell. He wondered how he could do it the easiest. An idea came to him and he sat down in the sheriff's chair, reached down and pulled out a bottom drawer where he remembered the sheriff kept the reward notices.

There was a drawerful of them, and Laredo dumped them all out on top of the desk, then set about looking through them. He kept Rosy's description of Crowell in mind as he leafed through the cards. Laredo could not read, but the picture was what he was after. Presently, he paused in his work and held up a card with a picture of a man on it. The printed matter might have been in Greek, but the face suited him.

He took the card and walked to the door, where he waited until a woman turned down the street at the bank corner. She was a middle-aged woman, in a hurry apparently.

As she drew abreast the door, Laredo greeted her: "Howdy, ma'am." He held the picture out. "Can you tell me the name of that jasper?" he inquired politely.

The woman's surprised look shifted from Laredo's face to the card. "W-w-why no," she stammered. "I don't know him. I never saw him before."

"I don't mean that, ma'am," Laredo said. "I mean, what does it say on the card? What does it say his name is? I can't read."

The woman sighed with relief and looked again at the card. "It says: 'This is the face that has terrified a thousand criminals and has trained a thousand detectives—J. J. Johns, Master Detective. The Continental Detective Bureau. He can teach you.'"

Laredo looked at her blankly. "Deteckative Bureau? What's that?"

"Some one's learning to be a detective from him—this Mister Johns, the Master Detective, I guess," the woman said.

"Well, I'll be damned," Laredo muttered. The woman passed on hurriedly, leaving him standing there. Laredo turned the card over and for the first time noticed it was the cover for a book.

"Hank Lowe astudyin' to be a deteckative," he muttered. "Well, I'll be damned."

He shook his head soberly and then began to laugh. Returning to the desk, he leafed through the cards again until he found the same type of face as the one on the book cover.

The next passerby he stopped was Pearson the banker.

"Howdy, Mr. Pearson," Laredo drawled from the doorway. "Reckon you can tell me what this poster says?"

Pearson, stiff and unbending, looked briefly at the placard Laredo held out for him to read. " 'Wanted for murder,' " he read aloud, " 'in El Paso, Texas. Simon Henry. Reward: five thousand dollars. Last seen—' do you want me to go on?"

"Nope, that's enough. Much obliged," Laredo said. Pearson bowed stiffly, resumed his leisurely pace toward the corner, Laredo watching him. "Durn. It didn't take him long to savvy it."

Laredo kept this placard out, put the rest in the desk and sat down, cocking his feet up on the desk top and slowly building a cigarette.

He had just thrown away the cigarette butt when Sheriff Lowe entered, a scowl on his face.

"What do *you* want?" he growled at Laredo. "Ain't I got enough trouble without havin' you swarm in here?"

"You ain't had any trouble compared to what you're goin' to have, Deteckative Lowe," Laredo observed dryly.

A slow flush suffused the sheriff's face. "So you been lookin' through my stuff, huh?"

"Me?" Laredo asked innocently. "Why, Deteckative Lowe! I wouldn't be that low-down."

"What I shoulda done is sent you out on that posse," the sheriff growled.

"Posse? What for?"

"Why, Buck Hammond's gal has been kidnapped—took right out of their place. Ain't you heard? I just got the posse off. I'm too danged busy to ride on one myself."

Laredo stared at him. "Well, I'm damned. Which way did they go?"

"Tracks out behind Hammond's barn looked like they was travelin' south, but you can't tell."

Laredo shook his head slowly. He reached in his pocket for the note Rosy had given him and offered it to the sheriff.

"That's from young Rand, and he give me some instructions to you to go with it."

Laredo told the sheriff what Rosy had told him. As he progressed, the sheriff sank into a chair, his mouth open. When Laredo was finished and the sheriff had read the note, he threw his hat on the floor and cursed bitterly.

"And he wants me to arrest Crowell—the jasper that's behind all this grief of mine and his, and not even tell the danged coyote what I'm arrestin' him for. Damned if I will! I'm double, ring-tailed damned if I will!"

"Yes, you will," Laredo said gently.

"Where is Rand?" the sheriff stormed.

"Gone."

"Gone? Where? And am I supposed to think up somethin' to arrest Crowell for, when I danged well got enough to hang the coyote on now."

"Yes, you will," Laredo repeated gently. "You don't know what Rand knows. Neither do I, but he knows enough to know what he's talkin' about."

"Say!" the sheriff said suddenly. "And I'll bet this Crowell was behind the kidnappin' of Buck Hammond's gal!"

"Why?"

"If he'd dynamite a lake, he'd steal a gal, wouldn't he?" the sheriff said.

"He might," Laredo conceded. "But what are you gettin' so red-headed about? You'll have Crowell in jail, won't you? All Rand wants you to do is to keep Crowell iggerant of why you're arrestin' him."

The sheriff thought this over a minute and could make no objections to it. He was vaguely resentful of Rosy's orders, but he had learned to respect Rosy's hunches.

"All right," he said finally, "but how we goin' to do it?"

Laredo explained his plan, showing Hank the placard he had saved out. "This looks considerably like Crowell, from what Rand said. I'll go over to the hotel and throw a gun on him and bring him over here and tell you his name is Simon Henry, and that he murdered some jasper in El Paso. You bring out the card." He grinned. "It can't help but work."

"But damn it," the sheriff objected. "He'll want a lawyer, and the lawyer will get him out on bail. He'll jump bail then and won't show up."

"I've thought of that, too," Laredo drawled. "Who's the prosecutin' attorney here? Benning, ain't he?"

The sheriff nodded.

"How many other lawyers is there?"

"Two, I reckon. Hartwick and Scoggins," the sheriff said.

"All right. You go to Benning and tell him to hire Hartwick and Scoggins to help prosecute the Henry case that's comin' up. Pay 'em enough and they'll side in with you. Then arrest Crowell and there won't be any lawyers in town to hire, because they'll all be hired by the prosecution. Don't that make sense?"

The sheriff thought a moment. "Plenty. Only, who's goin' to pay for all the advice they don't give? Them two will ask high fees."

"Let them argy that out between themselves," Laredo said calmly. "That's what lawyers is for."

The sheriff shook his head wearily. "Danged if it might not work at that. I'll go see Benning."

When the arrangements were completed with the lawyers to the sheriff's satisfaction, Laredo went over to the hotel. The same old man was back of the desk and Laredo quizzed him.

"Gent by the name of Crowell registered here?"

"Sure."

"Is he in?"

"Come in a couple of hours ago. Want to see him?"

"I'd sure admire to," Laredo said.

The clerk called a small boy from a back room and sent him upstairs to get Crowell.

Laredo leaned on the desk and waited. Presently, Crowell came down the stairs with the boy. Rosy had been pretty accurate in his description. Crowell was short, dynamic, and he was wearing a scowl on his dark face as he approached the desk.

Laredo noticed idly a gun in a shoulder holster. He was dressed in neat black, and his voice was resonant and confident as he addressed the clerk.

"Some one want to see me?"

"This gent," the clerk said, indicating Laredo.

Crowell looked at Laredo coldly. "Well?"

"I been lookin' for you a considerable while," Laredo said. "So you're registerin' under the name of Crowell now?"

Crowell's dark eyes glinted coldly, but not a muscle in his face moved. The two of them were about the same size, except now Laredo was lounging on the desk.

"Who are you?" Crowell asked.

"Jackson's the name," Laredo drawled. "I saw you on the street a couple of hours ago and I been wonderin' ever since where I saw you before. I got it now. You're Simon Henry." He paused. "Are you goin' over to the sheriff's office without a fight?"

"Who do you think you're talking to?" Crowell asked quietly. "You've got the wrong party. My name is Crowell, A. J. Crowell. I'm here on business."

"Your name is Henry, Simon Henry," Laredo repeated flatly. "Wanted for murder in El Paso. Are you comin' to the sheriff's office or am I goin' to have to take you?"

Crowell turned to the clerk who had overheard the conversation. "You heard this, didn't you, clerk?"

The clerk nodded. Crowell turned to Laredo. "I'm not going."

"I reckon you are," Laredo said.

He saw the flicker of Crowell's eyes and the muscles tense through the upper part of Crowell's sleeve. Laredo's gun blurred up from his hip to settle in Crowell's midriff before the taller man got his hand well inside his coat to his shoulder holster. "Think again," Laredo drawled. He reached up and took the gun from Crowell.

Crowell shrugged.

"Take me to the sheriff, then. Either you're a madman or else mistaken—I hope honestly."

Sheriff Lowe was seated at the desk when the two entered.

"I got a prisoner for you, Sheriff," Laredo said. "Name of Simon Henry. Wanted in El Paso for murder. I was tryin' to think all mornin' who he was and finally it come to me. Simon Henry."

"Look here, Sheriff," Crowell said heatedly. "This man approaches me in the hotel and sticks a gun in my ribs and orders me over here with the pretense that I'm a murderer. What's it all about?"

"I dunno," the sheriff said heavily. "Just keep your shirt on. I'll see if we have anything about a jasper named Henry." With deliberation, he pulled the bottom drawer of his desk out and dumped its contents on the desk top. His slowness was maddening as he shuffled through the notices, finally extracting a card which he viewed critically for a full minute, then looked at Crowell. "Here's a picture of Henry. It looks mighty like you."

"Let's see," Crowell said. He studied the card the sheriff handed him, then shrugged. "I've seen forty people like you, Sheriff, one a horse-thief. That doesn't make you out one, does it?"

"I dunno about that," Laredo said innocently.

"About what?" the sheriff said coldly.

"About that not meanin' anything," Laredo said. "If you looked like a hoss-thief and somebody accused you of it, you'd have to prove you wasn't, wouldn't you?"

"I reckon," the sheriff agreed slowly. He addressed Crowell. "This here says you murdered a cattle-buyer for Lynch's, name of Louis Peyton, on the night of August seventh, last year. Where was you then?"

"How should I know?" Crowell replied heatedly. "I don't keep a diary."

"A what?" the sheriff asked.

"I don't keep track of where I was every day and night of the year. Where were you on August seventh last year?"

"He was courtin' a old maid by the name of Lizzie May that was visitin' Robbie Blackman's wife's sister," Laredo said. "Ain't that so, Sheriff?"

Sheriff Lowe glared at him and squirmed in his seat. "I reckon. Well, Henry. What about it?"

"I'm not saying a thing," Crowell retorted. "I want a lawyer."

"Why sure," the sheriff said. "I reckon you got a right to have a lawyer. We got two here in town. Which one you want?"

"Either of them. No, get them both," Crowell said.

The sheriff turned to Laredo. "You git 'em."

Laredo shook his head. "And let this desprit criminal out of my sight? Not me. I'm stayin' here until I see him locked up."

The sheriff swore and hoisted himself to his feet. When he opened the door to the back room, voices drifted in. Soon he returned with a deputy who went out the street door on the errand for the lawyers. Crowell paced the room nervously under the eyes of the two men.

"What did you kill this here Payton for?" the sheriff asked suddenly.

Crowell stopped and stared blankly at him. "Payton? Oh, I—"

"See there," Laredo said. "Any one could tell he was just pretending."

Crowell glared at him, but kept his tongue, and continued his pacing. Suddenly, he stopped short and snapped his fingers. "I know where I was August seventh last year. I was in North Dakota. Aspen Wells, North Dakota."

"Where's that?" the sheriff asked.

"Western part. Near the badlands."

"Got a railroad?"

Crowell remembered his mistake too late. "No," he growled.

"Well, we'll have to lock you up until we can hear from the marshal or sheriff there. Who seen you there?"

"Moore, a storekeeper," Crowell growled. "Look here, Sheriff. Do you mean I have to stay in town until you can get word from the marshal that I was in Aspen Wells?"

"I reckon that's it," the sheriff said.

The deputy entered the street door, alone.

"Well?" Crowell asked.

"They won't take the case," the deputy answered. "They say they been engaged by the prosecutin' attorney to help put Henry in jail."

Crowell stared helplessly at him. "You say—" he turned to the sheriff. "Does this mean I can't have a lawyer, Sheriff?"

"Why no. I reckon you can have as many as you want if you can find any."

Crowell glared at him murderously. "I want a hearing and I want it right now," he stormed.

The sheriff shook his head sorrowfully. "The jedge is in Walpais. Won't be back until tomorrow night."

"And I've got to stay in jail until then?" Crowell asked slowly.

"I don't see no other way," the sheriff explained. "If you had a lawyer, maybe you could get out. But there's nothin' for me to do except lock up all the murder suspects that come my way."

Crowell cursed savagely.

"Now, now," the sheriff said soothingly. "We got a right nice jail. I'll get a telegram off to the nearest railroad town to Aspen Wells. I reckon when the jedge comes, you can get out on bail." He reached into a drawer and drew out a pair of handcuffs which he handed to the waiting deputy. "Take him over to the courthouse, Van, and turn him over to King." He looked at Crowell and shook his head. "You ought to confess, Henry. It'd save us both trouble."

Crowell was led out, still cursing. Laredo stood in the doorway watching him and two deputies go up the street to the courthouse. He turned to the sheriff.

"Well?"

"I hope they don't meet the jedge on the way," the sheriff said. "He ain't left town for three years. And if they do meet him, that danged fool of a Van will call him Jedge right in front of Crowell."

16
Boot Trail

Quinn was dealing faro when Laredo handed him Rosy's note. The gambler put it in his pocket and played a few minutes longer, then called a house-man to take over the table. This was allowed in the afternoon when gambling was slack. Quinn went to a corner of the bar, ordered a beer and read the note. He already had half a notion to take the afternoon off and this decided him. He'd go get a shave and a bath, then hunt Winters up and arrange a game for tonight that would keep him away from Mary.

He got his hat and left the Free Throw, heading for Sam's place, the only place in town where a man could get a bath in hot water. He entered the shop and found Winters stretched out in the single barber chair getting a shave. One other customer was waiting and Quinn took a seat.

Winters saw him and raised a careless hand in greeting. "Hello, Quinn. How'd they pry you away from that faro table?"

"I took the afternoon off," Quinn said. "I'm getting too rich."

Winters laughed easily. "I was hoping you'd be there this afternoon. I was coming in and take a heap of money away from you."

Something in Quinn's mind told him to be cautious.

"I never turn down a game," he said quietly.

"Then you'll be at the table in an hour or so?"

"If you want me to."

"Good. I'll bust you and your bank today. I feel lucky."

Quinn smiled and said nothing. He waited a moment, then stood up. "I'll be back later, Sam, when I don't have to wait."

Sam's black face creased into a grin and he nodded. Quinn

left the shop and headed up the street. Something had jogged his curiosity and he was going to satisfy it. Last night was the first night since Quinn had been working in the Free Throw that Winters hadn't come in and lost money. To Quinn, that meant one thing: Winters was strapped at last. But now, fresh and confident, Winters had boasted about breaking the bank. Evidently, he had money enough to throw away again.

Quinn went into the hardware store, one corner of which was walled up into a large room which was the post-office. Murphy, the hardware man, was behind the wicket when Quinn approached it.

"Hello, Murph," Quinn greeted him. "Has the mail for the Turner spread been called for yet?"

The store-owner looked up at the rows of pigeon holes.

"No. Winters come in and got his mail, but he never took the rest of it. Why?"

"I just wondered if I'd have time to get a note out there. Thanks," Quinn said.

On the street again, he headed for the bank. He had come to a decision about Winters at last. According to Murphy, Mary Winters had not received the money he had mailed her anonymously the night before, so she had not given Winters the money he now had. And yet he had money. Twenty-four hours ago he was broke. Where was it coming from?

He entered the bank and asked for Pearson.

"The president? Yes, sir. One moment," the clerk said, and walked forward to the frosted-glass cage. He returned in a half minute.

"He's busy," the clerk said shortly.

Quinn snorted, swung open the gate and strode past the clerk to the office door marked "Private." He swung it open brusquely. Pearson was seated at a flat desk, pencil in hand. Looking up and seeing Quinn close the door, he frowned.

"Didn't my clerk tell you I am busy?" he asked coldly.

"So am I," Quinn retorted.

He sat on the desk, reached in his billfold and drew out a card which he flipped carelessly on the desk in front of Pearson.

The banker studied the card and his rather stern features settled into more genial lines. He leaned back in his chair and nodded.

"I see," he said. His eyes traveled shrewdly, searchingly over Quinn, and the beginnings of a smile creased his face. "What can I do for you, Mr. Quinn?"

"I want to know about Winters, Mr. Theodore Winters," Quinn said without preliminaries.

Pearson's forehead puckered and he looked out of the window at the top half of the Free Throw across the street. "Winters. Yes. He married Mary Turner, Dick Turner's daughter, didn't he?" It was less a question than a statement, as if he were thinking out loud. "What about him?"

"Does he bank here? I'd like to take a look at his account if he does."

"Certainly." Pearson rang a bell which lay at the corner of his desk and a moment later the clerk opened the door cautiously.

"See if we have a Mr. Theodore Winters banking here," Pearson ordered. "If we have, bring me his account."

The clerk disappeared and Pearson settled back in his chair again. "Very interesting work you're in, Quinn," he commented pleasantly.

"So-so," Quinn admitted. As far as he was concerned the conversation was finished.

The clerk returned with a sheet of loose-leaf paper which he handed to Pearson, who, in turn, handed it to Quinn. The gambler scanned it swiftly.

"He banked twenty-five a week for three months, then stopped. That was two years ago." Quinn put down the account sheet. "He was married about that time, wasn't he?"

"Some time around there," the banker said.

Quinn rose. "Much obliged, Pearson, I'd appreciate it if this" —he tapped his billfold—"didn't get around."

"I understand perfectly," Pearson said.

Outside again, Quinn hesitated a moment, then walked across to the Free Throw. He knew a little more now, anyway

—knew that Winters didn't have any money in the bank and hadn't had any for two years, so that wasn't where he got it.

Quinn strolled through the main room to the dance-hall beyond. There was a small bar here to serve the dance-hall patrons and a door behind this bar opened into the aisle behind the bar in the main room. He strolled behind the dance-hall bar and gossiped with the bartender. He could look into the gambling room from where he sat and still not be seen by anyone in the main room.

He had idled away a half hour this way before he saw Winters come in, look around the room and walk over to the faro table. He began playing. Occasionally, he would look around, as if searching for some one, and Quinn smiled. The gambler stood in the doorway and caught the eye of one of the housemen, who came over.

"Mix around at Joe's table and see how big Winters' roll is, will you, Tom? Do you know him?"

The house-man nodded and left. In five minutes he was back to report.

"He's got a wad so big he can't get it in his billfold."

"Thanks."

Quinn left by the side door of the dance-hall, rounded the corner and walked down toward the station. At a shoe shop a few doors below the bank, he entered and was waited upon by a near-sighted and beaproned old German.

"Anybody called for a pair of ridin' boots during the last hour, Dad?" he asked him.

"Blendy," the German said. "Wass dey yourss?"

"No. Not half-boots, not cowboy boots. I mean riding boots, army boots," Quinn corrected himself.

The old German shook his head. "Only dey wear dese dancig bumps here dey gall gow-boy boots."

"Is there another shoe store in town?" Quinn asked.

The old German puffed out his cheeks. "Dere iss a man from me four doors down who sess he rebairs boots. Dey are from cartboard and wallpaper paste made, and mit stove polish colored."

Quinn thanked him, suppressing a smile, and went five doors down the street to the other boot shop. He asked the same question of an old Mexican who assured him fluently that he had not seen such a pair of boots since he fought in the Mexican army and, God willing, he never wanted to again.

Outside again, Quinn rolled a cigarette and crossed the street to the barber-shop where he had seen Winters. Sam, the Negro, was seated in an empty chair, half drowsing. He got up immediately when Quinn entered, a broad grin on his face.

"No. I don't want anything, Sam," Quinn assured him. "Where's Winters' room?" The question was asked casually, lazily.

A slight change came over Sam's face, a mere flicker of the eyes.

"Winters? Who's 'at, boss?"

"The gent you were shaving when I was in here a while back," Quinn said.

"He lives on a ranch, don't he?" Sam asked.

"He lives here," Quinn said quietly. "Better show me his room, Sam, and save yourself trouble."

The Negro's mouth gaped open. "Here? He don't live here, boss. No one lives heah but me an' the missus. Upstairs." He pointed a finger at the ceiling.

"He had slippers on, Sam. Men don't travel this country with slippers," Quinn said.

"Yassuh. Them's mine Ah give him to wear. His boots was pretty thin and he ast me to send 'em out an' git fixed while Ah was barberin' him."

"Where'd you send them?"

"That old Dutchman fella," Sam replied glibly.

"I asked there, Sam," Quinn said patiently. "He hasn't had any ridin' boots brought in today."

Sam blinked. "Well now, Ah sent 'em out by that littlest kid of mine. Mebbe he took 'em over to Garcia's."

"I asked there too. He hasn't seen boots like that since he was in the Mexican army."

Sam fidgeted nervously, settling into a stubborn silence.

"Better come across," Quinn said. "It'll save you trouble."

"Ah don' know nothin' about it, boss," Sam said sullenly.

Quinn regarded him dreamily. "Sam, where did you come from?"

"Texas, boss."

"Then you've seen a bunch of hard-cases hurrah the town, haven't you?"

"Yassuh. Too many times," the Negro answered.

Quinn's hand flicked to his holster, nosed up a gun from his hip. It exploded and a spider web of shivered glass surrounded a black hole in Sam's biggest mirror.

"Did you ever see one hurrah a colored man's barber-shop, Sam?" Quinn asked softly. "Think before you answer. I'll bet Winters hasn't paid you your room rent yet. I'll shoot up your shop, Sam—maybe you too, and get nothin' out of it but a fine." Pausing, he regarded the man with a slow inscrutable smile, extending in his other hand a ten-dollar bill. "What about it?"

Sam's hand reached slowly for the bill. "You go upstairs and turn to the right. It's the back room. Ah ain't got no key," he said.

Quinn swung open the loading gate on his Colt, shucked out the shells and threw the gun to Sam. "If anybody's curious about that shot, tell 'em you were cleanin' the gun."

He disappeared through the door in the rear, found the stairs to his left and mounted them. The door to the single room in the rear was locked, as he had suspected. He put his shoulder to the door and broke the lock.

Shutting the door behind him, he looked around the room. It was a mean affair, mussed blankets on a rickety cot, a sagging dresser, a dirty ragged rug on the floor; and a wash-bowl and pitcher on an up-ended soap box comprised the furniture of the room, all lighted by a single small window so dirty the room was almost dark.

Quinn's experienced eye noted a shoe box that was used as a wastebasket. It was full. That would come later if nothing turned up.

His examination of the room was thorough, starting with the dresser which revealed nothing but some soiled shirts and towels, and ending with the rug. Nothing.

"The wastebasket it is," he muttered. He dumped the contents of the shoe box on the floor near a window and began to sort out and smooth the crumpled pieces of paper. Half way through, he rose with a paper in his hand and went closer to the window.

The letter was sent from a well-known smelting company in Tucson dated two days ago. Its message was brief.

Enclosed are banknotes as you always direct with your shipments, $893.00 in payment for twenty-seven ounces of gold, quoted at the current market, refining costs deducted.

Quinn let the paper slip from his hands. "So that's it. Gold," he muttered. He plucked his lower lip thoughtfully, his forehead wrinkled in a frown. Picking up the letter, he reread it.

" 'As you always direct'—means that isn't the first shipment he's made." He shrugged. "Well, that's a clue. Not mine, though. Maybe Rand would like to know that."

Putting the paper in his pocket, he glanced around the room. Cigarettes littered the floor and rug, even the dresser top. Quinn lighted a match, touched off the paper in the shoe-box and waited for it to burn down, careful to see that nothing else in the room caught fire. Finished, he closed the door behind him and went downstairs.

Sam was waiting, his face sweating. "Boss, what am Ah goin' to tell Mistuh Wintuhs when he comes in? Who am Ah goin' to say broke that lock?"

"I took care of that, Sam," Quinn told him. "I set the paper in the wastebasket on fire, then put it out. Tell Winters you smelled smoke and had to break down the door to put out the fire."

Sam grinned happily. "Yassuh. He's the smokinest man Ah ever seed. Ah reckon he'll believe that."

Quinn gave Sam another ten. "Buy a new mirror, Sam. And just forget that I was ever in here."

"Ah ain't even likely to want to remember that, Boss," Sam said fervently.

17
Death in the Canyon

When they woke Dave it was by sticking a gun in his midriff.

"You got the hobbles off you. Come on," Reilly grunted.

Dave was a little weak from hunger as he rose to his feet, and his hand was stiff and throbbing, like a raw nerve. Lew and Reilly escorted him out to the table, where Sayres was waiting with a rope, a thin smile on his face.

"You're goin' to take a trip, Turner," Sayres said. "Put out your hands."

"I heard it," Dave said quietly, as he extended his hands to be bound.

As Sayres reached out, Dave lunged for his throat, wrapping his long fingers around it, his thumbs at the windpipe. Sayres slid off the table, clutching with his big hands at Dave's wrists as Dave felt a skull-shattering blow on his head. He held on doggedly, feeling another blow on the other side of his head, and yet another. As he sank into unconsciousness, he put every ounce of effort into the vise of his hands, feeling remotely the soft flesh give and swell under them.

It was daylight when he regained his senses, brought back by the steady jogging of his horse. He realized his head was lolling from side to side, his face in the mane of his horse. He could feel blood caked on his face, and his head throbbed maddeningly. About to look up, he suddenly checked himself. Around the saddle-horn his wrists were laced tightly and his hands were numb from the shut-off circulation.

Raising his eyes he could see through a screen of blood-matted hair that a horseman was leading the horse he was riding. Behind him he could hear the rhythmical clopping of a second horse. It was Lew ahead. They were threading their way through a broken, up-ended country, barren of any growth save an occasional piñon and a hardy yucca. It was a desert of rocks, jagged, gaunt, stark and sun-seared. The sun was beating down unmercifully on his head, and he felt as if his skull were a smashed egg, held together only by his hair.

Relaxing, he let his body sway loosely, as if he were still unconscious, and pulled his thoughts together as best he could. He dimly realized that he was mounted on his own horse and he fondly imagined the sturdy little beast was stepping lightly, trying to make it easier for him.

He knew the horse had not been unsaddled since yesterday, for it quivered its skin continually, as if to drive off the irritation of the wet saddle-blanket. Hanging his head a little, Dave looked beneath his arm and saw that his slicker, with the sheriff's gun inside, was still behind the cantle. A lot of good it would do him, he thought bitterly, manacled as he was, like a beef led to slaughter.

Reilly's thin whistling stopped suddenly and he called to Lew. The leader drew up and Dave's horse stopped willingly.

"Give us a drink," Reilly called.

Dave, slumped over his horse's neck, heard him dismount and the gravel crunch as he walked up to Lew.

"God, but I'm dry," Reilly said. He drank noisily from Lew's canteen.

"Reckon that jasper is alive?" Lew asked.

"I dunno. I been watchin' him and he acks just like he was dead. Rolls around on that saddle until you think he'd tip that damn nag over."

"Take a look," Lew said.

Reilly walked back and, seizing Dave's forelock, yanked his head up off the horse's neck. He shuttered up Dave's eyelid, saw the eye gazing blankly into space, then let his head flop back. He felt his chest too.

"He's alive, all right," Reilly grunted. "Damned if I know why, though. I slugged that skull of his till my arm was tired and he still hung on to Sayres."

Lew laughed shortly. "That kickin' Sayres give him didn't help much."

Reilly laughed too. "God, but wasn't Sayres mad? I bet he won't git a clean lungful of air for three weeks." Dave heard him spit. "Say, Lew. Why the hell are we ridin' over to Mimbres canyon when all we got to do is to stick a gun in his ear, dump him off here and lie in the shade for a couple of hours?"

Lew's answer was prompt. "Sayres said dump him over there and start a rock slide. If we leave him here, some ranny might blunder onto him and know him and we'd have to jump the country sure as hell."

"Hell," Reilly scoffed. "Who comes up this way?"

"You can't tell," Lew insisted. "Mebbe a posse after that gal. Mebbe some jasper cuttin' signs for some strayed beef from over north. Anybody spots buzzards, they'll take a *pasear* over here to see what's the bait. Huh-uh. We better do it."

"It don't make sense," Reilly insisted.

"You seen how bad Sayres can get," Lew told him significantly. "If he ever found out we never took this ranny to Mimbres, I reckon I'd hit the grit and ride for a week. And I ain't smart, but I know when I got a good thing. Not me. If you ain't hankerin' to sweat a few hours more, I'll take him myself."

"I'll go," Reilly growled.

"Besides, you git back too soon and Sayres'll know we ain't been to Mimbres. Reckon we better ride on."

Reilly growled something and walked back to his horse. They started out again. Dave opened his eyes, feeling sick. If he hadn't known before that they were going to kill him, he was sure of it now. And Mary back there alone with those killers. He tried desperately to think of a way of escape, but he was helpless and sick. He could not even struggle to free his hands or Reilly would notice it and shoot him in the back. Besides, it would do no good, for the reins of his horse were tied together, looped over the horse's head and fastened to a long rope which trailed from Lew's hand.

A high, jagged-edged hog's-back rose before them and Lew nosed his horse into the trail that ascended its side. The trail was narrow; to the left there was a sheer wall, to the right a long talus or windrift that sloped abruptly to the canyon bottom three hundred feet below. Lew looked back and hauled up the rope a little, so as to bring Dave's horse closer to him. He held the lead rope in his left hand, next to the wall.

"Wonder now, is that hoss spooky?" Lew asked. "If he is I reckon I'll let this rope go and you drive him up."

"Naw. He's dead on his feet," Reilly replied.

Lew said: "I hope so," and swung up into the sharply ascending rocky trail which was less than three feet wide.

Suddenly, Dave stiffened and smiled grimly through cracked lips.

"Maybe it'll work," he told himself. "The worst I can do is break my neck and that's better than gettin' shot in the ear and buried under a mountain."

He sagged loosely in the saddle, head bent down as his horse swung into the ascent. The steepness of the hill raised the horse's forequarters, letting Dave's sagging head slip down on the shoulders. He rode low this way for perhaps three minutes, letting Reilly become accustomed to it.

The three horses made their way cautiously up the steep trail making quick-footed recoveries as they slipped on pebbles.

Dave, his head hanging along his horse's neck between the wall and the horse, could not see how steep the grade on the other side was. He did not want to. Time enough to worry about that later.

"Look at that hombre, Lew," Reilly called. "Ten more minutes and the horse'll be ridin' him."

Lew glanced back briefly and grunted. His attention was taken up with the trail ahead of him.

Dave steeled himself. "Here goes, old horse. Sorry." And he sunk his teeth in the horse's withers, ripping away a large piece of skin. Electrified by the searing pain in its neck, the horse lunged and let out a shrieking whinny. Dave bit again, savagely.

On that narrow ledge, the horse, frantic with fright and pain, started to pitch. Lew's efforts to snub him with the rope were savage but fruitless. The horse reared back, then landed in a stiff-legged hump, and started to pitch in earnest, ears back.

"He's wild!" Reilly yelled. "Let go and ride up."

The pitching seemed to shake Dave into a thousand splintery fragments of bone as he tried still to keep the appearance of being relaxed. His head snapped back sickeningly, then whipped forward as if it were going to fly off his neck. His wrists, tied to the saddle-horn, were almost snapped in two. Whenever he could, he ground his knee into the raw place where he had torn the skin loose with his teeth. Gently, but firmly, he pressed his left knee against the spot, hoping that reaction from training added to the pain would swing the horse to the right.

Crazed with pain, the horse jarred down stiff-legged again, humped its back for another pitch and Dave savagely rubbed the raw flesh. Half-way up its arc, the horse started a sunfish, and when it landed Dave felt as if he were going to be ripped out of the saddle with the sudden fall.

The horse had gone over the trail edge.

With Dave's weight on its back, the horse started to plummet down the steep slope, its four legs spread in a futile effort to check its speed. Dimly, Dave realized that in the quick descent, Lew who had doggedly held to the rope trying to fight the horse down, had been swept from his saddle by the swift yank on it.

Dave heard a shot behind him and felt the horse shudder as if hit. Desperately, he guided the horse with his knees as best he could while behind him he could hear the gathering rumble of the rock and dirt slide he had started. The canyon bottom seemed to be rising steadily and swiftly to meet them. He hoped savagely that the horse would be able to pull out of the slide without help from the reins as he worked excitedly to free his wrists.

"Steady, boy," he called to the horse.

The last fifty feet of the slope was almost straight. Dave leaned as far back as he could in the saddle, careless of what Reilly and Lew might think.

The horse hit the arroyo bottom, legs spread, with an impact that was stunning. It staggered, stumbled a few steps, then fighting madly came out of it and trotted clear of the oncoming avalanche. Dave guided it behind a huge sheltering boulder.

"Steady, steady," he muttered soothingly and part of his calm was communicated to the horse, who stopped, trembling.

He had to be quick. Closing his eyes and clamping his jaws, he pulled savagely at the thongs binding his wrists to the saddle-horn. A sickening rip of skin and one hand was free. Soon the other was able to help him as he turned in his saddle, ears primed for pursuit, and struggled with blood-dripping hands to free his slicker. Hands and fingers were numb, aching. He did not try to free his feet; they would be on him before he succeeded.

The slicker free, Dave unrolled it swiftly and found the gun Hank had given him. Then, reaching down and seizing the bridle as reins, he spurred the horse slowly from behind the rock, looking up at the trail. A glance told the story. Both men were gingerly picking their way down the trail and were now close to the bottom. They had to climb to the top before they could turn around. A deep furrow was plowed down the talus where Dave's horse had slid. A distance away from it was another furrow, smaller, where Lew had been dragged from his horse and had fought his way back up the slope again.

"Good fellow," Dave whispered, stroking the neck of the trembling horse and backing it gently behind the rock again. He massaged his fingers, wet with streaming blood, and listened for the sound of horses in the canyon bed.

They were coming, both cursing savagely, at a gallop. Dave pulled his roan close in to the rock and balanced his gun lightly in his bloody palm, his eyes thin, flinty slits in his face.

Lew was the first to charge by, and Dave yelled. Reilly, close on Lew's heels, lunged into sight, already checking his horse, his hands whipping to his guns.

Dave coolly wheeled his horse broadside, in a high arc, stooping low over its neck as his gun dropped down slowly, hesitated, crashed and bucked up jarringly. Reilly screamed as he catapulted from the saddle across his horse's neck and to the ground, but Dave did not see him.

Lew's gun was clear, flashing its bright steel wink in the sunshine as it traveled up across his body. Dave deliberately fanned every shell in his gun at Lew's side. The first shot seemed to stand the outlaw up in his stirrups, but did not stop the ascending gun. The second knocked his leg free so that it drew up to his stomach in a gesture of pain. The third snapped his head to one side and seemed to melt him off the saddle and sprawl him quietly between the feet of his horse in the dust, dead.

Dave's gun sank slowly and the bleak, twisted smile on his face faded.

"Two," he muttered thickly. Spurring his horse over, he looked down at the two men. Lew was dead, drilled through the head. Reilly's mouth was a fountain of welling blood and Dave knew he was dying, if not dead. He stared at the men dully, sunk in a stupor of pain and fatigue and thirst.

He shook himself. This couldn't go on: he'd have to pull himself together. The first thing to do was to free himself of the saddle. The knots to the ropes were under the horse's belly where he could not reach them; so, loading his gun again, he shoved the muzzle of his Colt against the rope beside his foot and cut it with a shot.

Dismounted, he was so weak his legs gave way under him.

"I've got to drink," he thought dazedly, sitting on the ground. Crawling over to Lew's horse, he pulled himself up by the stirrup and slung the canteen from the saddle-horn. After the first slow drink he paused, then took a deep draught, which strengthened him. Then he lay down in the shade of the rock, tore the slicker into strips and, after washing his wounds, bound them. He found he could move his fingers easily, though with much pain.

"That's all I want," he told himself. "Just so I can hold a gun."

Seated by the rock, he considered his course. They had Mary there at the cabin and had been careful to remove him before she got there. God knows what this gang of renegades would do to her: he could not let himself think of it. There was only one thing to do. Go back and get her, selling his life as dearly as possible. His thoughts of the ranch were secondary now. If he was alive, no man would dare to claim the D Bar T, deed or no deed.

He tried walking and found that the water had given him a degree of strength. Collecting the guns and belts of the two dead men, he tested the six-guns for their balance. Lew's suited him best and he strapped them on. Reilly's guns and his own borrowed one he rolled up in what was left of his slicker and strapped on his saddle.

He considered the two dead men. They could not be left for buzzards and coyotes to pick, even if they did deserve it. He pulled them over a way to the opposite side of the canyon so that cloudbursts sweeping the canyon floor would not dig them up. Laying them side by side, he piled a cairn of stones over them. When he was finished, he looked at the grave and laughed grimly.

"That's more than you would have done for me, gents, but I reckon you deserve it."

He turned to the horses standing hip-shot in the sun. Dave mounted Lew's pinto and cut Reilly's horse across the rump with his rope. Dave had no idea where the cabin lay, but he knew if given their heads the horses would take for it.

Then he settled down into steady riding, keeping his eyes and ears alert, riding close to Reilly's horse. His own mount followed wearily behind.

Dave tried to figure out some plan of rescuing Mary. He could not guess how many men would be at the cabin. He judged he would get there in mid-afternoon. How would he approach? The dark of the night previous and his unconsciousness of this morning had prevented him getting any idea of how the place was situated. He would have to wait, trusting to luck.

The first two hours he relaxed, letting the riding wear out the stiffness of his body. His ribs ached and he knew without feeling that some of them were broken.

As the time went on, he became more wary and moved closer to the lead horse, watching it. When he heard it whinny and saw it increase its pace, he spurred his horse and headed it off.

Dismounting, he haltered the horses to the ground, laying heavy rocks on their reins. He looked around. Ahead of him, the land rose, broken and rocky, to the lip of a ridge.

Dave took a lariat from the saddle and made his way up the hill. On the ridge, he squatted inconspicuously by a boulder and looked the country over. There a little to the south of him, perhaps a half mile away, lay the cabin in a deep pocket of the valley. It was a log affair with log outbuildings. Beyond them, the country stretched in parallel rocky ridges to the mountains, perhaps six miles away. The outlaws had chosen their hideout wisely, Dave thought. Unless a man was on one of the rustler's homing horses, like himself, he could wander the badlands for years and only by accident stumble on the place tucked away in the hills.

There was a low ridge of gaunt rock just behind the buildings and a peninsula of rock jutted out from it at right angles.

"I'll have to get close," he thought; "close enough to see if I can set the barn on fire, anything to draw them out of the house."

He worked his way down to the low ridge, keeping in the shelter of the rocks as much as possible, until he had reached the finger of rock. He wormed his way out on this almost to the end, then rose and surveyed the place. The back of the cabin faced him, perhaps forty yards off. It was roughly rectangular but the storeroom addition placed a little off center to the rear destroyed the symmetry and also made windows impossible. Its low roof sloped up to the roof of the cabin proper.

Directly below Dave lay the barn nestled snugly against the

rock out of the wind. In the corral adjoining it, he counted six horses, but Mary's was not among them. He calculated swiftly how many men were apt to be at the house.

"Sayres sure. Cassidy will stay at the pass on the lookout for a posse. Fat may be back. He probably took two men to get Mary. That will be four at least."

Watching the house for a long minute and seeing no signs of life, he decided that no one was likely to come out and surprise him.

He looped the lariat around a point of rock, tested it, then let himself down hand over hand the twenty feet to the barn roof. Flipping the rope loose, he let himself down to the ground behind the barn.

Edging his head around the corner of the barn, he made a more careful examination of the shack. He could see the padlock gleaming on the back door of the addition, inside of which was Mary, bound and helpless probably. If he rescued her, it would have to be by the front entrance. He drew back thoughtfully, making his way around to the corral and climbing through the bars. The horses watched him closely, their mild unblinking eyes incurious and trustful. He let himself in the stable door and looked around.

Now that he was here a dislike for setting the barn afire came over him. It was a rancher's distaste for the waste of property, feed, saddles and labor. But some way, somehow, he had to get at least two or three of the men out of the house.

His eyes roved the barn, finally settling on a bearskin lying dusty and neglected in a far corner under some empty sacks. A plan formed slowly in his mind and he decided to try it.

Going through the stable door out into the corral again, he hugged the barn wall sheltered from sight in the house and moved toward the corral gate, which consisted of loose poles. Keeping a careful eye on the house, he removed the poles. The horses watched him, silently wondering at his strange actions.

In the barn again, Dave opened the huge barn door a foot or so. He picked up the bearskin and, after taking a last look at the house, went to the stable door.

He sailed the bearskin out into the middle of the corral, then dodged back in the barn and out the door, running as quietly as he could for the back of the addition.

The horses, smelling the bearskin, seeing it sail of itself out into their midst, milled wildly from it, finally boiling out the gate in a stampede.

"It's kill or die now," Dave muttered to himself as he watched them go.

The horses had fled past the south end of the house, heading down a narrow canyon to the east. Dave crawled softly around the north end of the shack, bending low before the one window in that end. At the corner he stopped and listened.

He heard chairs scrape, feet pounding, a voice from the door.

"Goddlemighty, it's them horses scatterin'. Who left that corral gate down?"

Dave did not recognize this voice, but he did the voice that answered. It was Sayres.

"You did, Ed, damn you! You were the last one in."

"But I never," Ed protested vehemently.

"Shut up and go round 'em up," Sayres ordered. "You help him too, Lafe."

"But we ain't got a horse left in the corral," Ed protested.

"They'll run themselves out," Sayres said. "My horse answers to a whistle anyway. Get along."

Dave edged his head around the corner of the house in time to see two men he didn't recognize file out and head down the canyon afoot.

He gave them time to get out of sight among the rocks, then he edged around the front door on his hands and knees, listening. He heard the conversation between two men, one of them Sayres, as it seeped past the closed door.

"Fat'll send word where the posse's headin' for. If they come down the valley, we can spot 'em. If they come up behind, Fat'll know. He'll have some one in the posse, don't you worry. If they crowd us, we better take the gal back to the line camp in the timber, north. They'll hunt a year before they kick up that place."

"She's a pretty gal," the second voice said suggestively.

"Ain't she, though?" Sayres drawled.

Dave lost the rest. A violent surge of rage blinded him momentarily. He straightened up and swung the door open.

Both men were seated at one end of the table, a bottle before them. They looked up to see a tall, lean, blood-spattered man standing in the door, leaning a little forward on the balls of his feet, bloody hands loose at his sides.

"Fill your hand, Sayres!" Dave drawled in a low voice, almost a whisper.

But Sayres had already started. And so had Dave and so had the stranger.

In the least part of a second Dave divined what Sayres was going to do. Seated, the outlaw could not get at his guns. He made a leap to place himself behind the stranger, his hands clawing at his guns. Dave's shot was quick, hasty, hardly allowing time for his Colts to clear leather. The shot caught Sayres in the side and pitched him into the stranger who was half out of the chair. The impact sprawled them both on the floor. Then Dave's rage broke as, feet planted solidly to meet any lead that reached him, he emptied his guns, the other nine shots, into the writing mass of arms, legs and bodies that was Sayres and the stranger. Only one shot came from that mass and it sang harmlessly into the ceiling.

A feeling of sickness and weariness and disgust enveloped Dave as he let his gun sag, and waited while the blanket of smoke drifted away from him to the door. He felt weak as water and he took two steps forward to lean on the table. Sayres lay sprawled over the upset chair, face down, his guns fallen out of his lifeless grip onto the floor, one side of his shirt cut to ribbons and slowly soaking up blood like a blotter. The stranger lay peacefully on his back, gunless hands crossed on his chest.

Dave shook himself. He shucked cartridges into his guns as he strode across the room to the padlocked door.

"Mary!" he called.

There was a sort of muffled cry for an answer and Dave shot

the lock off. He knew the two men after the horses would have heard the shots and would probably be running back now, but it was important that Mary be freed so she could escape while he held them off.

Once in the dark room, he made out a figure sitting tensely on the cot, a sack over her head. Dave fumbled with the strings and finally yanked the sack off.

Dorsey Hammond looked up at him with frightened, frantic eyes.

"Dave!" she said.

She was in his arms sobbing before he could recover from his surprise. She wept bitterly, her whole body shaking as Dave held her closely, pity welling up in his heart. At last he held her from him and shook her gently.

"Dorsey. Mary isn't here?"

"N-n-no. I don't think so."

"Who has the keys to the leg irons? Quick! We've got to hurry."

"I don't know their names, but it's the boss."

"Sit down," Dave snapped. "I'll be back in a minute."

He ran over to Sayres, rolled the body over and fumbled through the pockets. His hands paused and he listened, hearing the pounding of running feet. Slowly, his hand left Sayres and settled to his gun butt, his eyes narrowing. The running ceased, and a man stepped through the door hesitantly, guns already drawn, his eyes swiftly taking in the scene. Dave was behind the table, crouched by Sayres, but the newcomer saw him, for he went into action, guns blazing. Dave laughed silently and whipped a shot under the table where the man's legs were visible. Another and another he sent at the legs while he crouched behind Sayres' body, using it as a parapet. The outlaw sagged to his knees, still blazing away blindly.

Dave shot just once more and the man pitched forward on his face, slowly straightening his knees into a spasmodic sprawl and lay quiet. Dave waited for the second man, silently loading his gun as he watched the door. Suddenly, a window shattered and Dave laughed.

The second outlaw had chosen wisely. He was forted up behind a rock sixty yards in front of the house in the middle of the dry wash.

Dave found the keys on Sayres and returned to Dorsey who, white and trembling, had witnessed through the open door the duel with the outlaw.

"Are you hurt?" she whispered.

"No." Dave stopped to unlock the leg irons. "I'm sorry about that door. I should've shut it. It's been a bloody day."

His white, drawn face looked up into hers and she nodded dumbly, the look of horror still on her face.

"We kill coyotes because they kill our cattle," Dave said softly, "And we have to kill these *hombres,* or they'll kill us."

"I know."

"No, you don't," Dave said, "but you will when you understand. It's just bloody and cruel."

"Do you feel that way about it too?" Dorsey asked wonderingly.

"More than you," Dave answered. "More because I'm the one that's got to kill and kill," he added grimly.

"Then this isn't the end?" she asked.

Dave shook his head grimly. The outlaw in front of the cabin was still to be accounted for, although now he had ceased shooting.

Dorsey stood up, free once more. She shuddered.

"Can we get away?"

Dave nodded. He stepped to the back door of the addition and shot the lock off. Then he returned to Dorsey.

"Step through here and wait for me outside."

"What are you going to do?"

"A dirty job," Dave said slowly, "but a decent one, I reckon, at that. I'm goin' to fire the place."

His eyes were cold and flinty and Dorsey looked away from him. When she had stepped outside Dave went into the main room and scattered lamp oil on the floor and blankets. Then he touched it off and stepped outside to Dorsey as the first wisps of smoke swept out the door and up into the bright sunshine.

"That *hombre* out front has only got a six-gun," Dave said. "He can't hit us—I don't think he can even see us. Make a run for the barn and I'll follow you."

"But—" she began, then closed her mouth.

Dave watched her run to the barn. He leaned against the wall, thinking. Should he leave the place with the one outlaw alive, who would be sure to spread the word? And yet the man did not know that it was Dave who had caused the shooting. All the men who had seen him were dead in the burning house. He could still get away without being identified. What did it matter if this man carried the word to town of the shooting and burning? He would carry along with it the news that Dave had been half killed in a fight and buried in Mimbres canyon. He would not wait for the return of Lew and Reilly before carrying the word to Fat.

His reverie was interrupted by a shout from the barn.

"Look out! Dave."

Dave dropped on his face as a shot blazed from the corner of the cabin. He landed on his stomach, rolling on his side, his free arm whipping out his gun. Only the edge of a hatbrim and a gun showed, but Dave emptied his gun at them as he watched the other gun explode. He felt a hot searing pain in his arm and then the shooting ceased. He leaped to his feet, lunged for the shelter of the cabin as he drew his other gun.

Flattening himself against the wall, he waited. No more shots came and he made his way cautiously to the corner. He poked his gun barrel around it to see if it would draw a shot but it didn't. He swung out, gun ready, and saw the outlaw kneeling, his guns resting idly on his knees, leaning against the wall as if asleep. Dave lifted his hat and saw a neat purple hole just above his right eyebrow. The man had died like a tired child.

Dave shuddered and looked away. In the course of a few hours he had made himself a killer six times over. He shrugged wearily, and dragged the body into the burning house.

In the barn Dorsey was waiting, sitting on the floor. Her face was in her hands and she was sobbing quietly when Dave entered. He stood above her awkwardly, wondering what to say.

"I reckon we better hightail it," he said finally, and added slowly, "I'm sorry about that, but there was no other way out."

Dorsey stood up suddenly and made an effort to control herself.

"Take me home, please," her voice was low and toneless and her eyes lowered.

Dave remembered the stinging scorn in her voice when he had seen her in Dr. Fullerton's. He started to speak but the words died. "They're all dead," he said soberly. "We'll get the horses."

"Where are they?"

"About a mile from here, just over the lip of this hog's-back. Can you walk it?"

"Yes, I—" Dorsey at last lifted her eyes to his set white face. "You're hit," she cried. "Are you—"

"I forgot," Dave answered wearily. The last shot of the outlaw had seared his upper arm. Dorsey bandaged it expertly while he watched her, trying to read the thoughts back of her somber eyes.

"How did you get here?" he asked. "I heard 'em talk about a girl and I thought it was Mary."

They left the buildings and started slowly up the hog's-back.

"I went home a little after dark, dead tired. I'd been up all the night before. I put Pancho in the stable and went in the house. In the kitchen a man grabbed me and told me not to make a noise. There were two of them and one asked the other if they'd left the note. Then they put a sack over my head and tied me on my horse and we rode all night, it seemed. They treated me all right." She looked at Dave, her eyes puzzled. "What's this all about? How long is this madness going to go on?"

"I dunno," Dave answered. "I was forced to sign over my half of our ranch to the jasper named Crowell."

"Crowell? The man you and dad are looking for? The one behind the dynamiting?"

"Yeah," Dave nodded. "I thought he was behind it but there's some one else. Some one they all call the boss. He's

payin' Crowell for gettin' the ranch an' mine; Sayres and his
gang for the dynamitin'—" A wave of anger swept over Dave
as he recalled all the suffering that had been caused. "I'm goin'
to get out of here an' track him down like—"

"Yes, that's your way, isn't it?" Dorsey's quiet voice broke
in.

Dave swung around to face her. "Why, what else should I
do? What would any man—" he caught himself. "Here's the
horses," he said quietly.

They swung on them in silence and rode to the west. Dorsey
sat straight as an Indian, her face was white and remote. Dave's
thoughts were dark and bitter. He handed her a gun which she
received in silence and stuck in the belt of her skirt.

"That's in case I'm not lucky enough to reach you next
time," he said. They rode swiftly, each wondering what was
next, and if this all hadn't happened too late to save them.

18
The Fight on the Ridge

It was close to dusk when Dave and Dorsey neared the pass.
Dave had been scanning the rocky ridge ahead of them that
barred their way to the valley. Surely, in this interminable
stretch of rock outlined against the sky, there would be some
way of getting across without resorting to the pass. But when
Dorsey looked at him, this question in her eye, he smiled
crookedly and laughed a little.

"It's a prison," he pronounced. "Sayres, in some ways, I
reckon was a smart man. A twenty-foot pass for a front door
and the whole Sierra Blancos for a back."

"What will we do?" Dorsey asked.

"A little more butcherin'," Dave said quietly.

"Do you have to?"

"We've got to get by the guard at the pass," Dave said, "and he'll shoot. There's no other way."

They pulled in at a small draw and dismounted. Dave took the carbine from the saddle-boot, not looking at Dorsey until he had to. Then he said: "I wouldn't build a fire. It won't take long."

Dorsey came close to him and laid a hand on his sleeve. He could see that her eyes were searching him, trying to read something in his face that could not be read.

"Isn't there any other way besides blood?" she asked quietly. "You've had enough of that, Dave. Enough to last out five lives."

He shook his head somberly. "It's us or them. It's gone too far now to settle with words—or with law."

Dorsey's voice was edged with bitterness. "If I had killed like you have today, I'd turn back and wander through these mountains until I found a way out that didn't mean blood."

Dave winced, but his eyes held hers steadily. "It's too late for that."

"It's never too late not to kill a man!" Her voice rose a little.

"We've got to get out of here," Dave said slowly. "God knows what they've done to Mary. And Rosy is probably dead, lyin' somewhere in a dry gulch. My ranch is ruined. Everything is gone." His eyes smoldered as he strained to keep his voice calm. "What kind of man would I be if I didn't fight for those I love? And shed blood for them, too?"

She stepped back a little from him. His eyes seemed to sear her. "Then you owe it to yourself to go somewhere where you don't have to kill," she replied.

"I did. I was in prison for eight years—for killin' a man," Dave said. "It looks like that's the only place a man don't have to."

"If that's it, I'd go there," Dorsey said in a low voice.

Dave shook his head patiently.

"I didn't make this war. When I got out of prison, I swore it would take plenty to rawhide me into goin' for my gun." His eyes narrowed and he looked off to the far horizon. "But that's not the way the world gives a man what belongs to him, I reckon. It's fight or die. I died for eight years. I'm goin' to live now for a little while."

"And think about it the rest of your life?"

"It's better than thinkin' back on how I run from it. Nothin's worse than that. Not to a man anyway."

Dorsey caught her breath. "Then it is true," she said slowly, "you are hard. You're cruel and ruthless. You're a—murderer!"

Dave flinched as if struck with a whip. Her words hurt more than any he had ever heard. Why couldn't he make her understand?

"Dorsey," his voice was pleading, "can't you see?"

"Please go," she said quietly.

Dave's lips were a grim line as he turned on his heel and strode off into the gathering dusk. "She's right," he thought wearily. "If things worked out that way, nothin' should be bad enough to make you kill a man. But they are. And I'm payin'. This is what I spent eight years for and to hear her say it—" He shook his head to drive away these thoughts. He had work ahead of him. Unless Cassidy was out of the way, they would be shot down like sheep when they tried to go through the pass.

Ahead of him, the ground rose gently, announcing the steep ascent to the notch. Dave stopped and in the shelter of a rock scanned the country before him. He saw the rock ramparts, black against the fading sky, gaunt and waspish guardian of evil lives. Cassidy had been on the right rampart the night before. Was he still there? Maybe not Cassidy, for even a guard had to sleep sometimes, but there would be some one in his place, a silent, keen-eyed watcher, a rifle folded across his arms and a case of shells at his feet. On him depended the success of Sayres' job.

Had the man heard the shooting or seen the smoke? Probably; but he would be wise enough to bide his time. His orders were to guard the pass and he'd stay there until Sayres told him to leave.

The skyline showed Dave that the right rampart would be

the easiest to reach. Jagged boulders on top of the ridges, black
against the sky, led up to the rampart and this meant shelter
from sight and gunfire. If the rampart was occupied, the rocks
would afford him the best fighting vantage. If it was vacant,
with the guard on the left rampart, then it would afford shelter
from a searing rifle duel which would end in death for one of
them.

Making a wide detour and keeping hidden as best he could in
case the guard was using glasses to search out the back road,
Dave reached the top of the ridge about dark, perhaps a quarter
mile to the north of the rampart. Then began his slow and
cautious journey forward, through the gaunt, up-thrown rocks.

The silence of the night fell around him with a suddenness
that was ghostly. Far off down the slope he could hear the owls
hooting. A far whippoorwill announced its spurious message of
death and the coyotes quavered their mournful and defeated
wail to each other from mountain slope to mountain slope.

Dave paused to remove his boots. In this stillness, they
seemed to make the noise of an army on the march. Paused, he
suddenly jerked erect and listened. Behind him, farther down
the ridge he could hear the crunching of bootsoles on rock.

"Some ranny saw me and is followin'," he thought savagely.
In the dark he felt the rock around him and found a crevice
that would hide him and keep his body from showing against
the skyline.

He knew some rattlesnake might have sought this crevice
against the cold of the night, but he had to take the chance.
Letting himself down into it, he raised his head above the edge
of the rock and waited.

Slowly, the man was making his way forward against the
skyline. Dave saw him raise up and listen. Dave drew a bead on
him, then let his Colt slack. A shot would alarm the guard for
sure and give him away. If the man came closer and was still
unsuspecting there might be a chance to get him before he
could cry out.

He thought of Dorsey's bitter, accusing voice. Well, this
would be another one that he need never tell her about. Listen-

ing to the sound of the footsteps, Dave knew the man was close now. He could hear the quiet breathing of the man as he paused by the rock, apparently listening. Strangely, then, the man seated himself on the rock behind which Dave was hidden. Dave could only see the stars blacked out in a vague shape of a man.

With noiseless effort, Dave hoisted himself out of the crevice, got a toe-hold on the rock and lunged at the sitting figure. The force of his spring took them both sprawling on the ground. Dave's hand was on the stranger's throat, but the force of the man's great strength was not easy to calm. Dave felt a fist driving into his face time after time and he lowered his head to take the blows on the skull.

Suddenly, the man ceased struggling and Dave eased off his hands. A sudden soughing of wind came to his ears as the man inhaled deeply.

Then: "Dave Turner, you damned, jug-headed, murderin' fool!"

Dave slid off the body and knelt beside it.

"Rosy! My God—I thought you'd be dead."

"Hell, I damn near am," Rosy muttered. He sat up and rubbed his throat.

"How'd you know it was me?" Dave asked.

"When you lowered your head, I hit that place where the bushwhacker slammed you, but you was hanging on to me like a burr. I aimed to play dead so's you'd take your hand off my throat, but I damned near bugged my eyes out doin' it." He laughed ruefully, inhaling deep draughts of air as he talked.

"How'd that fat jasper happen to miss you? He was headin' for town to gather you in last I saw of him."

"I'll tell you later," Rosy grunted. "What are you doin' here?"

"Same thing you are, I reckon."

"The guard?"

"Uh-huh."

"Me too," Rosy growled. "I been crawlin' on my belly all afternoon and I waited another hour for the sun to go down."

"Did he see you?"

"I don't think so."

"And he's on this rock?"

Rosy said he was. They sat a moment listening to see if they had alarmed the guard, but the night was soundless.

"Dorsey Hammond's here," Dave said tonelessly. "They kidnapped her."

"Dorsey Hammond?" Rosy asked incredulously. "Why—I never heard about it. Are you sure? Is she all right?"

Dave told him about it.

"And I'll bet Mary was the one that found it out," Rosy said.

"Mary?"

Rosy checked himself. "Let's get on. We got some work ahead of us. Near as I can make out, this here rock he's on is cup shaped, maybe twenty feet across and a little higher than the rest of the hill. What's your idea to get him?"

They decided that Dave was to go down the slope, circle around, hide himself and open fire on the ground. Rosy was to approach the rampart from the ridge, as before.

"Then let's go," Rosy said.

Dave disappeared down the side of the scarp and Rosy continued ahead. Worming his way forward for nearly twenty minutes, pausing to listen occasionally, Rosy finally achieved a round knob of rock which he had noted from below as being close to the rampart. Edging his head around it, he saw the rampart, some four feet higher than the knob, outlined against the sky. It was twenty feet across to it, down a slight slope and up a steep one to the rampart edge. He took off his boots and socks, unholstered his gun and rammed it in his belt.

He could smell cigarette smoke, hear the slight movements of the man on top in the cup. A veering of the wind carried the smell of cedar smoke to him and he guessed the man had built a small fire.

He smiled. "Damned fool," he thought. "If he looks out into the night from that fire he couldn't see a cavalry troop."

Rosy waited impatiently. Dave would have to have time, he knew, but the minutes dragged by interminably.

A shot from below electrified him and he knew Dave was cached cosily behind a rock, shooting at random. Rosy heard the loud hiss of water on coals as the guard extinguished his fire. The answering shot was loud and close. The guard had returned the fire so he must be on the other side of the rampart, Rosy thought.

He waited for Dave's second shot, which slapped against the rock with a brittle report. Then noiselessly he ran down into the bowl-like depression to gain momentum and ran up the smooth rock of the rampart wall. By stretching his arms, his fingers just reached the top edge and he hung there patiently, waiting for Dave's next shot. From below, a volley of shots rang out and Rosy could hear their vicious slap as they smacked against the rock. A man evidently wise in the ways of warfare, the guard shifted his position before he returned the fire.

At this signal, Rosy hoisted himself up. With a stifled curse he heard his gun butt scrape loudly on the rock.

He could see the guard now lying against the sloping far wall. The guard whipped around, raised his rifle and a lance of orange licked out. Resting precariously on one elbow, Rosy clawed at his gun. In that cramped, awkward position he fanned the gun desperately, blindly, waiting for a bullet to pick him off and send him careening down among the rocks. Nothing happened. As his eyes washed out the color of the gun flame, he saw the limp body of the guard inch down the wall until it rested, huddled up, almost in the smoking fire. The guard's rifle had gone over the edge of the rampart.

Rosy pulled himself over the rim and hullooed loudly. Dave answered him dimly from below. Then he turned the body over, struck a match and saw the man was dead, three bullets carefully spaced in the middle of his chest.

"You get a pilgrim's burial, fella," Rosy muttered softly. "That's part of the game you play."

He loaded his Colt thoughtfully, shrugged and let himself down the slope. Finding his boots and socks, he put them on and made his way back and down the slope.

Dave was waiting with Dorsey at the pass when he reached it. Dorsey's greeting was spiritless and dull and in the dark he tried to see her face, wondering at the explanation. Dave sat wearily on his horse a little distance from Dorsey.

"Where's your horse?" Dave asked.

"It has probably run from the smell of blood," Dorsey said bitterly.

Rosy looked at her, but he could see nothing.

"A mile or so down the hill, I guess," he told Dave.

"Where are we going now? To kill more people?" Dorsey asked.

But the irony of the question was lost on Rosy.

"We're goin' back and clean up the rest of them red ants," he said grimly. "If we don't blow up the town tonight, then I ain't Mrs. Rand's son Rosy."

19
Gold Bits for Every Horse

It took Laredo three minutes to get a saddled horse from the livery stable after he had left the sheriff's office.

He rode slowly north up the valley, leading the horse. When he was out of sight of the town, he left the road and started up the mountains to the east. As soon as he was hidden in the timber, he cut back again in the direction of town. Where the mountains broke for the railroad tracks in a deep pass he turned east again and, still clinging high up on the mountain-side, he paralleled the tracks for three miles or so.

Presently, he swung down the hill to the tracks, hunted a wide draw bridged by the railroad trestle, hid the horses in some tall mesquite and, rolling a cigarette, stretched lazily on the ground.

When he heard the freight train come slogging up the grade and into sight, he watched it quietly. It swung past over the trestle and crawled into the deep cut of the pass, where it was hidden from his sight. As the last three cars disappeared, Laredo saw a man swing off the caboose, run a bit with his momentum, then stop and wave to somebody on the vanished train.

Then the man turned and surveyed the country around him. Laredo stood up and waved an arm and the man walked over to him. The newcomer was dressed in laced boots, clean but faded breeches and an open-necked khaki shirt. He was a middle-aged man, broad of face and quiet of eye. He smoked a pipe set comfortably in a wide mouth.

He greeted Laredo quietly, a glint of amusement in his deep-set eyes.

"Hullo, cowboy."

"Howdy, Chuck." They shook hands. "Can you still ride a horse?"

"Try me."

They mounted and started back over the same trail Laredo had come. Laredo's companion studied him often, his steady eyes reflecting an unspoken curiosity. Finally, he spoke.

"When are you goin' to tell me what this is all about, Laredo? I had to buy that brakeman a bottle of whisky to get a seat in the hack. Why all the secrecy?"

"It's a long story, Chuck. A lot of it I don't know, and I'm dependin' on you to tell me."

"What about?"

"A ranch," Laredo said simply.

Chuck scowled pleasantly.

"A ranch. Hell, man. I'm a minin' man. I don't know a cattle ranch from a fruit ranch, except they ride horses on a fruit ranch."

"And brand their apples," Laredo said.

Chuck laughed. "What's it all about?"

"I dunno," Laredo persisted. "That's what I got you up here

for. All we got to do now is to ride for a while and then you can tell me."

"Ride how far? I should catch the night train out."

"Fifteen miles or so. You can catch it at Soledad."

Chuck stared at him. "It'll be dark by that time."

"I got lanterns there," Laredo said earnestly. "I reckon you can see all you want by lantern light."

And after that Laredo did not talk. When they had passed the lake on the way to the D Bar T, Laredo left the trail that angled down to the ranch and picked his own. The two horsemen skirted the base of Old Cartridge which jutted down to the lake and headed north toward the mountains.

A half hour's ride led them into a maze of canyons, a jagged tortuous mass of upthrown and worndown rocks that seemed a fitting guard to the forbidding Sierras behind them. As dusk settled into dark, Chuck gave up trying to keep directions and let his horse have its head. With the precision of years of practice, Laredo went deeper and deeper into the canyons, pausing now and again to get his bearings.

It was like the bottom of a jagged floored well, Chuck thought. All he could see were the stars overhead and the pitchy blackness of the rocks around him. There were no landmarks, nothing by which to go except the patient clopping of Laredo's horse and the brief stretch of sky above the canyon tops. They had ridden an hour in this when Laredo drew up.

"Know your way out?" he asked Chuck.

"Huh-uh. I don't think you do either."

Laredo laughed and dismounted and Chuck heard him go off a short distance. When he returned, something clanked at his side.

"Here's a lantern," he said. "Light up and come with me."

Chuck did as he was bid and in the flickering circle of light cast by the lantern he followed Laredo. He saw now why the little foreman had left the horses, for the floor of the canyon was of black basalt rock made up of myriad sharp and flinty pieces that would have cut the hoofs of a horse. The canyon narrowed until its width could be spanned by stretching the arms, and a cool, dank smell of wet rock surrounded them. Suddenly they stepped out of the bottleneck on to the sparse grass of a little amphitheater. The walls fell back and he could see footprints on the ground.

"Here's the place," Laredo said.

"For what?"

Laredo squatted on his heels by the lantern and rolled a cigarette carefully before he answered.

"For a month, off and on, I been watchin' a *hombre* dig here." He jerked his thumb over his shoulder to somewhere in the darkness. "What I want to know is, what is it he dug?"

He picked up the lantern and moved over toward one of the walls. A tight-mouthed tunnel appeared before them and Laredo motioned Chuck inside. His lantern before him, Chuck crawled into the shaft followed by Laredo. The shaft itself was low, of a rubble containing much quartz. Five yards in, the shaft turned at right angles, bumped into a different stratum of rock which it punctured for nearly ten yards, then stopped abruptly.

Chuck set his lamp on the floor at the end with a smothered oath. A single, short-handled pickaxe lay on the floor. Laredo was smoking calmly when Chuck turned on him, seeking his eyes in the glow of the lantern.

"My God! Have you been lookin' at the walls here?" he asked Laredo slowly, unbelievingly.

Laredo nodded. Chuck pointed to the end of the shaft and laughed briefly. "Hell, he don't need a pick. You can pick those nuggets out with a pocket-knife."

"So it's gold?" Laredo asked.

"We've passed fifty thousand dollars' worth in the last twenty-five steps," Chuck said slowly. "Man! Somebody's so rich they can use solid gold bits for every horse in their stable." He glanced shrewdly at Laredo. "Who owns it? Not you?"

Laredo shook his head and spat precisely. "Not me. Not the jasper that's been minin' it either."

"You mean somebody that doesn't own it has done this work?"

Laredo nodded. "He figgered it would be his some day, so it wasn't wasted."

Chuck shook his head and studied his pipe. "If it was daylight, I could tell you more about the formations and the land."

"That's all I want to know," Laredo said. "Suits me."

"How did you run across it?"

"I was cuttin' trail in a canyon over to the west lookin' for strays. I heard the pick working, so I got out of the canyon and edged along the rim until I could see what was doin'. I laid doggo and saw this *hombre* workin' at the shaft. He never belonged there, but I didn't say anything. It wasn't none of my business then. But every once in a while I'd take a *pasear* up this way, sneak up on the rim and look over and I could hear him diggin' away. One day, I waited until he'd went, then I come down and looked."

"And you couldn't tell it was gold?" Chuck asked incredulously.

Laredo shook his head. "I never seen the stuff in my life. I could build a brandin' fire on a pocket of it and wouldn't know it."

"But you guessed."

"Mebbe it was that," Laredo conceded. "I saw money bein' spent where it shouldn't be and I got to wonderin'." He looked up at his companion. "Anything wrong with that?"

"No. Only I don't see how you kept it a secret," Chuck said, still puzzled. "A man would pay you fifty thousand dollars for telling him this—if he's got any conscience."

"That's it," Laredo said dreamily. "About fifty thousand dollars."

"You're a queer little runt," Chuck said slowly. "I don't savvy you."

Laredo smiled. "Hell, money ain't nothing to me. All I want is a little string of horses, a job, three days off every two weeks to git drunk and a lot of space to stretch out in."

Chuck laughed. "And you're getting that now?"

"Uh-huh. Just that." He stood up. "Let's git to town."

Chuck took a last look around. "Who owns this land? Is it owned outright?"

"Every foot of it," Laredo laughed softly. "C'mon. We still got a long ride to Soledad."

Chuck shook his head at Laredo's secrecy, but he knew his friend would tell him in good time.

When they were clear of the canyons again, they headed south for Soledad. Neither of them talked. They picked up the trail that led past the D Bar T and Laredo let his bay make the pace. Tonight, Laredo had learned something for certain that might explain a lot of the happenings of the past few days.

Chuck's voice yanked him out of his thoughts.

"Listen! Weren't those shots?"

"Shots? I never heard them. Where from?"

"To the south and a little west. Quite a bunch of them."

That would be the Turner place. Laredo scowled. Mrs. Winters was in town, Rand was out, and so was Dave. Who could be shooting around there? Laredo spurred his horse into a long lope.

"We'll take a *pasear,* Chuck. C'mon," he called.

When they approached the D Bar T, the place was dark. Laredo reined up by the corral and waited for Chuck.

"Think them shots came from here?" Laredo asked.

"It's the right direction," Chuck said, "but the place is dark."

"Let's look around anyway."

They dismounted and approached the house. The house loomed blackly, silently, before them. Laredo came up to the back door and listened. Nothing. He walked off to the side and listened again.

"I guess it wasn't from here," he told Chuck quietly.

Chuck was about to answer when a soft groan came from the front of the house. Laredo drew a gun and warily walked around to the corner of the house and stopped. Again the groan. He could make out its source now, a black blotch out under one of the cottonwoods. He walked over to it, Chuck following.

"A man," Laredo said. He knelt down and struck a match. As it flared, he saw a man lying sprawled in a wide pool of blood, face down. He turned him over.

"Rourke," he said quietly. "One of them nesters down on the corner of Turner's place."

Laredo turned the man over, and struck another match. "He's done for," he told Chuck, but the nester moved a little.

"Who—who is it?" the nester asked in a weak frantic whisper.

"Laredo Jackson. What happened, Rourke?"

"Water, water—"

Chuck went to the lean-to for some water while Laredo bent over the bleeding figure.

"What happened, old-timer?" Laredo asked him.

"They tried—to fire—house," Rourke whispered faintly.

"What happened, old-timer?" Laredo asked him.

"Who?"

"Dunno. Two of—'em. I—come—see Turner—about lake. Dark. Saw—both scatterin'—coal oil—leaves. They cut down —me. Took my—gun. Heard your horses—rode off. —Water."

"It's comin', old-timer," Laredo said. Chuck had found some water and Laredo poured it in Rourke's mouth. It seemed to strengthen the nester a little.

"Which way did they ride?" Laredo asked him.

"I couldn't tell," Rourke whispered.

"Hurt bad?" Laredo asked gently.

"Bad as hell," Rourke whispered. "I'm done for."

Laredo looked off into the night, cursing softly. "What kind of a gun was you carryin', Rourke?"

"Smith and Wesson .38. Had a chip off the butt," the nester whispered.

"And you never saw 'em? Never saw their horses? Never heard what they said?"

"I thought it was Turner. I spoke right out, and they both opened up on me. Don't remember much, except a pain in my guts. One of 'em kicked me in the face, and laughed, and took my gun."

"Didn't he say nothin'?"

"Somethin' about . . . wonderin' if they'd take it—at a faro table—instead of money."

"What did he call the ranny he spoke to?" Laredo asked.

There was no answer. Laredo reached out for the dipper and poured more water down Rourke's open mouth. The man did not move.

Laredo laid him down softly and struck another match.

"He's dead," he said quietly. "That poor old man that never harmed a soul."

The little foreman stood up, walked over to the house, struck another match and found that Rourke had been right. A window was broken and the rank smell of kerosene drifted around it. Leaves had been raked up in a pile from under the cottonwoods and soaked with kerosene, then stuffed through the window.

Laredo went back to Chuck.

"Reckon you can find your way to Soledad tonight alone?" he asked.

"I'm going with you," Chuck said softly.

"You got a wife and kids at home. Better not," Laredo said, then added: "Where I'm goin' tonight, there's goin' to be gunsmoke."

"I'm going with you, wherever that is," Chuck told him, and there was an edge of stubbornness on his voice.

"It's Single Shot. That's the only place there's faro tables close."

"Do you believe that about the faro tables?" Chuck asked.

Laredo nodded in the dark. "They thought he was dead, so they likely talked pretty loose. They was aimin' to finish the job of firin' the place after they shot him. They heard our horses and hightailed it. They likely thought we was Turner or Rand, so they won't come back. They could've rode west a ways, then circled up the hills ridin' hell for leather for Single Shot, because that's the closest."

"And you think they're there?"

"That's my guess," Laredo said softly, "but it won't be a guess long. I aim to find out."

20
Gambler's Trap

Martin Quinn stood among the curling pennants of tobacco smoke, his back to the wall, ringed by silent men, their faces intent as they watched the cards leaf out of the faro box. His face was still, impassive. His quick eyes looked up occasionally in a sweeping glance around the table. It was a big night for the Free Throw and the saloon was noisy with the crowd.

He felt a hand on his sleeve and looked up to see one of the house-men beside him holding out a folded slip of paper. Unfolding it with one hand, he read:

"Come to hotel room at once.

RAND."

"Who gave it to you?" he asked the house-man, his face still immobile before the curious glances of the table patrons.

"Dunno. Somebody left it with Mike at the bar."

"Get Royer," Quinn said quietly.

Royer was the owner of the Free Throw. The man studied Quinn a moment before he melted through the crowd.

The game was resumed. Presently, a bald, heavy man past middle age with a big diamond on the checked tie that he wore with an even gaudier suit, made his way to Quinn's side.

"Want me?" he asked, removing a cigar from his mouth. He glanced around the table belligerently. "What's the matter? Trouble?"

Quinn did not look up from the box. "No trouble. Do you want to take this table?"

There was a slight pause before Royer answered. "If you want to step out, give it to a house-man."

"Against rules," Quinn said. The game had stopped now and the men around the table watched the two. "I'm quittin', Royer," Quinn continued. "Check me out."

Royer's cigar came back into his mouth from a pudgy fist and he stared at him. "What's the matter? Ain't I treatin' you right?"

"No kick at all," Quinn said casually. His glance roved the table. "Better get a house-man even if it is against rules. I want to talk to you."

The owner shouted for a man and he and Quinn sought a quiet corner.

"Now what's this all about?" Royer asked. "This is a hell of a time to let me down."

Quinn pulled out his billfold, took out a card and silently handed it to Royer. The great bushy eyebrows of the owner raised as he read it.

"Well, I'll be damned," he muttered. He gave Quinn a searching look. "What is it, trouble?"

"I think so," Quinn answered quietly.

"Want any help?"

Quinn shook his head.

"I can do it alone, Royer. Thanks."

The saloon owner cursed, not without a grim smile however. "Well, go ahead. I don't see how the hell I can stop you."

"I won't leave before tomorrow," Quinn said. "I'll look you up before I leave."

He sauntered through the crowd into the dance hall, skirted the floor and stepped out the side entrance. By the dim light of the hall, he took out the note and read it again.

"If I hadn't seen his writin' twice, might have bit on that," he mused, for the writing was not the same as that on the two notes Rosy had sent him.

He walked slowly over to the hotel, a scowl wrinkling his forehead. The clerk greeted him and reached for his key.

"Seventeen, isn't it, Mr. Quinn?"

"Is sixteen taken?" Quinn asked, accepting the key.

The clerk looked at him, puzzled, then looked at the register. "No. It's empty."

"I want it," Quinn said. The clerk was about to speak, but a look at Quinn stopped him.

"I want the key to the door that connects seventeen and sixteen, too," the gambler said.

The clerk shook his head. "I'm afraid it's lost, Mr. Quinn."

Quinn nodded, took the key to sixteen, and headed for the stairs, leaving the clerk scratching his head in bewilderment.

At the head of the stairs, Quinn paused and removed his shoes. Then he loosened his guns, tried out two swift practice draws, and satisfied, continued down the hall.

Room seventeen, his own room, was on the back corner around a small L in the hall. He tip-toed down the corridor and let himself noiselessly into room sixteen, which was next to his own. He did not light a lamp, but went to the door which connected the two rooms, then knelt down to see if there was a light in seventeen. Unable to see, he rose and walked to the window. For a full minute, he looked out into the night, finally smiling a little.

Then he set about working. He put on his shoes, because the carpet covering the entire floor made his movements noiseless. Then, still working in the dark, he got a towel and soaked it in the pitcher of water on the washstand. He then took the pitcher of water, went over to the connecting door and poured the water slowly and quietly on the rug where it disappeared under the door. The rug soaked the water up like blotting paper, and spread it into the adjoining room. Then he rose, got the lamp, unscrewed the wick, knelt at the door again, and poured its kerosene slowly on the rug at the bottom of the door. Like an oily snake, the kerosene floated on the surface of the wet rug and slid under the door into the next room. Quinn got a wet towel, struck a match, lit the kerosene and watched the flame flare up and crawl under the door. It worked. Swiftly, he laid the wet towel against the door, extinguishing the flames on his side of it, then rose and went out into the hall.

He quickly took the ten steps in the corridor to room seventeen. He listened a moment, and could hear the tense mutter of voices inside. He inserted the key softly, unlocked the door, swung it open and stepped inside.

The room was dark except for the kerosene flame burning brightly against the connecting door. A tall rawboned man in range clothes with nearly white hair was kneeling before the flames trying to slap them out with his bare hands. Behind him stood Winters, holding out a wet towel.

"Good evening, gentlemen," Quinn drawled.

They both whirled instantly, forgetting the guttering flames on the rug.

"You sent for me, I believe?"

It took a half second for the two men to realize the situation. The tall man slid a glance at Winters, who nodded imperceptibly. As if this were an appointed signal, Winters, with a snarl, hurled a towel at Quinn's head. But the gambler had anticipated that half second. With a cat-like pluck of his quick hands, his gun butts were braced against his hip-bones, bucking solidly against him as they exploded at Winters.

Then the wet towel struck Quinn in the face and wrapped around his head. He plucked at it frantically, waiting for the shots from Winters' companion, but they did not come. When he wrenched the towel off, the room was in darkness. He waited a tense second, then threw caution to the winds and struck a match. By it, he saw that Winters had fallen against the door, slid down it and extinguished the flames. His hand was inside his coat, clenched on the butt of the gun in his shoulder holster. A ragged hole in his forehead had begun to trickle blood.

But the second man was gone. Quinn whirled and strode out of the room. He paused at the door and looked up and down the hall. The end of the corridor was just to his left. The window was open, and from a solidly embedded hook in the window frame, a rope trailed out the open window. The man had fled by the fire-escape. Quinn saw the rope move and ran to the window. He heard a body drop, then the sound of running feet.

"Hah," he said softly, and swung out the window and disappeared down the rope.

21
"Fill Your Hand!"

In Town, Laredo paused just long enough to tell Chuck: "You stay outa the way. I'm handlin' the shootin' irons tonight."

They swung into the crowded hitchrack in front of the Mile High. Laredo stopped here because it was the closest faro table. He could hear the saloon running full blast, but he set about his work.

He started at the corner and worked up, examining every saddled horse at the rack. The horses eyed him warily, but he spoke soothingly to them. Far down the line, he came to a blue horse and he stopped. The horse was breathing hard. Laredo swung under the rail, stroked the horse's nose to soothe it, then rubbed his hand on its coat. It was wet with sweat. The horse was lathered. Laredo saw that a slicker was tied on behind the cantle. He felt it, but there was nothing rolled in it.

But he persisted. He struck a match, knelt down and began to examine the ground under the horse. Some shiny object caught his eye and he picked it up. It was an empty .38 caliber shell.

"Rourke might have got that shot," Laredo mused. "Maybe this coyote shot Rourke with his own gun. Well, it don't matter. He was careful to shuck the empty out before he showed the gun."

He straightened up. In front of the saloon doors at the

hitchrack, a team and buckboard stood. Laredo walked around in back of the buckboard and swung up over the end-gate and faced the saloon.

Above the swinging doors the lights stretched out in a diminishing row of three.

Chuck, on the sidewalk, saw Laredo draw a gun, then the little foreman lifted his head and opened his mouth.

"Yee-o-ow-e-eee!"

His blood-curdling cry split the night air and he punctuated it with three swift shots through the door of the Mile High that winked out the lights, leaving pandemonium inside. For good measure, he threw some more shots through the two front windows, then leaped off the buckboard as the horses lunged frantically to free themselves.

A tentative shot coughed out of the Mile High, then the din began. Yells, shouts, curses and shrieks welled out of the door, just as the first customers came boiling through the door.

Laredo calmly loaded his gun as he walked down the road to the blue horse. He took one of his battered Colts and wedged it into his belt at the small of his back. He took his other gun and slipped it into his right holster, leaving his left one empty. Then he untied the blue's reins, looped them over the horse's head, and mounted. The blue did not offer to pitch as Laredo sat there, motionless, talking soothingly.

Laredo saw the running figure swing under the hitchrack, then come to an abrupt stop before the blue. A pause, then the man said: "Get offa that horse! That blue is mine!"

Laredo hesitated. "Why, so it is," he said mildly. "I reckon I was in such a hell of a hurry to leave that place that I got your horse."

He swung off slowly, then pivoted around to ram a gun barrel in the belly of the man standing beside him.

"Jest git on the walk," Laredo ordered softly.

The man started to protest but Laredo shoved the gun hard. On the sidewalk, in the dim street-light, Laredo saw that he did not know the man. He was a head taller than Laredo, unshaven, vestless, dirty and scared.

"What is this?" the man growled.

Laredo looked the man over, then reached out and pulled a gun from where it was wedged in the man's belt. It was a Smith and Wesson .38 with a chip off its plated butt.

"Ain't two guns enough for you?" Laredo drawled softly.

The men who had swarmed out of the saloon stopped now and formed a loose circle about the two men. Chuck was against the wall, watching.

"I won that in a poker game," the man blustered.

Laredo backed away from him slowly, his gun steady and ominous. "Now tell 'em you lie," Laredo drawled thickly. "Before I cut you off pocket-high, tell 'em you got the gun from Rourke, a man you killed and then kicked in the face."

The man did not answer.

A voice from the circle of men addressed Laredo and he recognized it as that of Petersen, one of the nesters on D Bar T land. "Do you mean Rourke, over on the D Bar T, Laredo?"

"That's who I mean," Laredo said softly, not taking his eyes from the killer.

"Why, you—" Petersen began.

"Cut it, Petersen," Laredo said sharply. "He's mine." The crowd was slowly backing away out of the line of possible shots.

"Now, you yellow-bellied, murderin' coyote, fill your hand!" Laredo snarled.

But the man did not move. The crowd flattened against the buildings. Not a word was spoken for a full five seconds, then Laredo said:

"Yellow, by God!"

The killer's eyes slid wildly over the line of hostile faces as he cringed alone on the sidewalk, an outcast among men.

Laredo threw Rourke's gun down on the sidewalk, then threw his own gun down beside it.

"Now, whippoorwill," he drawled. "Maybe them odds suits you better."

With that last cry of a cornered rat, the lone killer streaked for his guns, terror written on his face.

Laredo was laughing a little. He hunched his back and whipped his Colt that had been wedged at his back around his side in a tight, swift arc that, completed, lanced out its five shots in one roaring pencil of orange.

As the killer's guns cleared leather and exploded half drawn, he took a step back to brace his stagger and his guns dropped, out of clawing hands. Agony stamped his face; he tried to scream and slavered up a mouthful of lung that channeled down his shirtfront. Then, legs planted wide, his knees buckled slowly and he pitched forward on his face.

Laredo spat noisily and looked around the crowd, his gun trailing a wisp of acrid smoke up into the night. "Any one else want to buy in on this fight?" he asked the crowd.

"Ain't nobody but me goin' to buy in on it," a flat uncompromising voice announced. Through the circle which had formed again, the sheriff shoved his way. He looked at the figure sprawled in a pool of blood on the sidewalk, then shifted his gaze to Laredo. His unblinking shallow eyes held a question, but he did not ask it.

"Anybody know him?" he asked, instead.

"Name's 'Chinch' somethin'," a man in the crowd said. "I heard he rode for Sayres."

The sheriff nodded. "A coupla you men take him across to Murph's."

The hardware store was also the undertaking parlor. Two men volunteered for the job. The sheriff turned to Laredo.

"Come on over to the office. I got to talk to you."

"If you're arrestin' me for killin' that sidewinder, I'm damned if I will," Laredo said stubbornly. The murmur of the crowd backed him up.

"It ain't that," the sheriff said: "I just want to talk to you. Bring your friends along if you want."

Petersen, the nester, and Chuck fell in behind Laredo and the sheriff. They went over to the sheriff's office.

Inside, they found the lamp lit. Rosy and Dave were seated watching the door when the sheriff opened it.

"Well, I'll be damned!" the sheriff said. He glared at Rosy and started to speak, when Rosy raised his hand.

"Save it," Rosy drawled, and grinned. The newcomers found seats, but the sheriff stood in the middle of the floor, still glaring at Rosy.

"You better start talkin'," the sheriff said ominously. "I got Crowell in jail and I ain't said why we really want him. Now you tell me. It looks like every one in San Angel County knows the sheriff's business but the sheriff."

Briefly and bluntly Rosy told them what he had overheard Crowell say to Winters at the D Bar T. Dave sat quiet, his eyes hard and bitter. He had heard it all on the way to town. Then Dave told them about his capture by Sayres and what he had heard Sayres say about the boss. He finished with the fight with the outlaws and his escape with Dorsey Hammond. Laredo explained his killing of Chinch and the reasons, but he did not explain how he and Chuck happened to be within hearing distance of the shots. When he was finished, they were silent, each locked in his own thoughts.

"What I can't figure out in the whole thing," Rosy said, presently, "is what it's all about. Why do they want the ranch and the mine? Why? They ain't worth a damn as they stand. They ruined both places when they blew out that lake. It just don't make sense."

"I reckon I can tell you," Laredo said. "At least I can tell you why they want the D Bar T."

Dave looked up. "Why?"

"You tell 'em, Chuck," Laredo said.

"Gold," Chuck said bluntly. "Plenty of it."

"Gold," Dave repeated after him. "Not on our place. You must mean the Draw Three."

And then Laredo told him of his discovery of Winters' working the gold, and how he had brought Chuck up to make positive.

"You mean," Dave said slowly, when Laredo had finished, "that Ted Winters was tryin' to get the place out from under his own wife?"

"It looks that way," Laredo said softly.

Dave rose to his feet and looked at the sheriff. "I'm goin' out and I'm not comin' back till I find that coyote. I'm warnin' you now, I'll kill him."

"Mary," Rosy said softly.

Dave looked at him and nodded wearily. He seemed to sag. He couldn't kill his sister's husband, for Dave thought Mary loved Winters. Rosy had carefully omitted any mention of Winters striking Mary, for he knew Dave would go wild with hatred if he did. Rosy wanted to follow the wiser course and let things work out as they inevitably would. For Rosy too was not sure that Mary did not love Winters. Women were queer. Dave sat down again, his eyes filled with pain.

"There's just one thing left to do, now," Rosy announced quietly.

"I been wonderin' what it was," the sheriff said dryly.

"We got to turn Crowell loose and let him lead us to the boss," Rosy said.

Then the sheriff exploded. He took two strides over to Rosy and shoved a blunt finger in his face. "The hell I will!" He stood glaring at Rosy, his face red with anger. "You got him in jail now, and I'll fight the hull crowd of you before I let you turn him loose. He stays there!"

But Laredo's anger matched the sheriff's.

"You fat knothead," he said scornfully, whirling the sheriff around to face him. "Crowell ain't behind all this! Can't you understand that after Rand and Turner tellin' you? There's somebody bigger than him that's runnin' it. And Crowell will tip the hand. Keep him in jail and what have you got? A measly understrapper! The big boss will hire the best lawyers in the country to keep Crowell from bein' convicted. You damned well can't prove anything on him anyway. He's seen to that. But let Crowell go and what does he do? Likely the first thing he'll do is try to buy Hammond's mine again. Hammond won't sell it. All right. Crowell's up a danged tree. What does he do?" Here Laredo paused dramatically and tapped the sheriff's chest. "He takes us right to the big augur."

The sheriff groaned and sat down. "I got to risk all this work by lettin' a criminal loose."

"What work?" Laredo jibed scornfully. "Who's done the work? Rand and Turner and me and Chuck! You've sat on that fat tail of yours and we done the work. It's our deal, dang you, and you'll do what Rand says. You got a posse out here fifty miles south lookin' for that Hammond gal, when Rand and Turner brought her home safe!"

The sheriff blushed. "How in hell was I to know where she was?" He pointed an accusing finger at Laredo. "You told Rand where to find Sayres and you had a danged good hunch that was where Hammond's gal was, but you never said anything."

It was Laredo's turn to look sheepish, and he did.

"I done one thing, anyway, that I ain't got credit for," the sheriff fumed. "Buck Hammond has been lookin' high and low for Crowell, so he could sell him the mine and git the money to ransom his gal. I never let his man see Crowell, I never even told him where Crowell was."

"All right, all right," Rosy said pacifically. "Let it go. We got to get to work." He stood up. "We're goin' to let Crowell out," he told the sheriff, "and we all got a job to watch him."

He gave instructions. Laredo was to go warn Hammond to act as if he were ignorant of the man behind his daughter's kidnapping when and if Crowell came to try and buy the mine. Then Laredo was to go back to the hotel, and keep a check on Crowell if he went there. Rosy gave Petersen a minute description of Crowell, then gave the nester some money with the injunction to watch the station and if Crowell boarded the night train to follow him and wire back for help. The sheriff was to go let Crowell out of jail with apologies, and the explanation that he had arrested the wrong man. Dave and Rosy were going to follow Crowell and not let him out of their sight.

"And now," Rosy said, turning to the sheriff, "you're first in the loadin' chute. Go let Crowell loose."

22
Crowell Sees His Boss

The San Angel County Courthouse was a sorry affair of board and adobe brick so slapped together as to form a crude, barren courtroom and a lynch-proof jail.

Across from it on the top bar of a corral, Dave and Rosy lounged. In silence they were watching the dimly lighted rectangle which was the jail door.

When the sheriff's fat figure appeared in the doorway, followed by a small and slim one, they slid down off the corral bar together, crossed the street and fell in behind the sheriff some thirty yards away. The night was inky, so they could not be identified.

"But hell, man," they heard the sheriff say, "give us a chanst. You looked like Henry. The only way we could prove it was to wire El Paso and that's what we done. They said Henry was caught and already hung."

"If I ever see that little runt again that brought me over to your office, I'll break his neck for him," Crowell stormed, punctuating his statement with a string of bitter oaths.

"I wouldn't," the sheriff advised quietly.

They walked a way in silence, nearing the saloon corners. As they drew abreast the sheriff's office, Hank stopped. Rosy and Dave drifted off into the shadows. "I'm right sorry about all this," the sheriff said earnestly. "If I was you, I'd dye my hair or somethin'. Might save you gettin' picked up again."

"Bah!" Crowell snorted, and turned on his heel.

He crossed to the Mile High corner and disappeared. By hurrying Rosy and Dave saw him enter the hotel. In three minutes, he was on the street again, where he cut across to the Free Throw corner and headed down the side street.

Rosy and Dave followed him on the other side of the street,

hanging back just far enough not to draw his attention. They saw his shadowy figure turn into Dr. Fullerton's. The lamp burning in the glassed-in porch signified that Hammond was awaiting him.

"Ain't he goin' to get a jolt when he sees Dorsey settin' there talkin' to Buck?" Rosy asked.

"I hope Buck keeps his temper," Dave said.

"He's got to. It means more to him than the rest of us."

Crowell's visit to Hammond was short. When he came out of the doctor's house he walked swiftly toward the hotel. From the corner of the Free Throw, they saw him enter it.

"He looks spooked," Rosy observed. "I bet he hightails it, now that he's found his plans have gone haywire."

Crowell came out of the hotel, a piece of luggage in his hand.

"What time is it?" Rosy asked.

"Train time for him," Dave replied.

Rosy whistled softly as they drew back in the shadows. "So that was his hurry? Only ten minutes to catch a train."

Crowell's destination was plain. He was striding down to the station, looking behind him occasionally. As they fell in behind him, they heard the night train whistle just outside of town. By the time Crowell reached the station, the train had pulled in.

"C'mon," Rosy called.

He walked around the rear of the short train. On the other side of the tracks, they kept in the shadow again, and walked a few hundred feet past the panting engine until they came to the stock pens. They hid here.

"Feel like runnin'?" Rosy asked.

"Let's get on now," Dave said. "We can hook on the rear end and watch him through the door."

Rosy shook his head. "I dunno. I got a hunch he ain't ridin' as far as he did the other mornin'."

He left Dave and walked back until he could see into the car. Petersen was already on the train. Crowell came in and deposited his bag in the front end of the car, then opened the front door of the car and stood in the doorway, looking out at the few loafers gathered on the station platform.

Rosy walked up and tapped on the window of Petersen's seat. The big nester looked out, recognized him, looked to see if Crowell was watching, then grinned at Rosy.

Rosy faded away in the shadow. When the engine bell started to clang, he was again squatting with Dave.

Slowly the train lumbered out of the station, pulled abreast of them and passed them. Rosy's body was tense with waiting. In a few seconds, they would have to make a dash for it.

Then Rosy chuckled and settled back on his heels. Something hit the cinders ahead of them and slid harshly a distance. It was a piece of luggage. Then the dark figure of a man could be seen as he swung down from the car, ran a bit, drew back into the shadows of the stock pens and let the train pass.

"He's a careful ranny, ain't he?" Rosy asked softly. "If that nester has any brains, he'll ride on to Soledad."

They crouched motionless in the shadow as Crowell neared them, picked up the bag and retreated to the stock pens again.

Dave started up, but Rosy held him down. They listened and soon heard the footsteps behind them to the rear of the pen. Rosy edged his head around the corner and saw it was Crowell. He was headed back toward the station.

Using piles of ties, tool sheds and a horse trough as shelter, Crowell swung wide of the station, walked beyond it a way, then crossed the tracks into the alley which ran behind the buildings of the main street.

In the alley, with the dim light of the town at the upper end, they followed him easily. At the rear of the Free Throw, he peered out cautiously into the street, making sure there was no one in sight, before he dashed to the alley behind the hardware store.

They let a moment pass, then followed him across the street and flattened themselves against the store wall. Rosy saw his figure midway up the alley, his back to them, walking swiftly; and they swung into the alley behind him.

At the end of the block, Crowell drew close to the dark corral of the livery stable. Rosy and Dave moved up on him a little. He swung right at the corral and streaked down a narrow path that skirted the edge of town. Tall buck-brush lined the path and they moved closer as Crowell's pace slackened a little. Once he stopped, listening, then turned again and made his way forward. The path led into an alley which ran behind a row of barns. This part of town was a residence section.

Suddenly Crowell swerved out of the alley, climbed over a small, neat hedge, moved around to the front of a house, mounted the one step of its low porch and knocked on the door. Evidently a voice bid him enter, for he disappeared.

Dave's amazed eyes sought Rosy's in the dark.

"Know it?" Rosy asked.

"God, yes!" Dave said huskily. "That's Pearson's!"

They stood up and surveyed the lawn, enclosed by the hedge. The house was small, one story, almost square, a neat New England board affair, painted a light color.

"Here's the dehornin'," Rosy muttered. "Come on."

They vaulted the hedge and stepped on to the porch cautiously. Testing the door, Rosy found it unlocked.

He drew a gun, as did Dave, and swung against the door. It opened readily, letting them into a low-ceiled, half-darkened room.

Sprawled in an easy chair on the other side of the wide fireplace, at the far end of the room, sat Quinn. One of his guns pointed at the door. The other pointed at the two men, Pearson and Crowell, seated together on a davenport. Both men were holding their hands over their heads.

"Quinn!" Rosy exploded, and he grinned from ear to ear.

"Howdy," Quinn drawled, and grinned back. He nodded to the two men on the davenport. "Pearson seems to think I shouldn't have come here tonight."

Rosy was the first to find himself and he chuckled. "Reckon he'd like to tell Buck Hammond that?"

"I don't intend to tell Buck Hammond anything!" Pearson snapped. His face was stern and unyielding. "I'm putting my hands down now. I'm tired."

"I didn't tell you to put them up," Quinn said mildly.

Pearson's hands settled to his knees, but he kept silent. Rosy glanced briefly around the room. It was luxurious for a frontier town, and reflected the banker's taste as well as his money. Quinn drew a pair of handcuffs from his pocket and handed them to Rosy.

Pearson straightened up. "I'll not wear those things. There's no use asking me to. This whole thing is preposterous!" he declared sternly.

"I won't wear them either," Crowell declared loudly.

"Nobody's askin' you to do anything," Rosy said grimly, approaching them with the cuffs. "We're just tellin' you. Put your hands out."

They hesitated stubbornly and Rosy lifted his gun. "Pearson, you may not have been in the West long, but I reckon you've heard of gun-brandin'."

"The sheriff will hear—"

Rosy's brief laugh was a scoff. "The sheriff, hell! I'm goin' to have a hard time keepin' him from shootin' you already. Put your hands out!"

They obeyed and were handcuffed together.

"Reckon you and Quinn can take them over to Doc Fullerton's?" Rosy asked Dave. "I'm goin' to get the sheriff. We'll make this legal, anyhow."

It was a grim and silent group that collected on the sunporch of Dr. Fullerton's at Rosy's behest. He had gone to the hotel to waken Mary, and had been told by the clerk that Winters was found dead in a hotel room. The clerk had informed the sheriff, who immediately started a search for Quinn, in whose room Winters' body was found.

"Did you tell Mrs. Winters?" Rosy asked swiftly.

"Sure. He's her husband, ain't he?"

"Aw hell!" Rosy growled.

He had no desire to face her now, so he had sent a note up to her room with the clerk, asking her to come to Hammond's. Then he picked up Laredo, Chuck and the sheriff, and they went back to Hammond's.

Mary was there ahead of them, and apparently she had told Dave of Winters' death, for Dave's face was strangely calm.

Pearson and Crowell were sitting side by side on an empty bed. Dorsey was sitting on the far side of Hammond's bed. The mining man's face was grim and merciless, but he held Dorsey's hand in his with the gentleness of a child.

Quinn was seated in the corner near the door. Hank eyed him suspiciously and asked him to move away from the door. Quinn nodded affably at the request and changed his seat, a smile of inner amusement on his face.

As the newcomers took their seats, Rosy avoided Mary's eye. He needed only to glance at her and all the senseless cruelty of the thing made him rage inside again.

The sheriff started in without preliminaries. "Pearson, we've got all the goods on you," he announced bluntly.

"I haven't any idea what you're talking about," Pearson replied.

He was still the banker, unruffled, precise, unbending, his stern, not unhandsome features composed. In this group of roughly dressed men, his quiet manners and dress were a silent defense for him. Of all those present, he appeared to be the least capable of being a criminal. Rosy realized this, and he realized that the sheriff's blunt methods would get them nowhere.

"Wait a minute," Rosy put in.

He lounged off one of the beds and sat on the foot of Hammond's across from Pearson and Crowell. Hammond had not said a word, except by way of greeting. Rosy built a cigarette, lighted it, and inhaled deeply, watching Pearson.

"Matter of fact, Pearson," he drawled at last, "we haven't got a thing on you." In the background the sheriff winced, but held his tongue.

"Then let me go," Pearson said coldly. "I haven't any idea what this is all about, except that I have no connection with it."

"What connection have you got with Crowell?" Rosy asked mildly.

"Banking business," Pearson said.

"The kind that would make Crowell get on a train in front of five or six men to make it look like he was leavin' town and then jump off as soon as he was out of the station?"

Pearson was unruffled. "What Mr. Crowell does is no business of mine. We had an engagement tonight. He kept it. That's all I know." His voice rose a little. "I insist that you free me!"

Rosy laughed quietly. "What makes you think we have to?"

"Because I'm innocent of any crime. The law requires it!"

Rosy leaned forward a little, his face unsmiling. "Forget you have any rights under the law, Pearson. There's no lawyer here. The only law is the sheriff, and"—he smiled a little wryly at the banker— "like I told you before, for your own good, I wouldn't want to leave you alone with him. I don't think you'd be able to tell any one what happened."

A gasp came from Mary in the corner. Pearson slid an uneasy glance at the stolid and phlegmatic face of the sheriff across the room.

"You see," Rosy continued softly, "he knows you're behind this bushwhackin' and dynamitin' and stealin' the same as we do. Only he don't have what they call the 'judicial temperament.' Maybe you've wondered what's happened to Sayres."

Neither of them answered, but they looked at Rosy closely.

"He's dead," Rosy said. Pausing, he watched the two faces before him. "Trials are expensive, the sheriff thinks."

The lie was drawled slowly, convincingly. He studied the end of the cigarette, glancing up at them occasionally. Their faces were set, impassive.

"I'm talkin' to you now, Crowell," Rosy said. "I was under the davenport when you were talkin' to Mrs. Winters and her husband. I heard the conversation you and Winters had when Mrs. Winters went out of the room. Dave overheard from Sayres that you ordered the kidnapping of Dorsey Hammond, and the deed signed was in your favor. More than that, you left orders before Hank arrested you to burn the D Bar T, so as to make Mary sign away her half the spread. What've you got to say?"

"Prove it," Crowell said calmly.

Rosy made an impatient movement with his hand. "That's just what I'm tryin' to tell you. We don't have to. It's proved to us, because we heard you. We ain't interested in what a jury's got to say. We know."

"I demand to be placed in jail and have this go through the regular channels!" Crowell said heatedly.

Rosy sighed and turned to the sheriff. "Hear that, Hank? He demands a trial."

"Yeah. I heard it," the sheriff said. "Better let me take him to jail."

Rosy shrugged. "All right. Dave'll go with you. I'll talk to Pearson."

"I can handle him alone," the sheriff said. There was a quiet menace in his simple speech that swiveled Crowell's face to him. "Gimme them keys," he said to Quinn. The gambler reached in his pocket and brought out the keys.

Rosy leaned back and watched the sheriff unlock the cuffs. The color had fled from Crowell's face, but his lips were a thin line of determination. "You're a fool, Crowell," Rosy drawled. "Here you get it in the neck while Pearson, the man behind it all, goes free. He never took any risks, did he? It wasn't him that talked to Mrs. Winters while I was listenin', riskin' his neck by openin' his mouth. It isn't him that gets a bull—gets locked up in jail I mean, with no bail and no chance, is it?"

Suddenly, Mary cried out. She took three swift steps and faced Rosy. "Rosy, don't do it! Don't do it! You know what will happen!" The room was deathly still.

Rosy shrugged, avoiding her eye.

"I ain't the sheriff, ma'am," he muttered.

Mary wheeled to face Dave. "Dave, are you going to let him? Are you—are you that callous?" she finished, turning to every man in the room, and none of them could meet her eye.

Dave's voice was cold and dead. "There's more than one way to arrive at justice, Mary. I reckon that's why the cottonwoods are so popular in this country."

Mary sank into a chair, sobbing quietly.

"You better be careful, Hank," Hammond said cautiously.

"Yeah. I will," the sheriff grunted. "Come on," he said to Crowell.

Crowell's face was parchment-colored, frozen tight in terror, but he got to his feet and followed the sheriff out of the room without a word.

No one spoke as they heard the front door shut. Rosy watched Pearson's face. The banker sagged, his stern face suddenly weary and years older. Mary's sobs throbbed throughout the room and no one looked at his neighbor. Pearson's tight voice suddenly broke the silence.

"If there's a law in this land, every one of you in this room will hang for this."

"That's it. There ain't," Rosy said briefly.

Two muffled shots from some distance came to them, and they looked at each other. It might have been shooting down in the town. And it might have been what they all thought it was.

Rosy shrugged and his eyes sought Pearson's face again.

"It's easier to talk," he said quietly.

"Mr. Pearson," Dorsey broke in from Hammond's side, "if you know anything, tell it! It's—it's awful!" She shuddered, and Pearson's gaunt face with its burning eyes looked at her beseechingly, but he was silent.

"For God's sake, yes, Everett!" Hammond broke in gruffly. "Anything is better than that. Let's have it and we'll keep you from Loew if we have to ride over into the next county with you."

Pearson hung his head. Rosy noticed his knuckles were white as he clenched his fists, but even that could not keep his hands from trembling.

The outer door opened and heavy footsteps trailed through the house. The porch door opened to let the sheriff in again. No one looked at him as he took a seat.

"A quick trip," Laredo said quietly.

"Uh-huh." The sheriff rolled a cigarette and lighted it, then looked at Rosy. "Well?"

"No go."

The sheriff smoked his cigarette down, every one watching him now. When he rose, Mary could not control a little gasp.

He walked over to Rosy's side and stood looking down at Pearson. There was a faint smell of gunpowder on his clothes.

"Better come along, Pearson," he growled.

"I'll go with you," Rosy said hurriedly.

"Huh-uh. I reckon he won't be much trouble," the sheriff said.

"I better go," Rosy insisted.

"Hell, no!" the sheriff exploded. "I'm sheriff around here! I can take care of my own prisoners!"

"One's enough, Hank," Hammond put in curtly.

"Enough, hell! It might be for you, but it ain't for me. I got elected on a oath that I'd do my best to prevent crime." His hard, unblinking eyes stared at Pearson speculatively. "If you think I'm goin' to let him go and have this to go through all over again, you better take a longer guess."

"How you goin' to cover it up?" Hammond asked.

"Crowell's over at Pearson's place now, lyin' on the floor with a gun in his hand," the sheriff said brutally. "Pearson can be across the room with a gun in his hand when I come in with my deputy in the mornin' after the bank asts me to find him. Just a plain case of two men shootin' each other."

Dorsey hid her face in her hands and the sheriff snorted. "Why not say it? I reckon he knows what's happened to Crowell." His challenge did not bring an answer from any one in the room. He turned to face Pearson, but the banker had crumbled.

"Oh, God, get him away!" Pearson moaned through his hands. He crawled down the bed against the wall, where he huddled like a small boy fearing punishment. "I did it! I did it! Get him away!"

"Get out, Hank!" Rosy said, winking at the sheriff.

The sheriff made his way out of the room while Pearson fought his terror.

"Better spill it," Rosy said quietly. "We'll see you don't get what Crowell did."

"Where do you want me to begin?" Pearson asked weakly.

"I reckon it begins with the train hold-up, don't it, Pearson?" Dave asked.

Pearson nodded. "How did you know that?"

"That ranny by the name of Chinch out at Sayres' place," Dave said.

Quinn frowned, then turned to Pearson. "The money in the ,baggage car was goin' to your bank, was it?"

Pearson nodded. "Crowell gave Sayres the order to stick up the train. Part of the money would be given to Sayres, and the rest turned over to me. You see"—a gleam of shrewd cunning came into his eyes—"that money was insured. I would get that same amount back from the insurance company—"

"And about three-quarters of what was stolen back from Sayres through Crowell. Is that it?" Quinn said.

"That's it," Pearson said.

The porch door opened and Crowell stepped into the room, prodded by the sheriff's gun.

Pearson's jaw slacked and he stared at Crowell, then at the sheriff, then glared at Rosy.

Rosy grinned at Pearson. "Worked pretty slick, Pearson. You haven't the guts for the kind of game you play."

Crowell walked to his seat by Pearson, glaring at the sheriff.

"Want to go on?" Rosy said to Pearson.

The banker shook his head.

Rosy grinned. "It's a little too late to stop, now, I reckon. You've confessed to robbin' a train and falsifyin' reports to the insurance company. That ought to be worth about twenty years apiece in the pen." He paused, watching Pearson. "You'll be dead before the time's up, Pearson."

Still Pearson said nothing.

"Maybe it's that you don't want to mix Crowell in this? Is that it?" Rosy asked. He laughed softly. "I reckon you will, though, Pearson. To begin with, you couldn't stand to see Crowell turned loose, freed, while you were servin' a life term in the pen, could you? He did all the dirty work, was responsible for all the crimes and he goes free. It isn't fair, is it?"

Pearson slid a glance at Crowell.

"With his brains," Rosy continued, "he'd be a rich man pretty quick. But it was you who gave him his start. Your brains. He committed all the crimes and you go to the pen." He laughed again. "Maybe he'll send you some tobacco around Christmas time," Rosy taunted.

"He will not!" Pearson suddenly snarled. "He'll go with me!"

Crowell's fist drove into Pearson's face and Rosy leaped on the two figures. Crowell struggled as if insane, clawing Pearson's face in a maniacal rage, kicking, biting and cursing impotently. Laredo stepped in to help Rosy and after a mild clubbing with gun barrels, Crowell gave up.

Rosy and Laredo sat down again. "Let's have it, one of you," Rosy said.

Both men began to babble at once and Rosy silenced them with his hand.

"Pearson, let's hear from you first. No. Wait," Rosy's eyes sought Dave, and he leaned over him. "What about it?" he asked softly, motioning to Mary.

Mary was in a corner by herself, watching the scene with a quiet curiosity. Dave spoke to her in a low voice, excluding the others. "Maybe you'd rather hear all this tomorrow."

"Is it about Ted?" Mary asked calmly.

Dave nodded.

"I'd rather hear it now," Mary said. "I've suspected it all along."

"All right," Dave said to Pearson.

Pearson drew a long breath and began. "It starts when I offered to buy into the Draw Three, Buck," he said to Hammond. "You remember when I had the expert come look at it?" Hammond nodded. "He told me there was gold there, lots of it, but that you were missing most of it. He said it would be over to the north more, in the quartz, and that any good mining man could put you right. So I tried to loan you enough money so that the control of the mine would be in my hands. It didn't work."

"And there's gold there now?" Hammond asked incredulously. "Lots of it?"

"Enough to make you rich," Pearson said. He addressed

Rosy again. "Then I got hold of Winters. He tried to forge a check once and I caught him."

Rosy looked at Mary. Her eyes were moist but her chin was up. "Was that before he was married?" he asked.

"Yes."

"Why didn't you prosecute him?"

"I can always use men that have brains but no courage," Pearson said. "I was repaid, all right. A little while after he had been married, he came to me with the story of gold on the Turner place. He wanted me to buy the place from his wife and Turner, and then we'd work it together. That was when I conceived my plan." The banker's face was aglow once more as he thought of the daring of his scheme. "I wanted a man with brains, with courage, with resourcefulness—and who was poor. Crowell fitted that order. He was out to get rich, and when I found him in Walpais, I knew my scheme would work. Crowell was a gambler—and a poor one."

"A fool, you mean," Crowell said.

"So I was careful to work it all out," Pearson said. "I knew that Sayres was a blackguard, and that he could be bought. So I put Crowell up as my front, for I was to remain unknown, the Mystery Man." Again he smiled exultantly. "Crowell tried to buy the D Bar T from Mrs. Winters. She wouldn't sell. He tried to buy the Draw Three. Hammond wouldn't sell, although he was barely paying expenses. I knew of the quarrel over the lake, and that fitted into my scheme to perfection. I thought if the lake was blown out, both the ranch and the mine would be ruined, and that Turner and Hammond would both sell to Crowell. Winters was to persuade Mrs. Winters."

"And he was cheating you all the time," Quinn put in quietly. "He was mining that gold on the sly and selling it, and gambling the money away." He told them of his discovery of the room Winters kept in the barber shop and the source of his money. "That's why I went to see you this afternoon, Pearson. And"—he smiled slightly—"that's what's goin' to get you hung."

"Why?" Rosy cut in.

"Because Pearson told Winters I was snooping around and Winters decided to kill me before I found out too much and told Pearson." He told them of the note, and the killing in the hotel room. The sheriff listened intently, nodding his satisfaction. "And when I caught this jasper that was with Winters down in the alley," Quinn finished, "we had it out. I downed him. Then I knew Winters could have learned about me from only two people—Sam, the barber, and Pearson. And Sam was too scared to talk. So I headed for Pearson's."

Rosy looked at him for a long moment, then turned to Pearson. "Go on."

"I'll go on," Crowell rapped out, sneering at Pearson. "Let me tell about this Eastern genius. The lake was ready to blow when Dave got home. When Pearson heard about Turner coming home, he lost his guts. He hired Freeman to bushwhack Dave, and make it look like Hammond did it. Then he had Sayres blow the lake out. When Hammond wouldn't sell, even then, he ordered Dorsey Hammond kidnapped. Hammond would have to sell the mine to get the money to ransom her, and of course, Pearson's money that I would give Hammond for the mine would go to Sayres and back to me and then to Pearson again." Crowell sneered, and smiled evilly at Pearson. "He even ordered the D Bar T spread burned, so Mrs. Winters would be frightened into selling her half the place."

"And I was to be murdered," Dave put in quietly. "Murdered by those whippoorwills of Sayres' after they tortured me into signing away my half."

"That's it," Crowell gloated. "His orders! He thought of it all! Once I was in, I couldn't back out, or he'd have me killed like a dog! You were to be killed, Rand was to be killed—any one who stood in his way!"

Laredo stood up. "I'd always heard that polecats carried a white stripe," he said quietly, "but I reckon I've lived to see one that runs a bank too." He gazed at the sheriff mildly. "Hank, sometimes I wisht you was a mean man. You'd save the county the cost of a double trial." Although he drawled this quietly, Laredo was raging inside. He drew out his guns and handed them to the sheriff. "You better take these," he said, his voice quavering a little with suppressed passion. "I'm gettin' so old I can't trust myself no more."

The sheriff accepted them stolidly and stuck them in his belt. Pearson looked at his captors fearfully. Their quiet questions had prodded him out until he had taken a kind of pride in the recital of his villainies, but now that he was finished he could see the loathing and contempt in their faces. He was afraid.

"C'mon," the sheriff said stolidly to the two of them. "Put out your hands." He leaned over his fat belly to handcuff them together.

With the swiftness of a striking snake, Crowell whipped one of Laredo's guns out of the sheriff's belt and pointed it at the sheriff. Crowell backed away a few feet across the bed, his gun nosing steadily at his captors.

He was laughing quietly, a little insanely, in the still room.

"You'll never make it, Crowell," Rosy said softly. "You'll only get one of us before we cut down on you."

Crowell laughed again, that soft, insane laugh that struck chills to Rosy's spine. Crowell turned to Pearson, who had not moved in the last minute. The banker's face was gray with fear.

"Let's get out, Crowell," Pearson said.

"You damned, squealing swine," Crowell said tonelessly, a kind of secret mad delight in his voice. "I would have died for you and you turn me in." Slowly his gun swiveled to Pearson, but his eyes were on Rosy and the sheriff. Pearson backed away against the wall, uttering small, unearthly cries of terror. Crowell slid his eyes to the gun and shot twice at Pearson. The banker's scream was cut short and he folded up like a tired child. Crowell's gun was trained again on Rosy and the sheriff, who did not dare move.

"A good job, wasn't it?" Crowell asked, listening to Pearson's death retching. Mary moaned a little in the corner.

Suddenly, Crowell laughed a high, frenzied laugh of a maniac, turned the gun to his chest and pulled the trigger. The impact of his own shot bumped him against the wall and he sagged to the floor.

"Prob'ly the first good thing he ever done," Laredo said softly.

23
Tangled Trails Turn Straight

Rosy fell in beside Mary as they left the doctor's. Laredo and Quinn were ahead of them. The rest had stayed behind a moment.

"Let's walk slow," Mary said.

"I reckon I feel that way too," Rosy answered. "It come a little too fast."

The silence was long.

"Rosy, do you mind telling me things?" Mary asked presently.

"Anything you want to know," Rosy said gently.

"Did you know that Ted was mixed up in this when you came to the house this morning?"

"I was pretty sure."

"And you didn't tell me. Why?"

"I—I couldn't," Rosy said huskily. "He was your husband."

"What would you have done if this—if Ted had been along with Pearson and Crowell tonight?"

"I wouldn't have been there," Rosy answered promptly. He amended this. "Yes, I would too. But I wouldn't have liked it."

"Why? Was Ted any more deserving of sympathy than the others?"

"Less," Rosy answered briefly.

Mary thought this over and asked why.

"Pearson was a lone wolf," Rosy explained. "Out for money

and he didn't care how he got it. Crowell was a gambler. He'd risk his neck for a stake. Winters? Well, he had more to lose than the rest. He carried more with him when he fell." He turned to Mary. "Why are you askin' me this?"

"I don't know," Mary answered soberly. "It's just—" She looked up at him. "Maybe you wouldn't understand me if I told you."

"I'd try."

"Well, it's hard to put in words. I can't remember very many men. Dave was taken away when we were both young. He was a good brother, but he didn't have much use for girls. Dad was —well, headstrong. Dave's arrest made him bitter and unjust. Dad was harsh, terribly harsh, even on people he loved. Sometimes he could be unjust too. Then after I married Ted, it seemed as if the same traits were in him. Harshness, even cruelty. Besides Ted and dad, I haven't been around men much— except the two hands that were working for us."

"And they weren't any different. Maybe worse," Rosy said.

"That's it. And when you and Dave came home, I saw you were different from the others I'd known. So when you were kind enough to hide all this for me, it was hard to believe. It was something new."

They rounded the corner and cut across the street to the hotel. Rosy's face was grim, his jaw set. Mary looked at him shyly; he did not look at her. As they entered the lobby, Mary stopped.

"I'm sorry if I've offended you," she said humbly.

Rosy smiled a little crookedly. "Bless your heart, you didn't," he said gently.

"I don't understand," Mary said. "You looked so cross."

"No. I reckon you don't." Rosy's eyes were somber and he found it hard to speak. "It's just that you've never had a man that loved you enough to be plumb decent to you. And because I treat you the way any jasper would that had two eyes in his head, you're grateful." He waited to see if she understood him. "It makes me plumb ashamed to wear a pair of pants."

"But they are not all like you, Rosy. Dave is, I think. I don't know him very well. But they're not all like you," Mary said earnestly.

"I reckon you'll find one some day that is," Rosy said quietly. "One that's like me that way and a lot more in the other things you want."

"I don't think I will," Mary answered.

Rosy flushed. "I reckon you didn't understand me."

"I think I did," Mary answered softly. "I still think I won't."

Rosy fumbled with his hat, not taking his eyes from hers. "Then some day, I'm goin'—I'm goin' to ask you somethin' and if you answer it the way I hope you will—" He bogged down, then began again valiantly: "When this is all over and you know your own mind, I'm goin' to—I hope—"

"I think I know what it is, Rosy," Mary answered simply. She placed a hand on his arm. "I think I know what I'll answer."

Rosy waited for her to go on. She only smiled and squeezed his arm a little. "And I think it will be what you hope it is."

She turned and walked across the lobby and up the stairs, her back straight, erect.

Dave was the last to leave the doctor's. He shut the door behind him and let Chuck and the sheriff go ahead. He stood on the porch a moment looking at the night, his body ready to drop with weariness. He thought over the events of the night. Winters was dead and Mary was free. They were rich, rich enough not to have to worry about water and alfalfa. Then he remembered the nesters and their plight now that the water was gone. He could take care of them. He'd hire them at good wages when he opened up the mine on his land, and they could earn enough money to buy good farms. And the quarrel with Hammond was over, finished. Hammond didn't need water now that he would start mining in quartz. He'd—but he was too tired to think. He wondered how quickly he could get in bed. He wanted to think about Dorsey but he checked himself.

"I'm going to sleep the clock around," he muttered as he descended the steps.

"Dave." It came from the opened door and he stopped. It was Dorsey. She came close to him.

"I couldn't let you go without telling you that I'm sorry I said what I did this afternoon," she said, her voice low and sincere.

"That's all right," Dave said.

"No, it isn't," Dorsey cried. "It was all wrong! I was wrong! I never understood how right you were until I heard and saw all this tonight."

"It was pretty bloody."

"But if a man doesn't fight for what he has and loves, people will take them away from him."

"I reckon that's right."

"And I was angry when you took to your guns to stop it," Dorsey said humbly.

"You were half right at that," Dave said. "I took to my guns once too often—a long time ago. I lost enough that time to make me think twice about goin' for them again." He looked down at her and spoke kindly. "That's what you were tryin' to remind me of, wasn't it?"

"No," Dorsey said simply. "I have never thought you lost anything in jail, Dave. I didn't know you before, but you couldn't have been any"—she hesitated, seeking a word, and feeling a slow flush come over her face.

"Any what?" Dave said.

"—any finer, more honest, brave," she finished.

She felt Dave's hand grip her arms, saw his dark face with its darker eyes looking down on her.

"It's worth eight years in the pen to hear you say that," he said huskily. "It—it makes a difference."

"What difference?"

"I can hold my head up now," Dave said softly. "I can go on thinkin' there's somethin' to life besides fightin', eatin' and sleepin'."

"Just because I said that, Dave?"

"You make it sound small," Dave said. "It isn't."

He looked down at her fondly. "It's like—well, like food for the way I've been. I guess I've been sick."

"Then you'll grow fat and sleek, Dave," Dorsey said with a little laugh.

Dave frowned. "I reckon I don't know what you mean."

"That was honest, anyway," Dorsey said. "It was like you."

"But I still don't see," Dave said humbly.

"If my saying I trusted you, believed in you, is food for you, Dave, then you will grow fat. There. Isn't that plain?"

Dave paused, suppressing a grin. "I reckon not."

But Dorsey did not see the grin. "I can't make it plainer without making it too plain," she said softly.

Dave did not answer and Dorsey sighed. She would be honest. "I'll be blunt, Dave. It's simply this: I love you."

With a low laugh, Dave caught her in his arms and kissed her. "And I've loved you from the first time I saw you."

When she spoke next, there was a note of gentle reproof in her voice. "You did understand, Dave. You led me into saying it. I—I—don't think that was honest."

"I reckon it wasn't," Dave admitted gently. "But I also reckon I can spend the rest of my life makin' it up to you for that one lie."

At the corner of the Free Throw, Quinn asked Laredo: "Think I could send a telegram tonight, Laredo?"

"Sure. I know Stanley. He'll take it."

They walked down to the station, both of them silent. Both the Free Throw and the Mile High were lighted brightly, a pleasant din issuing from their doors. Quinn cut his pace for Laredo. There was a strange communion between them tonight that both felt, even though they were practically strangers.

Laredo broke the silence. "What do you think of a jasper that don't mind his own business?"

"Sometimes I think he's got pretty good sense," Quinn replied, with a secret smile.

"All right. Here goes," Laredo said. "Just why in hell was you so worried about where Winters' money was comin' from? You ain't his brother, are you?"

Quinn laughed. "No. I'll show you in a minute."

They swung into the station and Laredo hammered on the lowered window. A mild man wearing eye glasses raised it and smiled when he saw Laredo.

"Hullo, Harvey," Laredo greeted him. "Reckon my friend here could send a telegram?"

"Sure."

The agent shoved the blank in front of Quinn, who wrote his message. When he was finished, he handed it to Laredo.

"I can't read," Laredo said dolorously. He swore. "It's the only time in my life I wanted to. What does it say?"

Quinn read aloud from the blank containing his message.

A. WINGERT
CATTLE ASSOCIATION
PHOENIX, ARIZ.
CASE CONCLUDED SUCCESSFULLY ALL PRINCIPALS
KILLED OFF NONE BY ME STOP SPLIT REWARD BETWEEN
DAVE TURNER ROSY RAND LAREDO JACKSON ALL OF SIN-
GLE SHOT STOP SUGGEST NEXT CASE YOU PUT ME IN
RANGE CLOTHES SINCE GAMBLERS LIFE NOT LONG STOP
WHAT WILL I DO WITH SIX THOUSAND I WON RUNNING
FARO TABLE IN SALOON.

MARTIN QUINN

"Principals?" Laredo repeated. "What are they?"

"Sayres' gang. We've been after them for two years now."

Laredo stared at Quinn. "So you're a range detective?"

"That's it," Quinn said.

"Runnin' a faro game at the Free Throw?"

"I was working on the town end of it," Quinn explained, "checking up on where the heavy money was spent and by whom. That's why I got curious about Winters. He was spending so much money that I began to wonder if he wasn't one of the Sayres' gang. You know the rest."

Laredo shook his head and waited while Quinn paid for the telegram. Outside, they turned up the street again.

"Like a drink?" Laredo asked.

"I wouldn't like one. I'd like about four," Quinn said.

He started to cross the street to the Free Throw. Laredo grabbed his arm.

"Huh-uh," Laredo said. "This is a celebration. And when I celebrate I head for the Mile High." His eyes lit up strangely. "Let's you and me go clean that joint out," he suggested soberly.

ABOUT THE AUTHOR

LUKE SHORT, whose real name was Frederick D. Glidden, was born in Illinois in 1907 and died in 1975. He wrote nearly fifty books about the West and was a winner of the Special Western Heritage Trustee Award. Before devoting himself to writing westerns, he was a trapper in the Canadian Subarctic, worked as an assistant to an archeologist and was a newsman. Luke Short believed an author could write best about the places he knows most intimately, so he usually located his westerns on familiar ground. He lived with his wife in Aspen, Colorado.

"One of the most important contributors to the history of the frontier ever published."
—*John Barkham Reviews*

DEE BROWN

Author of
Bury My Heart At Wounded Knee

___ **Action At Beecher Island**	20180-2	$2.95
___ **Cavalry Scout**	20227-2	$2.95
___ **The Girl From Fort Wicked**	20218-3	$2.95
___ **Showdown At Little Big Horn**	20202-7	$2.95
___ **Yellow Horse**	20246-9	$2.95

THE OLD-TIMERS

These two grizzled knights of the Old West never listen when folks say they're over the hill—they just use their true grit, their know-how, and a little luck to tame even the meanest young outlaws.

☐ **THE OLD-TIMERS IN THE SANGRE DE CRISTOS**
20032-6 $2.95

☐ **THE OLD-TIMERS OF GUN SHY**
16565-2 $2.95

☐ **THE OLD-TIMERS ON THE OPEN RANGE**
20033-4 $2.95